The Missing Person

The Missing Person
A novel

Alix Ohlin

ALFRED A. KNOPF, NEW YORK, 2005

THIS IS A BORZOI BOOK
PUBLISHED BY ALFRED A. KNOPF

Library of Congress Cataloging-in-Publication Data
Ohlin Alix.
    The missing person : a novel / Alix Ohlin. — 1st ed.
      p. cm.
    ISBN 0-375-41524-6
      1. Women art historians—Fiction.   2. Brothers and sisters—
    Fiction.   3. Albuquerque (N.M.)—Fiction.   4. Environmen-
    talists—Fiction.   5. Fathers—Death—Fiction.   6. Missing
    persons—Fiction.   7. Ecoterrorism—Fiction.   I. Title.

    PS3615.H57 M57
    813'.6—dc22   2004048879

Manufactured in the United States of America
First Edition

To David and Eleanor Rice

ACKNOWLEDGMENTS

I'm very grateful to the Michener Center for Writers in Austin, Texas, where I started this book, and to Portsmouth Abbey School in Portsmouth, Rhode Island, where I finished it. For their support and encouragement over many years I also owe big, big thanks to Amy Williams, Gary Fisketjon, my friends, and my family. All writers should be as lucky as I have been.

The Missing Person

One

Days started in Brooklyn with bright, compromised light. I'd been sleeping late. In the mornings, the blinds sending geometric stripes across the sheets, I kept willing myself to wake up, then slept again, fifteen minutes each time. Construction and conversation, dogs barking their greetings, the irritated beeping of vehicles in reverse—none of it could get me out of bed. By the time I got up, it seemed too late to bother doing anything; the day was almost gone. This was a problem I'd been having.

The phone rang early in the morning, early in June.

"Lynn," my mother said. She was panting slightly, as if she'd been running to the phone, though hadn't she placed the call? "I didn't think you'd be home. You're always at the library, or teaching, I thought."

"I almost always am," I said, pulling back the covers and pushing myself finally out of bed. I opened the blinds and looked out through the grate. Across the street from me, between the pet store and the souvlaki place, was a psychic's office. A neon crystal ball—blue pedestal, red base, under a pair of cajoling hands—stayed lit in the window twenty-four hours a day. The psychic herself was a stocky woman with long frizzy hair, given to flowery housecoats and red lipstick. I sometimes watched her sit in the window drinking coffee and smoking cigarettes, gazing out at the street. I never saw any-body go in there. What did she do all day, and how did she sur-vive? I'd lived across from her for three years, ever since I started graduate school, but still I often asked myself these pressing questions.

"Lynn," my mother said again. "So what do you think I should do?"

"About what?"

"I've been talking," she said. "By convention, on the tele-phone, one person talks while the other listens. People have agreed that this is the best way to approach it. Do you have a different idea?"

"Sorry. My attention must have drifted there for a minute. I just got up."

"It's ten o'clock!"

"I was up late, um, studying."

"I've been up for hours. I couldn't sleep. I'm worried about Wylie, and I thought, I'll call Lynn, she always knows how to handle him, she can communicate, and now you're not even listening."

"What's wrong with Wylie?"

"He cut off his phone. He lives like a monk and weighs about as much as a tin can. An empty tin can. Not only that—he won't speak to me. I have one child who won't speak to me in person and another who won't listen to me on the phone."

"I'm listening."

This she ignored. "I want you to come home."

"To Albuquerque?" I gave a shudder I hoped was inaudible and went into the kitchen to make coffee, cradling the phone against my shoulder.

"Don't take that tone," my mother said. She seemed to have heard the shudder, which was an uncanny ability of hers.

"What tone is that?"

"The I'm-too-good-for-Albuquerque tone. You've had it ever since you moved to New York."

"I hated Albuquerque just as much when I still lived there."

"I don't know why. You're just like Wylie, do you know that? You have all these objections that don't even make sense."

"Mom," I said, "I feel like we're not actually getting anywhere in this conversation." Across the street the psychic entered the window and stood with her arms folded, a cigarette tense between her fingers. The souvlaki guy, passing by her window, waved good morning. With slow elegance she raised her eyebrows and blew a perfect smoke ring, and he laughed.

"It's those eco-freaks," my mother said plaintively. "Wylie's friends. They've turned him against me. He won't call, won't come over for dinner. He says he's breaking away. He says I'm too complicit, but I don't think it's *complicit* to cook him a hot meal. I don't even know what I'm complicit in, do you?"

"I'm not sure. The dominant paradigm?"

"I'm a travel agent," my mother said, "not a paradigm." Sorrow and annoyance chimed together in her voice, a mother's chord.

"I know," I told her. We observed a moment of silence. Afterwards a gentle plastic rattle came through on the line, the sound of my mother's short manicured nails against her keyboard, and I realized she was calling from work.

"I'm booking you a ticket. We have some great deals through Minneapolis."

"Don't do that, Mom."

"I'm not taking no for an answer."

"No," I said.

"What did I just say? We've got great deals. Minneapolis is desperate for flights. They'll do anything. They'll pay you to fly there, practically. Listen, I'm pressing a button. I'm confirming. I'll e-mail you the reservation."

"Don't do that," I said.

"You're coming home."

Outside, summer heat was putting pressure on the day. My super, Guhan, stood by the door rifling through the building's garbage cans, sweat inking a line down the back of his Yankees T-shirt. He was very nosy and went through everybody's garbage, supposedly to make sure all the right paper got recycled. When he saw me he grunted. Originally he'd helped my old roommate—a dark-haired, six-foot-tall Swiss woman from my art history program—get a rent-stabilized apartment in the building. I moved in; then Suzanne finished her dissertation on a little-known Swiss surrealist and went back to Bern. For months afterwards Guhan kept asking me when she was coming back. Now he just sighed, eternally disappointed by what was left.

The street smelled of coffee in paper cups, car exhaust, perfume that had just been sprayed too strongly in the privacy of apartments, dog turds baking in the sun. I crossed the street and passed the psychic, gone now, and the pet store, where mangy kittens lay curled in the window in sad, scruffy balls. I bought a coffee and a paper to read on the subway. All the news involved natural disasters in faraway places: earthquakes, droughts, fires, floods.

A man wearing fake breasts under a black dress came on the train and sang a Spanish song while shaking his hips and holding his palm out for money, which nobody gave.

The woman beside me, middle-aged, short-haired, and suited, fell asleep, her tired face smearing makeup against my shoulder.

The Missing Person

I thought about Wylie, my baby brother, fat and jolly when he was little, tall and bony and righteous now. Our father had died two years ago, when his heart suddenly failed him; it was quick and painless, the doctor said. I went home for the funeral and stood with my mother and brother at the graveside, thinking that these were the most appropriate words for death I could imagine: "heart" and "failure." Ever since then, Wylie'd been getting both thinner and more radical. These days he was some kind of environmental crusader, a haranguing activist with a philosophical bent. He supposedly was finishing his biology degree at UNM, but only registered for one class a semester. My mother often said he took after my father, who was a scientist; but my father had a Ph.D. and a job at a lab, whereas Wylie was twenty-four and years away from any degree at all. Instead of doing course work, he devoted his time to writing his undergraduate thesis, a massive opus "about *all of nature*," as my mother told me on the phone when I asked why it was taking so long. The opus seemed to have more to do with ideology than biology, and sometimes he sent me chunks of it by e-mail, in the middle of the night, after too much beer: *The desert is deconstruction in practice, not theory; an experience that dismantles the border of the self and defies the human (frequently but not always male) sense of authorship, the idea that people create their own reality. In this Derridean context we can locate a species of alternative to the institutional structures of civilization. Not by fixing but by decentering us, wilderness puts us in our place in the world. It is a narrative that cannot be controlled by the participant.*

Usually I didn't make it much further than that. In my head Wylie was still a tousle-haired geek of around fourteen, camping out in a teepee in the backyard and building that science project where the volcano erupts. There was no way I could take him seriously. "Lynnie," he wrote at the beginning of one of his messages, "I showed this section to Mom, and she said, 'Have you ever thought about going to law school?'"

By the time I got to school it was past noon. Summer students with fluorescent hair and bad posture sat smoking on the concrete steps of the art building, where optimistic pigeons kept pecking at the discarded butts and dropping them, pecking and dropping, never learning their lesson. Inside, the hallways were almost empty, the classrooms silent and offices closed, my steps echoing against the linoleum. Bright shreds of posters on the bulletin boards publicized outdated events. I could hear a girl's shrill giggle around a corner, fading as she walked away.

In Michael's office there was yet another girl, this one young, very pretty, and Japanese, in a red miniskirt and matching high heels.

"But you don't understand the pressure I'm under," she was saying. "If I don't get an A my parents will kill me, seriously kill me!"

"I have to admit that I doubt your life is in danger," Michael said, his voice a low rumble, audibly amused.

"But everything will be ruined, and it will all be your fault! Who do you think you are?" the girl said, hysteria rising into her voice.

"It's my job to grade your work."

"You're the teacher," she said squeakily, "not *God*."

Michael's voice dipped even lower, practiced and reconciling, soft as felt. I stepped into the doorway and coughed loudly. It was a little phlegmier, actually, than I'd meant it to be. The girl barely glanced up, but Michael smiled broadly, lines creasing deeply around his eyes, his looks as excellent as ever. He was my advisor. He was married. We'd flirted my first year in grad school, slept together my second, broken up my third. It was something he did; I knew this now.

"Lynn. Give me two minutes."

I checked my mail in the department office, and by the time I came back the girl was promising to rewrite her paper over the course of the summer—making it the most "A-worthy" paper, she swore, he'd *ever* read—and away she went, tottering delicately on her heels.

"So," he said. "How are you?"

"Good." I sat down, pulling a pen and notebook out of my bag as if I expected a serious discussion, which I didn't. The pages were filled with absurd scholarship in my messy handwriting, copied-out quotations from famous critics, notes on the sexual proclivities of obscure artists, reading lists of books I never consulted. It was a documented history of wasted time.

"How are you, really?"

"Really good."

He smiled again. It seemed unfair that he was still so handsome. He crossed behind me and closed the door, then came back to face me. "I don't suppose you have anything for me," he said.

"You want gifts? If I'd known bribery would get me a degree, I wouldn't have bothered to sleep with you."

He didn't laugh. He was wearing a dark blue T-shirt and black jeans and a silver bracelet on his left wrist which he twisted around and around while he looked at me. "A chapter. Part of a chapter. An *abstract* for a chapter. An idea. A glimmer of an idea that might eventually, in the fullness of time, become something more."

"Oh," I said. "I didn't bring any of those." I looked over his shoulder at the window. Students bent practically double under the weight of backpacks portaged across the quad. Rangy dark squirrels rummaged for snacks in the trees. As I watched, a gust of wind freed sheets of paper from the trash and skipped them like stones across the pavement.

"I am concerned," Michael said softly, "about your progress in the program."

"Yeah, well . . . I guess it's been kind of a slow semester."

"It's been a slow *year*, Lynn. You haven't done anything, so far as I can tell, for at least a year. Quite possibly two. When are you going to take your exams? What's going on with this?" He opened a file folder on his desk—my dossier, I guessed, wondering what other information he kept in there—and held up a piece of paper, my supposed abstract of my supposed research for my supposed dissertation. We'd written it together one night in bed in my apartment, the laptop battery toasting my thigh, Michael's arms circling me from behind, his index fingers tapping with aggravating slowness on the keys. The abstract, and his endorsement of it, had gotten me the year of fellowship support I was living on now. I could tell that he was going to read it out loud.

"Please don't start reading it out loud," I said.

He peered at it as if he hadn't written it. "The Secret Modernists: Cultural Production and Practice in Women Artists, 1965 to 1980." He looked up. "Have you looked at those Eleanor Antin papers I was telling you about? Did you go to Philadelphia to see that show?" Then, after I didn't answer: "You know, Lynn, I've always thought this was an excellent topic. You have an opportunity here to do something potentially explosive. But if you sit on it for too long, somebody else will beat you to it."

I'd heard this speech before, though I couldn't remember where the idea had even come from originally, whether it was mine or his. The dissertation supposedly would re-evaluate the feminist art movement in modernist terms, arguing that even though the artists themselves rejected traditional barometers of quality, the work itself could nonetheless be evaluated and prized according to those terms. It was the perfect approach, Michael once said, one that dismantled previous criticism while elevating provocative work; it could push buttons, make enemies, resurrect careers. And, if nothing else, I did like the art of that period, which was populated by high-concept performances and fervent politics, women parading around naked in galleries, issuing manifestos, painting with their menstrual blood. I liked the physical and emotional extremity of it, the willingness of the artists to put their blood and guts, their pain and pleasure, on full display. My dissertation was going to make the case for the aesthetic value of this art, as opposed to its historical significance; I would use my skills as an art historian to situate this work in a broader context and, at the same time, situate myself in the job market. That was Michael's plan, and clear enough to me; I just hadn't gotten around to following it.

He was watching me, and I shrugged. His computer hummed its same monotonous song, and his office smelled of the pear soap he used at home. I didn't say anything. His area was contemporary art, his office littered with catalogs and announcements and letters and slides. He wrote for all the magazines and went to all the shows. That first year in graduate school, I believed that he was going to teach me something important, not only about art but also about how to live in the world as a sophisticated person. I'd felt my life, and myself, changing under his gaze. But it didn't last.

"Your grant runs through the end of the summer," Michael said. "You can take these next few months and then—well, make up your mind. Decide whether you're going to put out or get out."

"Not to criticize," I said, "but do you think that's the best choice of words?"

He sighed. "Look, Lynn, you might not believe this, but I'm only trying to help."

"Oh, you're a big help," I said. "You're massive. You're *huge*."

I could barely hear him saying good-bye as I walked out of the office and down the hall. All professors sleep with students, and then with other ones, and nobody is surprised. I wasn't surprised myself. It was amazing how unhelpful, in the end, lack of surprise could be.

On I went through the building's pale hallways. Other people in my program had finagled research opportunities in quaint medieval libraries or internships in plushly air-conditioned museums. Everybody was gone for the summer, and soon Michael would be off to Europe or California or Asia or wherever he was heading with his wife, who was a professor in the anthropology department. The two of them were always jetting off to deliver papers or consultations in exotic locales. I'd met Marianna several times at departmental functions. She was a stoop-shouldered woman given to scarves and shawls and wraps, anything soft to bundle around her angular body—whether to accentuate or to disguise it, I never could decide. I knew she knew who I was. She never gave sign of it, though, only smiled and talked politely about Santa Fe. When anybody in New York heard I was from New Mexico they talked politely about Santa Fe's galleries and restaurants, its clear light, the pink mountains. The rest of the state was invisible to these people. "I'm from Albuquerque," I'd say, and they'd smile, picturing the airport. In my head I saw Albuquerque's potholed streets and sweeping neon strips, and smiled too, glad to be gone.

. . .

The Missing Person

"Lynn," Wylie had written recently with digital urgency, another late-night message. "What if we aren't moving forwards in time? I have decided that progress is a lie."

During my first year of graduate school Wylie came to visit me in New York: his first, and only, visit to the city. He came off the plane stinking of sweat and pot smoke. My mother had given me orders to take him to the Metropolitan Museum and to a Broadway play. I left him at home one day while I went to the library and when I got back he and Suzanne were drinking tequila in the tiny living room with some Salvadoran waiters he'd met while taking a nap in the park. He never made it to the Met; but for weeks after he left, the phone would ring in the middle of the night, and someone would ask for my brother in Spanish, the sounds of a party ringing and dancing in the background.

I took the subway back to Brooklyn, where the world was overcast and no light glinted on the steel cages pulled down over the closed businesses of my street. The smell of exhaust and food being cooked in the Portuguese restaurant down the block rose and stalled in the air. At home I devoted some serious scholarly time to reading *People* magazine.

Past midnight, I'd just fallen asleep when the buzzer rang— a loud, old-fashioned buzz that always made me think of fire drills.

Michael came in wearing art-party clothes and an expression of drunken concern. "I wanted to make sure you were all right," he said, then lay down on the bed, his arm with its silver bracelet flung across my pillow.

"Where's Marianna?"

"Chicago. No, San Francisco. *Are* you all right? You seemed depressed today."

"I have a melancholy temperament," I said.

"I like your temperament."

I sat down on the bed and allowed him to hold my hand. This happened once in a while. He'd show up late at night, reeking sweetly of gallery wine and acting sentimental; in the morning, he was still married and we were still broken up.

"And you wonder why I'm confused," I said afterwards. A yellow line of streetlight poked through the window grate. I could hear the distant crash of traffic. There was no response; he was already asleep. I lay awake for quite a while, picturing a life in which Marianna fell madly in love with one of *her* students and moved to Prague or Berkeley or somewhere, and I moved into their enormous apartment on the Upper West Side with Hudson River views and book-lined rooms and copper pans hanging over the stove. Then the idea of me living in a place like that made me laugh, and then time passed, until finally it was morning.

He never disappeared in the early hours, like men do in movies. Instead he had to be prodded out of bed and served coffee. He even asked for eggs.

"I don't make eggs," I said. "Who do you think I am?"

He laughed, both hands around his coffee cup. No wedding ring, but Marianna didn't wear one either. They had some kind of agreement.

"Okay, no eggs." He stretched, running his hands through his shaggy black hair. His glance took in my tiny living room, and the former closets that passed for bedrooms, with something I took for nostalgia. "I'm going to France," he said. "Want to come?"

"What are you talking about?"

I stood at the window and watched the psychic sit at a table in her window, reach down, and then set something in front of her on the table, staring at it intently. Tarot cards, I thought, or runes. She started to move one hand over the other, rhythmically, as if performing some incantation. After a second I realized that she was painting her nails.

The Missing Person

"It'll cheer you up. Maybe get you excited about work again. In two weeks. I've got an extra ticket."

"Marianna's ticket."

"She has to go to Venezuela instead."

"You want me to go to France using your wife's ticket."

"I want to offer you an all-expenses-paid trip to Paris with a man whose company, based on recent evidence, I'm fairly sure you enjoy."

"Well, when you put it that way, it doesn't sound so bad."

"That's what I like to think," he said. "So you're coming?"

"I'll think about it."

And I did. I lounged around my apartment for those two weeks, committing several issues of *People* to memory and thinking about the two of us holding hands as we walked along the Seine by moonlight, et cetera. Then I thought about Melinda, the visiting assistant professor from Costa Rica whose year-long appointment in our department had precipitated our breakup and who I guessed had gone back home. I also thought about New Mexico, the blank astringency of the air and the bleak sunny streets sprawling with gas stations and chain restaurants. Finally I thought about my brother and his fervent midnight e-mails demanding, "How do we live decently in an indecent world?" It was true that I hadn't received any messages for a while, but knowing Wylie, he was probably just too busy writing his manifesto or picketing butcher shops or getting drunk with waiters or whatever else he did with his time.

In the end, I told Michael I'd meet him at his apartment— I wanted to picture him there, petty in my revenge, *waiting for me*—and boarded a plane to Albuquerque instead.

Long hours afterwards I stepped into the hushed boredom of the small, clean airport. My mother stood by the gate wearing a blue sundress, her hair clipped and neat; she was smiling broadly, as she always did when she'd gotten her way.

"How was the flight?"

"Fine."

"How was Minneapolis?"

"I only connected there."

"But was it efficient?"

"My flight was on time."

"That's what I mean," she said. "They're very efficient in Minneapolis. I think it's the cold weather. They have no distractions like we do here."

"It's June, Mom," I said.

We walked through the uncrowded hallways alongside men in cowboy hats and boots embracing their children and wives, their tight jeans cinched even tighter at the hips with large-buckled belts. Passing the airport restaurant, I smelled green-chile stew. I felt like I was on a different planet, in a separate, contrived dimension; a place created for vacations. The air outside was cool and dry, the lights of Albuquerque gleaming on a miniature scale against the blackness of the desert. Everything seemed very small. My mother drove through the familiar streets, past the gaudy neon, the Pop 'n' Taco, the Sirloin Stockade, then the brown shadows of adobe houses. Pink rays of cosmos and tall, nodding sunflowers bloomed in the yards. Everything was exactly the same, shabby and plain, as if I'd never moved away, as if New York were only a dream I'd had, an ongoing dream every night for years.

Lynn: We cannot return to the elemental things. There is no way to go back. But how to move forward when so much has been lost? How can we even think about the future when we are burdened by such an oppressive past and pessimistic present?

"Did you tell Wylie I was coming?"

"How could I tell him?" my mother said. "He has no phone, he's never at home, and God help the person who tries to get a straight answer from one of his so-called friends."

The Missing Person

We pulled up to her small condo. She lived alone now, in a two-bedroom place, having moved out of the house where I grew up, in the Northeast Heights, within a couple months after my father died. Sitting in the living room, I waited for her to say more about Wylie, to deliver my marching orders. But now that I was finally home she didn't seem to be in any rush. I closed my eyes—it was midnight in New York—as she puttered in the kitchen. The sounds of her movements were like my native language, the first I'd ever heard and learned: the hiss of water, her footfalls on a tile floor, a drawer being pulled out, spoons clinking against ceramic cups.

Her house was clean and spare. Unlike in my apartment, there were no stacks of anything anywhere, not a mote of apparent dust. On the white mantel above the fireplace she had arranged her collection of artifacts: Hopi kachinas, a storyteller doll, a bowl from Acoma. I thought about Wylie's contempt for the material world. *Lynn: We purchase our crumbling senses of self at the store, then try to mend the body politic with items advertised at attractive discounts during the President's Day Sale.* I sat there on the couch, my eyes still closed. Cicadas pulsed outside.

My mother came out of the kitchen and brought me a glass of water, touching me on the shoulder. "You're falling asleep," she said, and I realized she was right.

Two

Mid-morning I woke to an empty house, my mother gone to work early, at least in my terms; she'd left a note inviting me to lunch. I wandered around the house opening curtains. The sun was plangent and full, striking through the neighborhood's occasional pines, her street deserted except for a few cars parked neatly against the curb. It all seemed weirdly quiet. Wylie's old car from high school, a boat-sized, ivory-colored Chevy, sat in the driveway. These days, according to my mother, he'd abandoned gasoline transport and went everywhere on foot or by bike, but couldn't bear to actually sell the Caprice. The sun had bleached its paint, turning the ivory uneven and mottled as the keys of an old piano, and its wide red-leather interior was peeling and patched in places with duct tape. Nonetheless, it started right up. Despite his politics my brother apparently came back and serviced it regularly.

I drove around Albuquerque for a while, getting used to the feel of things. One-story buildings shedding turquoise paint, dirt lawns parked with old pickups. To the east, the bare brown mountains; to the west, the lone peak of Mount Taylor. Fast-food franchises brightened every block, a rainbow of reds and yellows, their white marquees advertising specials that were always misspelled or missing a letter or two: MIL-SHAKES, ROTBEER, FENCH FRIES. The colored shards of a million broken bottles glittered among wildflowers in abandoned lots and alleys. Every now and then, billowy clouds of grit rose in front of the car. It takes some kind of city, I thought, to make Brooklyn seem clean.

Among the adobes, here and there, stood the green landscapes of rich homes and corporate parks. I drove past the thickly watered emerald of a golf course, where men in festive pants lifted their clubs to the desert sky. Another green spot was the cemetery, where I stopped to look at the square, undistinguished marker I hated. It wore his name, Arthur Fleming, and the dates of his life, primly chiseled letters and numbers that seemed to have nothing to do with the fact that once this person, my own father, had lived in the world, and now did not. I pictured his face, with all its familiar crags and shadows, then shelved it in a corner of my mind, a gesture as physical and as habitual to me as folding clothes into a drawer. In the weeks after he died, I saw him everywhere on the streets of New York—getting on the 6 train at Union Square, buying a donut, waiting in line for a movie, not that he ever actually did any of these things—and knew that I had to put him away in order to keep going on. Now I spent barely a minute in front of his grave. I hadn't brought flowers or any other gifts, and felt that the moment was lacking in ceremony. Then I got back in the car and headed toward Wylie's.

On Central Avenue, opposite the low-slung campus buildings, a few summer students sat at the Frontier drinking coffee among the Hare Krishnas and the homeless. A man in tattered, abbreviated shorts, the rest of his body tanned to leather, had taken up a post outside the library, holding up a placard to the passing traffic: I'M A NUDIST AND I VOTE. A woman with an umbrella and many layers of clothing was muttering private endearments to the sidewalk.

Wylie lived on the second floor of a negligible apartment

building three blocks from the university. Out front, several old cars sat slumped in the gravel, two of them missing wheels.

I knocked on his door and waited for a good long time. "Wylie, it's Lynn." There was no answer, so I knocked again.

A middle-aged woman in a thin housedress opened the door of an apartment below and squinted up at me, the smell of long-standing smoke drifting into the morning air.

"I'm sorry if I—"

"I thought you was from the property management," she said, and slammed the door.

I knocked once more, without much hope. But as I was leaving, the door opened, and I turned to see a red-haired man standing there in nothing but blue boxer shorts. He had brown, freckled arms and a tanned face, but very white skin in the outline of a T-shirt, so that his paleness seemed to cover him like clothes. He smiled broadly, as if he were delighted to see me, and for some reason this surprised me more than anything. Finally I said, "You're not my brother."

"Probably not," he agreed. He ran a hand through his short red hair, which stood up straight as a field of red grass; then he opened the door wider and stepped backwards. "Would you like to come in?"

The apartment was dark behind him. "Is Wylie here?"

"No, ma'am."

"Do you know where he is?"

"No, ma'am."

"Or when he'll be back?"

"No, ma'am," he said, smiling widely.

His skin, even his pale chest, had a glow that reminded me I'd been inside an apartment in Brooklyn for most of the past ten months. He was possibly the healthiest-looking person I had ever seen.

"Would you like to come in?" he said again.

The Missing Person

I tried to look around him, into the cavelike apartment, but couldn't see anything. "All right," I said, brushing past him into the living room. I flicked a light switch, which did nothing. The power was apparently off. Boxer Shorts walked around the room pulling down sheets attached to the windows with duct tape, seemingly Wylie's favorite design accessory. The sun stormed in, and he turned around, covering his eyes.

"Excuse the mess," he said. "I just got up." He stretched his arms out from his long, pale chest and then went over to a sleeping bag in the corner and picked a pair of jeans off the floor. The jeans themselves were spotted with holes and showed a fair amount of skin.

"You sleep late," I said.

"I was up late, um, working."

"And where do you work?"

He squinted at me in the brilliant light. "I work for the good of Planet Earth," he said.

I burst out laughing. "Yeah, okay."

I took a clearer look around the apartment. Last time I'd been here, everything was pretty normal: small student desk, small student chair, small student bed. Now the walls were stripped of decoration. There was no furniture anywhere, only sleeping bags and backpacks tucked into corners. A shelving unit against one wall was stacked with wrenches, drills, emergency flares. The place was neat and empty, thoroughly impersonal, like an army barracks.

"So you're Wylie's sister? From New York City?" He crossed the room to the kitchen, leaned against the counter and smiled.

"How did you know that?"

He looked me up and down—at my black dress, my black sandals, my black leather purse—and shrugged. "Just a guess."

"Look, I'm trying to find Wylie. Could you tell me when you saw him last?"

He shrugged again. "Not sure."

"And you're not worried about him?"

"Wylie's a deep thinker," he said. "He's grappling with serious issues, and sometimes he needs to be alone."

"To grapple."

"That's what I said, yes."

There was a weird smell in the apartment—not unpleasant but vaguely acrid, layered, and chemical. I moved a foot or two closer to Boxer Shorts, who was still leaning, pale and shirtless, against the counter. It was coming from him. "I have to go now," I said.

"Come back anytime," he said, his broad grin showing very white teeth.

I turned on my heel and left, annoyed. Wylie'd been involved with causes and crusades for years, constantly enrolling in new student groups, petitioning, marching, bouncing from civil rights to homeless rights to animal rights. He could never find the right rights to hold his attention for long. But throughout it all, he'd never gone so far as to disappear.

I was unlocking the Caprice when I heard a voice shout, "Wylie's sister! Wylie's sister!"

Boxer Shorts, in his white chest and holey jeans, was running down the building's stairway. He ran like a soldier, his back rigid, knees high in the air; and although he was going pretty fast, he stopped on a dime in front of me and wasn't even out of breath.

"People usually call me Lynn," I told him.

"I didn't know," he said. "My name's Angus Beam."

We shook hands and stood there for a second, looking at each other, me smelling his weird, chemical scent.

"Was there anything else?"

"There's a meeting tonight, here, of our group," Angus said. "I thought you might want to come. Meet Wylie's friends. See what we're about."

The Missing Person

I nodded and thanked him, then got into the car. He stood there in the parking lot and watched me back out, which made me uncomfortable. Before hitting the street I rolled down the window and asked, "What *are* you about, anyway?"

"The meeting's at nine," he said, and waved.

After Wylie's I dropped by the campus to look for him in the biology and philosophy buildings: a long shot, but I felt I should check anyway. It was strange to hear my footsteps echoing in another set of academic hallways, these ones decorated with fake pueblo accents. I found myself walking into the library, where I stepped to a terminal and typed in, by habit, my father's name.

Fleming, Arthur: *The Temporal Dimension in Physics*. It was his doctoral dissertation, and only published work, which had sat on a shelf at home. In the acknowledgments he thanked my mother, who was then his fiancée, for all her help, support, and typing, and as a child I'd been fascinated by that; it was hard for me to grasp the idea that my parents had once been students together, living in a one-bedroom apartment in Chicago, drinking wine late at night, my father watching over my mother's shoulder as she turned his scrawled notations into typescript. What did they look like then? What did they say to each other? The vision was magnetic yet alien, like life on another planet. I'd thought that one day it would come into focus; in the same way, I'd always assumed that eventually I'd be able to read the whole book, decipher its diagrams and equations, resolve it into meaning just as I was learning to read harder, longer words as I got older.

But this never happened. As a teenager, I decided I wasn't interested in science. I didn't like math and especially hated physics, and my father's job was some unknown, boring thing he did for the government in a windowless office. The fact that he was a scientist was one of my many grievances against him, not because he was involved in anything sinister—although for all I knew, he was; I really had no idea what he did at work all day, and often into the night—but because of his scientist's geekiness, the knee socks he wore with shorts, his taupe-colored shirts that never seemed to fit right, the way he sometimes talked with his mouth full, all his embarrassing habits that potentially incriminated my own awkward teenaged self. After I graduated from high school and left home, this attitude mellowed, and I might even have got around to asking him about his work. Now there seemed no point. Yet it pleased me to think of him living on in the screen's digital glow, almost as much as the yellowing copy of the book itself in the stacks.

At noon I headed downtown to my mother's office. Around me sunlight glinted off lowrider fenders, cholos staring out from behind the steering wheels, their music pounding down the streets. Farther west, slender shadows bordered the boxy, old-fashioned buildings of the tiny business district.

Inside Worldwide Travel, the air was conditioned to a glacial level, and I had to stand still for a second just to readjust. Sweat cooled to ice on my skin. My mother was in her office explaining something to a large, burly man with an equally burly mustache. I sat down in the carpeted lobby underneath a poster of Greece, a bone-white beach against the turquoise Aegean, and waited for her to finish with her customer. I could hear their voices but not what they were saying. Francie Garcia, my mother's partner, sat talking on the phone behind the glass door of her office. Other phones rang distantly, were answered, rang again.

Francie came rushing out, jiggling car keys and smiling

mechanically at the top of my head. "Someone will be with you in a moment," she said, and then, "Lynn!"

"Francie, how are you?"

She smiled. She was in her late forties but looked younger, with long, curly hair and circles under her eyes. For reasons I never understood she always wore bright blue eye shadow.

"Well, I'll tell you, honey," she said, shaking her head and tucking the keys into her large black purse. "At least I have my health." She said this all the time.

"That's good, Francie."

"And how's life in the big city?"

"It's all right."

"You should come by and see Luis while you're here. He'd love to hear all about New York." Luis was her son, and around my age. During high school we'd had one disastrous, parentally induced date. "He'd love to see you."

"How is Luis? Is he married?" This was how I pictured everyone I knew from high school who'd stayed in Albuquerque: living in a prefab house in one of the new West Mesa suburbs, with a brood of children playing on a swing set stuck crookedly into the rock lawn. It was unfair to generalize, but on the other hand, it was generally true.

Francie threw me a sideways look. "Luis? No. I don't think he'll ever settle down."

I wondered what not settling down implied about someone who'd lived in the same town, surrounded by his entire family, for his entire life.

"Listen, honey, your mom's waiting for you with her friend, so I'll let you go." She kissed me on the cheek and left.

I went behind the counter to my mother's office, asking myself what Francie meant by "friend." Then, in the moment before she stood up, I saw her blush and knew the answer.

"Lynnie," she said, "you remember David Michaelson."

The burly man turned and smiled at me under his mustache. He was wearing a navy-blue suit whose jacket sported Western piping and pockets. He also had on cowboy boots, and it was the boots, for some reason, I remembered first. Before my father died we used to live next door to the Michaelsons. Their two boys, younger than Wylie and me, were sports stars of some kind.

"Hello," I said, shaking his large hand.

"I invited David to lunch."

"Good. Great," I said.

"New Mexican okay?"

"Excellent," I said, smiling hard.

We left the refrigerated offices and headed down the street to a restaurant, surrounded by the heat and noise of the traffic. Behind me, the thick heels of David Michaelson's cowboy boots made knocking sounds against the pavement, and I could hear him whistling under his breath, a sprightly, unidentifiable tune. I wondered if the real reason my mother wanted me to come home was to reintroduce me to David Michaelson. I wondered what had happened to his wife and his athletic children.

Inside, we sat quietly as our drinks were served. I'd ordered a frozen margarita, my mother an iced tea. David Michaelson sat back in his chair and took a large slurp of Coke, crunching the ice in his mouth. He was heavier than I remembered; his stomach strained against his light-blue, snap-button shirt and bulged over a square brass belt buckle that was practically the size of my head. With the belt and the mustache and the chest he reminded me of some early, imperious monarch: Henry VIII of the Wild West.

I took another long sip of my drink. "So you're a lawyer, right?" I said.

"Yes, that's right," he said.

My mother smiled at me.

"What kind of law do you practice?"

"Oh, a little of this, a little of that," he said with a shrug. "Corporate, mostly, but whatever I can get my hands on. A client's a client, that's what I like to say."

"We weren't sure if you'd remember David," my mother said.

"Of course I do."

Silence fell. I didn't know what to say about the wife and the athletic children. The waitress brought a basket of chips to the table. Half my margarita was already gone.

"What about Wylie?" my mother said. "Did you find him yet?"

"I went to his place, but he wasn't there."

"I don't like this," my mother said.

David Michaelson reached over and rubbed her arm, his expression at once sensitive and plastic. I remembered the boys' names, Donny and Darren, and their sport, hockey. Throughout the arid winters they'd get up at five in the morning and trundle out to the car, lugging enormous duffel bags with their pads and sticks and helmets, as if they were traveling to some distant part of the country, where such materials would be required.

"David thinks we should consider an intervention," my mother said.

"I thought that was for alcoholics and drug addicts."

"It's for anyone in trouble," he said, then picked up a chip and snapped it cleanly between his teeth. "And your mother seems to think that Wylie's in trouble."

"He doesn't eat, he quit his classes, he lives with nothing—you should see his apartment, Lynnie."

"I saw it."

"I thought you said he wasn't there."

"Some guy was," I said as the waitress arrived, balancing plates of enchiladas on a manhole-sized platter. I shoveled some food into my mouth and burned my mouth on the cheese, then gulped down the rest of my margarita in an attempt to ease the pain. The result was horrible, like an enchilada Popsicle, a bad idea for a food item if ever there was one. The waitress asked if I wanted another drink, and I nodded gratefully.

David Michaelson took a long, prissy drink of Coke.

"You should drink some water with that, Lynn," my mother said. "Or else you'll get dehydrated."

"I'll be fine, Mom."

"You'll thank me later if you drink a glass of water right now. You've forgotten how dry this climate really is."

"I *know*, Mom."

"Just drink some water to appease me."

I rolled my eyes and drained half a glass.

"Who was there—that Angus person?"

When I nodded, she leaned forward, ignoring her food. "He's the person I hold responsible." Anger lent her eyes a sharp, even light. "You should hear how Wylie talks about him. Or used to talk. He's changed since he got involved with that whole *group.*"

"What group?" I said. "Changed how?"

"Wylie used to be . . . well, you know how he was," she said. She began to fiddle with her food, teasing the sauce with her fork. "He had his ideas about the way things should be run, of course. But he was a good boy. I know that sounds like a motherly thing to say. But."

"What do you mean?" I said. "That he isn't a good boy anymore? What are you talking about, exactly? Has he turned to a life of crime?"

"You know what she means," David Michaelson said in an ingratiating tone.

"No," I told him, "I really don't. He might not have the loveliest apartment or be going to *law school,* but besides that I'm not sure I see what's so wrong with his life." I started in on the second margarita.

The Missing Person

My mother glanced down, wielding her knife and fork as if she were about to commence a delicate surgery; and then the muscles in her face contracted, bringing all her wrinkles into relief, the bones of her face growing prominent beneath her skin. She looked sad and fragile and old. "I wish he'd call me," she finally said, and took a bite of refried beans.

After lunch I once again shook David Michaelson's hand.

"Enjoy your visit here, Lynn," he said, leaning, it seemed to me, on the word "visit." I swallowed, with some effort, and thanked him. My mother squeezed my hand.

At a red light, the driver next to me sat lovingly picking his nose. The desert dropped away from the highway in pale brown layers, thin shrubs of cactus dotting the ground, dim blue mesas sleeping at the edge of the horizon. The world looked scorched and brittle in the glare of the afternoon sun. As the cars in front of me inched forward, I read from bumper to bumper. WICCANS HAVE MORE FUN, one sticker claimed; I also learned that GUN CONTROL MEANS HITTING YOUR TARGET and IT'S A DESERT, STUPID! I turned on the radio, listened to the weather forecast—hot and sunny and dry for the next week, for all weeks, for the indefinite future—and asked myself where the hell Wylie was.

I parked the Caprice in my mother's driveway. Without her in it, the condo had the vaguely liberated air of childhood days when I'd stayed home sick from school. Aside from the tchotchkes on the mantelpiece, my mother had mostly stored away the things from our old house, and I wondered what she'd done with it all. Not just the furniture or my father's books and clothes, but the smaller items: his diploma, say, or the Nambe dish he kept spare change in, and which I always stole from, and which he knew and tolerated. Other knickknacks also had been dispensed with: candlesticks and planters, the flower-shaped clock, even art that used to hang on walls. There was a kind of ruthlessness to her decorating scheme, as if she'd turned her life into a hotel room. But she couldn't have gotten rid of everything.

On a hunch I went into her bedroom and looked in her closet. Her clothes were neatly classified into sections of shirts, pants, skirts, et cetera. Her shoes, too, encased in a long plastic bag that hung behind the door, were divided by category: running shoes, loafers, flats, pumps. She was the Dewey of closet organization. I kept snooping around, feeling guilty about going through her things, though not guilty enough to stop. Somehow this made me feel closer to her than I did when talking to her in person. I kneeled down and looked under her bed, a space filled with large plastic bins. I pulled one out and discovered a mother lode of memorabilia: old report cards of mine and Wylie's, from kindergarten right through high school; school projects and drawings; home-made Mother's Day cards spastically coated with paper doilies and glitter. In the next, I found a few items from my father's office. A geode. One of those stands with a gold pen sticking out of it at an upright angle, a pen I never saw him use. A small framed photo of Wylie and me as little kids, grinning like idiots. Barely able to look at these things, I closed the bin quickly and slid it back underneath the bed.

Yet I didn't want to stop. I pulled out an even larger, rectangular bin, in which something flat was wrapped in towels and, beneath them, brown paper. Inside were two small paintings that used to hang in the bedroom hallway of our old house in the Heights. Although I'd forgotten completely that they existed, seeing them now was like running into a childhood friend or an old teacher or relative. I recognized their colors and dimensions right away, without thinking, the way you recognize a person's face.

They were oils, the paint thickly, even crudely applied.

The Missing Person

Studying them, I was almost surprised my parents had hung them in a house with young children; then again I'd never noticed the content, not until this moment. They were the same size, in matching brown frames. One showed a man and a woman seated across from each another at a dinner table. Both had straight dark hair, and both were naked, straight-backed, their postures less domestic than combative. The composition was awkward, perhaps purposefully so: the table was located on the right side, with nothing to balance it on the left, as if the pair of them were in motion, about to drift beyond the frame. Underneath the blue tablecloth, the woman's legs stuck straight out and her feet reached the man's knee; she might have been kicking or caressing him, it was impossible to tell. In the background was not a house but pink, unforested, hulking hills not unlike the ones around Albuquerque. I turned the painting over. Glued on the backing was a typed label: "Desert I (The Wilderness Kiss). 1978. By Eva Kent, rep. Harold Wallace."

The other picture was more disturbing. The palette of the first was largely blue and green, with the mountains turning pink in the background. It was a pretty scene, however odd, in jeweled colors. This, on the other hand, was ugly, its palette awash with reds and oranges and browns, the paint slathered even more thickly, almost violently. Again it was a man and a woman, naked, this time in a reverse pietà: the woman lying on her back in the man's lap, his hand touching her dark hair. This was clearly the same woman as in the other painting, but the man—though he, too, had dark hair—was different. His face was round-cheeked and cherubic, babylike, with a happy and wide-eyed expression. The woman, however, was miserable, her muscles tensed with fear, her scowling face turned away from him toward the viewer, as if she knew for a fact that he intended to harm her. Yet his arms weren't restraining her. She just lay there, limp, with a slash of red at her throat. Due to the roughness of the execution, it was impossible to say what this red was meant to represent; it could have been blood, or clothing, or makeup, or merely some play of light and shadow. The title on the back was "Desert II (The Ball and Chain)." Again 1978, by Eva Kent, represented by Harold Wallace.

If there was one thing I supposedly knew about, it was work by women artists of the 1970s—at the very least, I'd seen a lot of it—but I'd never heard of Eva Kent. I leaned the paintings against the wall, on top of my mother's bed, and gave them a hard look. This wasn't garage-sale art or a housewife's watercolors. Technically the work was impressive; not genius, maybe, but impressive. It seemed to have genuine authority, the force that gives you a shock of recognition and tells you that you're looking at serious work.

Michael used to describe this feeling in sexual terms. The magic of attraction: just as you can feel a jolt of electricity when you look at a person, so you can feel a jolt of understanding when you look at art. Then again, he used to describe almost every feeling in sexual terms, at least with me, at least for a while. I thought of him now, the smell and hum of his office, his voice telling me to put out or get out. When my old roommate Suzanne found her minor surrealist, she became the golden child of the department. She discovered he had a brain tumor, wrote about the relationship between neuroscience and creativity, and suddenly his work was profoundly interesting to everybody. She curated a major exhibit of his work in Bern, and the show was traveling to New York next summer. I put everything else away and carried the paintings back to my room, leaning them against the dresser, one at each end, a strange couple of couples. Eva Kent, I thought, rolling the sound of her name over my tongue. Neglected Artist, New Mexico Native, Lost Icon. If there was one thing I used to be good at, it was giving Michael what he wanted.

Three

Wylie as a kid was chubby and pale, with a shock of fine dark hair that was always falling in front of his eyes. One day, I remember, we were playing together in the front yard. Maybe we were six and four; it was before my mother went back to work. Wylie and I had just learned about April Fools' Day and were smitten by the prospect of pulling our own hilarious pranks, so I told him to lie down in the dirt and stay very, very still. I ran inside yelling my head off that Wylie was hurt. Our mother was in the kitchen drying dishes, and she threw her towel down and raced outside toward his small prone body.

But Wylie was too excited to wait, so he stood up and started jumping up and down. "It's a joke, Mom!" he shrieked. "April Fools' Day!"

She stopped in the driveway with her hands still reaching out toward him, then slowly let them drop. Her green dress had a full skirt, and with her apron on she looked like a pioneer woman confronting some early, primitive danger to her family. A hot and sickening feeling advanced from my stomach to the back of my throat. When she shook her head and went back inside, Wylie turned to me for explanation. "Why wasn't it funny?" he said.

That afternoon in my mother's condo I made myself a drink and sat in the cool living room, the glass sweating in my hand. I had no idea where Wylie was, or how to find him, and I felt tired and homesick for Brooklyn, my apartment, the psychic, those weird sickly kittens in the pet-store window. Michael stopping by late at night. When I first moved to New York for grad school, I had the sense that everyone there belonged to a club I'd always wanted to join, and Michael was inside the velvet ropes. People spoke to him at openings, with one or two others standing a few feet away, hoping to be invited into the conversation. Even sauntering across campus he was a star. Late at night, in some bar in TriBeCa, artists would sit at our table, drinking and laughing, and when Michael laughed at them, at some bald categorical statement or self-promotional ploy, they didn't seem to mind. I loved it when he talked about their work with me in private, evaluating its place in the river of art history that flowed cleanly through his mind. And I loved hearing him lecture in class; even now, my memories of the seminar room, the drone of the projector, his voice the soundtrack to every slide, were both drowsy and erotic.

Growing up, I'd gone to the art museum in Albuquerque all the time. I'd take the bus there after school and spend the late afternoon wandering through its deserted exhibits and historical dioramas, its paintings of local scenes by local artists. The art wasn't very good, but I didn't care. The lights were always dim and the air conditioning pumped on and off, regular and rhythmic. It was peaceful, the hush and stillness of it, the suspension of life outside. Sometimes it seemed that the main reason I decided to study art history was to gain the license to wander quietly through rooms, looking at pictures on the walls. Maybe not the best reason, but there it is.

It was Michael who made me think that this impulse was significant. Who wouldn't want a person like that to fasten his eyes on you, to compliment your work, to tell you your ideas were interesting and your eye for art acute? Which is exactly what happened, and how all the flirting began. Then, in a swell of urgency after my father died, I threw myself at Michael, and he caught me; we went from flirting to fixture. Out on the town on his arm, I was recognized as his current "companion" and knew it. Can an experience feel degrading and like an honor at the same time? Yes, of course it can. And the fact that I suspected I would be discarded eventually, that perhaps I'd even chosen him for this very reason, didn't make me feel better when it came to pass.

A latch clicked and my mother stepped through the door, dropping an enormous tote bag on the table in the front hall.

"Any word from your brother?"

I shook my head and she nodded, her shoulders sagging a little. Before I could say anything else she went into the kitchen and almost immediately set to work fixing dinner. I put my drink down and joined her, and before long she was giving me intricate details of a trip she was planning for a client, who for some reason wanted to visit every single country in South America.

"You wouldn't believe how long this takes. These places don't have faxes. They don't even have *phones*. I'm making reservations by letter, and they send back some dog-eared piece of paper that says, 'Everything okay, come now, pay later.' They must attach the note to a mule or something, then the mule trots down a dirt road that eventually leads by the post office. I do believe that mules are involved in these places, Lynn. I'll just be pleased if Dr. Trujillo comes back alive."

She kept this up all through dinner preparations. I thought about how people say travel broadens the mind, and what this meant for my mother, who was expert at organizing its every feature but never, ever went anywhere herself. She'd barely been out of town since I was in high school. There was something either heroic or insane about it. I set the table for our tidy, well-balanced meal: baked chicken, green beans, and rice. When my mother offered me a glass of milk, I laughed and shook my head.

"What?" she said.

I shrugged. "This is nice," I told her. I never cooked in Brooklyn and had almost forgotten people still did. I assumed the world had completely gone over to takeout. My mother sat down opposite me and smiled.

"So, how long have you and David been going out?"

She set her fork and knife down without touching her food. "Well, I wouldn't call it that, Lynn."

"What would you call it?"

"We enjoy each other's company."

"So, how long have you and David been enjoying each other's company?"

She cut her chicken into neat geometric pieces, took a dainty sip of milk, and carefully wiped her mouth with her napkin, an act of stalling so obvious as to be almost a parody of stalling. "A while," she finally said.

"I see. Where does he live, anyway?"

"Still in the same place, next to our old house."

"Oh." I looked at her, but she was intently focused on the task of spearing a green bean evenly on the tines of her fork. "What happened to his family?"

"Nothing happened to them," she said piously, then ate her bean and moved on to the next one. "Donny's still in high school, and Darren got a hockey scholarship to a college in Connecticut. They're both lovely boys, and David is justly proud. They both talk to him regularly. Darren calls home every Sunday evening at seven o'clock sharp."

"Yeah, well," I said, "that sounds great. So, excuse me for asking, but what's the deal with his wife? They got divorced?"

"No, they didn't." Her voice was tight and even.

"You're kidding."

"I'm not kidding." She kept on eating, one green bean at a time, the chicken in its orderly pieces.

"You're kidding," I said again.

"What did I just say?"

"You're having an affair with a married man."

"David's wife is very ill. She's confined to the house. We enjoy each other's company, and accept the situation, and I expect you to accept it too."

"You're kidding."

"Stop saying that."

"Mom," I said. She raised her eyebrows at me, and I opened my mouth but said nothing. Fortunately, I had chicken to fill the void. We sat in confused silence, cleaning our plates as if our lives depended on it.

When we finished, she cleared the table and took everything into the kitchen. "Lynnie, you do the dishes," she said. "I'm going out."

"It's eight o'clock."

"I know what time it is."

"Where are you going? To see David?"

At this she turned, her eyes narrow, and the look she gave me was frightening but familiar. It was the same look she'd given me in high school when I came home with my hair dyed green, and closely related to those she'd offered when I was in college in Pennsylvania, talking about feminist art all the time, hatching plans to move to New York and referring to Albuquerque as a cultural backwater.

"You've been here exactly one day," she said. "Don't start telling me what to do."

"You tell *me* what to do all the time."

"That's completely, one-hundred-percent different," she said.

. . .

I did the dishes, feeling irritable and put-upon. Afterwards, I went out into the suburban night. The air was warm, and the moon rose pale and low and clear above a gray bank of clouds. The enormous cockroaches that terrified me as a child scrambled scratchily across the sidewalks, great hordes of them glistening in the streetlights. For the second time that day I drove my brother's car to his apartment, though now the streets were neon-lit. The same cars as before were parked outside his building, amid a jumble of bicycles and skateboards. Wylie's door stood ajar, held open by a brick, and yellow light fell onto the landing. That's where the smell hit me: dried sweat, old clothes, and a crush of bodies, the smellable ideology of water conservationists. I held my breath and walked inside, straight into Angus Beam.

"Hello, Wylie's sister," he said, his smile as wide as ever. "I'm glad you joined us."

"I told you before, my name's Lynn."

"Lynn." He shook my hand and held on to it. He was wearing a faded T-shirt with a million tiny holes in it, as if he'd been attacked by kittens. Up close, his skin was covered with light freckles that disappeared from view when you were farther away—pointillist pigmentation. There were even freckles on his eyelids.

"Angus Beam," I said without thinking, "you should stay out of the sun."

He laughed. "Why is that?"

"Your complexion. You're extremely vulnerable."

"You're sweet to be concerned," he said. "I always wear a hat."

He stood aside and made a grand welcoming gesture. I remembered what my mother used to say when Wylie and I came in after playing outside all day: "Here they are, the great unwashed."

The great unwashed were gathered all around me in Wylie's apartment. The men wore khaki shorts, bright T-shirts with equally vivid logos in contrasting colors, and hiking boots with thick socks bunched halfway up their calves. The women wore dresses of flimsy, multicolored Indian fabric and their hair in long, loose ponytails. In fact there was hair everywhere, on chins and armpits and legs. From their belt loops or backpacks dangled Swiss Army knives, leather pouches, water bottles, lidded coffee cups. They looked like they either had just come back from camping or were prepared to set off at a moment's notice. A few people glanced at me and smiled inconclusively. Others conferred in twos or threes, whispering urgently or nodding fast as they consulted notepads and maps. I couldn't believe how many people had crammed themselves inside this one room. It was very hot. I was breathing through my mouth and hoping that it wasn't too noticeable.

In the back of the room, behind the kitchen counter, I thought I glimpsed Wylie. It was hard to tell in the swarm of people, and his back was turned, but he had the right slouching, skinny build and the right dark, floppy hair. I hadn't imagined there could be circumstances in which I might not recognize my own brother. Wylie, if it was him, was talking to a middle-aged Native American man with thick glasses and long, braided hair, his large hands sporting several bulky turquoise rings.

Angus Beam walked to the kitchen counter, turned around, and smiled. An automatic silence fell over the room. "I don't believe in rhetoric or public relations," he said, "but I believe a small group of individuals has the power to make real changes. So let's skip the speeches and get started."

A soft, satisfied whimper rose up from somewhere in front of me and I realized that a woman in the crowd was breast-feeding her baby. Otherwise the room was quiet. The man with glasses crossed his arms. Hidden behind his broad shoulders and large head was the one I thought might be Wylie. When we were little, Wylie and I spent hours trying to develop our telepathic powers, guessing which cards were being held up, picking numbers between one and ten. Wylie, I thought now, it's *me*.

Angus Beam looked around the room, smiling. "Time is of the essence," he said, raising his hands. "Sprinkler systems, this wall. Forestry, other side. Fuel economy, to the back. Gerald, you're with me, in the bedroom. Report on plans in half an hour."

The crowd nodded like a small, obedient congregation. The person who might have been Wylie and the middle-aged man—Gerald, apparently—headed to the back, out of my sight, as people clotted into groups and started talking. Sweat gathered on my forehead and armpits and trickled down the small of my back.

"I can siphon the gas out of a Ford Explorer in under ten minutes," said a man close to me.

"And then where do you put it?" a second man asked.

"It just has to be removed. One less SUV on the road, even if it's temporary."

"No, that's useless. You have to show the gasoline somewhere, in quantity. Or all the stranded SUVs."

A man next to me unrolled a blueprint and began pointing at it with a dirty fingernail. At his feet a brown lump I'd thought was a backpack uncurled itself and stood up, revealing itself as a dog.

"A revegetation campaign," he said. "Guerrilla horticulture. We go to people's houses and rip out, like, the California plants, right, and put in native vegetation. Free xeriscaping—those people will thank us later, man."

"Sure they will," somebody else said.

The noise level in the room throbbed and rose. I heard "industrial-agricultural complex" and "ranching subsidies" and "ecological catastrophe." The dog, a skinny brown thing with protruding ribs, shook itself and padded into the kitchen.

"REM," a man's voice said. "It stands for Radical Equality Movement. It covers animals, plants, and humans. Everything."

"That's for sleep, man. Not to mention the band."

"Shit," somebody said in another corner. "We produce it but we don't want to talk about it or deal with it. We take in whatever we want, then refuse to deal with the consequences of our own bodies. This culture is packed with philosophical and logistical constipation. That's the real issue. It's all about shit."

What if we aren't moving forwards in time? I have decided that progress is a lie. I stood up and tried to push through the crowd to the back room, but everywhere I turned was blocked. There seemed to be more people every second, murmuring and plotting pranks: digging up corporate gardens, taking stink bombs to shopping malls, spray-painting new subdivisions with antidevelopment slogans.

"Excuse me," I kept saying, but as one person would step aside, I'd walk into another bare shoulder or hairy arm. The heat was suffocating. Finally, feeling dizzy and faint, I just pushed myself through a final wall of people into the kitchen, behind the counter, with the dog. I looked to the side, but the bedroom door was closed. In front of it, chatting with a tiny, wiry woman, was a man with a football player's build, in a turquoise tank top that revealed thick armpit hair. He smiled at me politely. A moment later the wall re-formed. Three or four people sat on the counter, blocking my view. When I opened the refrigerator door, only bad-smelling air came out. There was no light, no cold, no food, nothing to drink. Suddenly I felt damp on my leg. The dog was licking my knee almost sadly, as if it couldn't help itself, its eyes pleading and chagrined.

"Stop that," I told it, but it kept licking and followed me as I backed up.

The woman who'd been nursing her baby broke through the people surrounding the kitchen. "Stop it, Sledge," she said sharply, to the dog. "Stop that right now."

The dog lay down instantly and hung its head in shame.

"I am quite sorry for that," she said to me. She had an accent, something European. She rehoisted the baby in its cloth sling and held out her right hand. Her face was wide and pale, with broad, slanted cheekbones, and strands of brown hair curled delicately around her ears. The baby crouched against her chest like a frog.

"I'm Irina," she said.

"Lynn," I said, shaking her hand.

"Welcome," she said. "Would you like something to drink? It is boiling with the heat in here."

I gestured to the fridge. "There's nothing in there."

She laughed, a gold tooth glinting in her smile. "I have something." She reached into the capacious sling where the baby was and fished around, then pulled out a glass bottle full of pulpy brown liquid and handed it to me. It was actually cold. "Apple juice," she said.

"Thanks." I drank some, and it was delicious, sweet and woody.

In her arms the baby gurgled happily. Its wide, pale face was shadowed and dimpled, like the surface of the moon.

"Are you one of these vandals?" I said.

Irina shrugged. "We all have different projects."

"What's yours?"

"Right now, to make sure you are doing all right."

"You guys don't seem very concerned about security."

"What do you mean?"

"You let me in, and I heard all about these felonies you're planning. I could turn you all in."

Irina laughed again, and the moon-faced baby did too. I drank some more juice, and seeing the bottle was empty, she took it back and stuck it somewhere inside the sling. I wondered what else she had in there.

"But you're a friend of Angus," she said.

"I don't know Angus. I'm here looking for my brother. Wylie."

"Yes," she said. "Wylie. I don't think he's here."

"I saw him."

"Did you? What I am thinking is he is not here."

Around us, the buzz of the room rose and hissed and began to roil. I saw a bottle passing from hand to hand. A woman's laughter sounded loud and shrill above the din, repeating at intervals, like a ringing telephone. In one corner a man strummed a guitar and sang a country song. It was turning into a party.

Then the bedroom door opened and Gerald walked out through the crowd and left the apartment without speaking to anyone. No one acknowledged him, but on the other hand they all moved aside so that he could get by. When Angus came out, the music stopped and the same immediate silence fell.

"Reports, to me, now," he said, then turned on his heel and went back into the bedroom, followed by three or four people. The door closed, and the party started up again. I thought I smelled pot. Irina was rocking her baby back and forth.

"What is this?" I asked her.

"Just people who want to be living differently," she said.

Still dizzy and hot, I leaned back against the counter and looked down at the floor, where a cockroach was nosing around the curling edge of the linoleum, its antennae languidly twitching.

Irina put a hand on my shoulder. "You would like to go outside in the fresh air?"

I nodded and followed her out of the apartment. After the press of bodies, the night air was blissfully cool. The moon still hung low in the sky, and the baby cooed at it. We walked slowly down the dark street, the sound of the party fading behind us.

"What's your baby's name?"

"Psyche," she said.

"As in Cupid and Psyche?"

"Yes, Cupid is the god of love, and Psyche is the soul."

"I see," I said.

"I'm going to raise her at home and teach her myself. Angus says that what they teach in schools here is useless. The only skill the children learn is conformity to a set of capitalist rules."

I had a sudden, obvious thought. "Is Angus—"

Irina tilted her head and smiled at me gently. She was very pretty. "Is he what?"

"Is he Psyche's father?"

"No," she said. "He is more in a nature of an uncle. He helps me very much, though." She turned to face me under the dim umbrella of a streetlight. "I think he likes you."

"We don't know each other."

"That doesn't matter."

A prickle started at the back of my neck and trailed down my back to my legs. Then I felt embarrassed. "What is this, high school?"

"Oh, he didn't say anything to me like that," Irina said. We started walking again, and turned right to make a loop around the block. "I can just tell. Because I know him."

44

The Missing Person

In the silence that followed I could hear the tiny hum and wheeze of Psyche snoring. Finally I said, "How well do you know Wylie?"

"Pretty well, I should say."

"When was the last time you saw him?"

"Oh, I don't know. He comes and goes. Sometimes he camps for long times in the mountains. He is a very independent person, you know."

I sighed. Nobody seemed to care that he wasn't around, except for my mother and me. I felt annoyed, and concerned, and lonely—whenever I came home, Wylie was supposed to be there—and tired from the combination of it all. "I'm worried about him," I said to Irina.

She shrugged and ran a gentle finger under Psyche's fat sleeping chin. "Why? I think he is happy enough."

"Happy enough? That's not exactly a ringing endorsement."

"It is probably more than most people can say."

I didn't answer this statement, which struck me as true. We made another turn and walked back toward Wylie's apartment. Ahead of us, a group of people was coming down the stairs of his complex. One of them stopped and blew his nose in a visible spray over the street. "That was no dog," his friend was saying. "It was a goat!" Then they all got onto bicycles and rode away.

I went back inside, hoping against all realistic hope that Wylie would be there, waiting for me and ready to talk. But the apartment was empty, and he wasn't.

Four

Life at my mother's house settled into a shaky routine, the tenuous reestablishment of an adult child come back home. It didn't feel right, but it didn't feel exactly wrong, either. In the mornings as I slept my mother left me notes, assigning me various chores—defrost the fridge, take out the trash—that I consistently ignored. She came and went day and night, to work and to go bowling or to the movies with David Michaelson, like some roommate I'd found through a classified ad. Neither of us mentioned his wife.

Daytime television kept me sane. During the long, bright days I closed the curtains and lay on the couch, eating ice cream and learning about celebrities' drug recovery programs, also their wedding plans, decorating styles, and diets. Sometimes I fell asleep to the Weather Channel, the calm swaths of cold fronts in the Rockies, the monotony of drought in the Southwest.

One evening, when my mother came home from work, I turned off the television and brought out Eva Kent's two paintings.

"Were you going through my room?" she asked.

"Sorry," I said quickly. "I just wanted to see some of the old things again."

She shrugged. "I don't care for those paintings."

"I like them. I think they're pretty good, actually."

We both glanced at the paintings—I'd set them against the living-room wall—as if they might have something to contribute to the conversation.

My mother raised one eyebrow, briefly. I could tell she put stock in my judgment, even though it contradicted her own, which was touching, if probably a mistake.

"Well," she said, "you would know."

"Where did they come from?"

"Oh, your father came home with them one day. My birthday present, I think."

I was surprised to hear this, and couldn't remember it happening. Then again, if he'd given them to her around the time they were painted, I would've been a baby. Still, my father always gave abstract and wildly impersonal presents: board games, magazine subscriptions, T-shirts. The popularization of the gift certificate was the best thing that ever happened to him, birthday-wise.

"Probably his secretary picked them out for him," she went on. "I hated them all along, to be honest with you. Those naked, unhappy-looking people. And what's happening in that second painting, with the woman lying on the man's lap? I don't even want to know. But I didn't want to hurt your father's feelings, so up they went."

"Do you know anything about her? Eva Kent, I mean."

She studied my face for a moment. "The artist? Why are you so interested in her all of a sudden? You never showed one bit of interest in those paintings before."

"I have more training now," I said. "I, um, know things."

This shut her up. "Well, I'm sorry I can't tell you more." Then she went into the kitchen and changed the subject. "What about Wylie? Have you made any progress on figuring out where he is?"

"Well," I said, and sighed. "I've decided that progress is a lie."

She came out of the kitchen to pick up my ice-cream bowl and carry it back in there, a gesture I interpreted as laden with reproach.

"Don't do that, I'll take care of it."

"You will?" she said.

"Eventually."

She picked the bowl up anyway, and I followed her to the sink, where she started scrubbing away as if at years of accumulated dirt. Still in her work clothes, a navy-blue skirt and a light-blue blouse with short sleeves, she looked like the head attendant on an exhausting flight. The flesh of her arms bounced and shook a little as she washed.

I opened the fridge and took out a bottle of beer.

"Lynnie," she said.

"The thing is, Mom, if you're so desperate to find Wylie, why don't you look for him yourself?"

She set the bowl gently in the drainer and turned around, water from the sink stretching across her abdomen, like a smile or a scar. "Do you think I haven't?" she said.

So in the morning I set off again in the Caprice, the radio turned up loud, and drove through the sun-addled streets. The city looked criminal: dust blew across the windshield, men leered at me from corners and from behind the wheels of their pickups, working girls paced beneath the bleached neon signs of fleabag motels. The Sandias were brown in the distance. The houses were brown. The highways were brown. Everything was brown. The car's wheezing air-conditioning blew a stream of tepid air over my right shoulder. I was sweating and cursing by the time I pulled up at Wylie's place.

The Missing Person

No one answered my knock. I sat down in a slice of shade on the landing outside his door and waited for someone to come back. A stray dog ambled down the block, head down, marking its territory here and there in the brown lawns. In this neighborhood dirt and weeds were fighting a winning battle against all grass. The dog lifted its head, sniffed the air, and looked at me.

When we were kids Wylie and I had a dog named Sycamore—Syc for short, which my parents thought was funny—that we took on hikes in the Sandias with my father. Hiking was our main activity together. During the week he got home too late for us to see him much, but on Saturdays or Sundays my mother would send the three of us packing so she could clean up or chat with her friends or talk to her mother on the phone. My father always wore the same thing, brown shorts and those too-high socks and a broad-brimmed hat, and he almost always took us on the same trail. It led to a cave, where we ate a lunch he'd carried for us in his knapsack. Sometimes he invited a friend, another scientist from work, and they'd walk too fast, talking shop and ignoring me and Wylie until we turned on each other and had to be yelled at. Other times, though, alone, he'd talk about his own childhood in Chicago, a place that sounded dramatic and foreign to me, with snowdrifts higher than I was and hot dogs as long as my arm. For years I dreamed about going there in winter to skate on the streets to my father's school, the way he'd done when he was a kid.

On one of our hikes, Syc came bounding back onto the trail, his tail wagging like crazy, with something in his mouth. My father bent down, sweat loosening his glasses from the bridge of his nose, and said his name softly. Syc just stood there, wagging. My father gently pried his jaws apart and a pale-gray rabbit dropped onto the ground, shiny ropes of dog saliva coating his fur. Wylie and I stood there looking at it. Then my father put the rabbit behind a tree and shooed Syc away. Wylie asked to keep it, but my dad said no, so he pouted all the way home. But I'd seen what Wylie didn't: that the rabbit just lay there, stiff, on the ground.

The shade had widened over the landing. In front of me, the stray dog snapped up a piece of garbage in somebody's yard, seemed dubious about it, then moved on. I watched it leave, shaking my head at myself. It had been over ten years since I'd gone on a hike of any kind. But if your brother held wilderness all-important in an overly civilized world, why on earth wait for him at an apartment building? Why would you, unless you didn't really want to find him in the first place? I decided I was an idiot and got back into the car.

I could remember only that one trail, which started in the western foothills by a water reservoir, a round white container that always looked to me like an oversized aspirin the mountain was trying, year after year, to swallow. At the trailhead, two mountain bikers in fluorescent gear were squirting energy food from tubes into their mouths. It was a weekday afternoon, and aside from a single jogger far ahead up the trail, there was no one else around: just the sky and the sun and the arid ground, with dry husks of burnt-out cactus making the skeleton shapes of bushes.

I started walking. Where the dusty foothills pulled steeply upwards into a bit more greenery, I saw the jogger disappear around a bend. Now there was really no one around. Gradually the trail took on a malevolent air. The dead cacti rustled and whispered; invisible animals scurried underneath. Fifteen minutes later I was exhausted. I could walk for hours on city blocks in high-heeled boots, but a quick stroll at Albuquerque elevation was killing me.

On a rock barely shaded by a juniper tree, I sat down and

wiped my forehead with my T-shirt. "I hate being hot," I said out loud. I hated being thirsty, too. I vaguely recalled there was some kind of stream on this trail, although maybe you weren't supposed to drink from it because of the bacteria. Or was that somewhere else? I was ignorant; my feet hurt. I thought about Wylie spending weeks at a time in the mountains, philosophizing or thinking or whatever it was that he did out here, and felt a profound wash of affection, even gratitude, for the attributes of civilized life, for apartments and stoplights and magazines and the steam that issued from manholes on the streets of New York.

But none of that was within my reach just now, so I stood up again. Somewhere up ahead was the cave where Wylie and I used to pretend, over lunch, that we were prehistoric man, if prehistoric man had had access to peanut-butter sandwiches and Nilla wafers. My father often began those hikes with a distant, preoccupied air, speaking about current events and the weather as if we were strangers he'd just happened to fall in step with; but gradually he'd relax into his more fatherly self, telling stories and jokes, every once in a while ruffling Wylie's hair. I always thought that it took him a while to get used to his family again, not because he didn't like us but because during the week, when he was at work, he just didn't think about us that much. We weren't the central focus of his life, and he was capable of forgetting us. When he died I thought: if he'd cared a little more, he would have fought harder to stay.

Birds muttered in the low bushes by the side of the trail. The sun shone on the back of my neck, the heat a pressure as real and finite as an iron flat on your skin. My shoes were covered in brown dust. I climbed up through rocky crags, heading up switchbacks, turning back and forth like a goat. I kept thinking the cave would be around the next corner, but it never was. On another rock I rested again, this time looking back toward the city, flat and undistinguished below me: the gray acreage of parking lots, the beige hulks of new malls, the streets hectic with tiny cars. In the distance I could see the small peak of Mount Taylor, floating in the desert like an island rising from a brown sea. My throat and feet and neck were dry and sore and sunburned, respectively.

I gave myself ten more minutes and finally reached the cave, though it was less the cave of my memory than a rocky overhang with the remains of a fire below it, charred rocks, scattered trash and paper, old beer cans and condom wrappers. It was a ready-made antidote for childhood nostalgia. I sat down in the shade, leaned my head against the rocky wall, and passed out.

When I opened my eyes the jogger I'd seen earlier was standing over me holding out a bottle of water. It was Angus Beam. I was almost positive I was dreaming. His skin shone thickly with sweat. He was wearing a light-blue T-shirt that was soaked and translucent, sweatpants, combat boots, and a Panama hat. His arms and neck were the color of persimmons.

"Drink this," he said.

I grabbed the bottle and drank almost half of it, undeterred by its weird taste, which was both chemical and citrusy. A layer of dust had somehow settled on my tongue as I slept.

He crouched next to me, balancing lightly on his heels, and squinted at my face. "You look terrible."

"What are you doing here?"

"Walking around," he said. "Wearing a hat and carrying water. Which is more than I can say for some people."

"Don't start."

"Water is the key to life here in the arid Southwest."

"Yeah, I know."

"Without it we'd all perish."

"I said I know," I said. "Can I have some more?"

I felt nauseous and stupid and annoyed. Every time I looked for Wylie, I wound up with this character instead. He took a folded handkerchief out of his pocket, dampened it with water, and gently wiped my forehead and cheeks. "Can you walk? Otherwise I'll carry you."

"Don't even think about it." I stood up and immediately sat down again. My calves were knotted and cramped, and some floating squares of color—red, blue, green, purple—hovered weirdly in my field of vision. When I pressed a hand to my face, one was hot and the other ice cold, but for a second I couldn't tell which was which.

"Let me help you," he said.

It took twice as long to get back down the trail as it did to climb up. I leaned heavily against his shoulder and stopped often to drink water, and by the time we got to the trailhead I was feeling almost normal. The sun was lower now, drooping densely in the flat sky, and hikers with dogs and children spilled from their cars in the parking lot. I could see far below us the sparkle of traffic on the highway. I had no idea how long I'd been on the trail. Without saying anything Angus steered me to the Caprice, took the keys I offered, opened the door, and sat me down in the driver's seat. Then he leaned against the door and asked if I was all right to drive. Suddenly his smell hit me: the stinky pheronomic nastiness of male sweat, plus that chemical odor I'd noticed before, and, on top of that, a general odor that was strangely but recognizably clean. It was impossible, but he smelled like *water*.

"I think so," I said. "Where's your car?"

"I walked."

"From Wylie's apartment?"

"As modes of transportation go, it's both safe and reliable," he said. "Listen, would you care for a drink?"

"What time is it?"

"It's five o'clock somewhere," he said, and smiled. Under the brim of his hat, sweat was gathering in drops and preparing to trickle down his face.

"So you want to get a drink," I said slowly. "Right now."

He reached into the car and placed his hand flat against my forehead.

"You're sure you're all right to drive?"

I glared at him, and he grinned widely, his teeth gleaming against his dusty skin, and then sprang away from the door with a light, quick step. A millisecond later, it seemed, he was sitting on the passenger side.

The streets were crowded with traffic, and I rolled down the windows and sighed, asking myself what the hell I was doing. Angus gave me occasional directions and fiddled constantly with the radio, listening to ten seconds or less of every single song, ten words or less of talk. It was basically the most annoying thing ever. I kept glaring at him, which only made him laugh. This went on for fifteen minutes as mothers in minivans cut me off, truckers barreled down on top of me, and packs of teenage girls stared at us and giggled for no reason that I could see. I was sweating a lot and hating it. Finally Angus reached behind him into the backseat of the car, leaning far over to rummage around on the floor, his sweatpanted butt perilously close to my shoulder.

"What the hell are you doing?"

He turned around clutching a fistful of cassette tapes in his hands and sorted through them quickly before sticking one in.

I heard strings.

"The sweet sounds of Frank Sinatra," Angus said. "They've always been a favorite of mine."

"Is that right?"

"It is. Take this left on Indian School, please."

The sweet sounds seemed to calm him down, and he sat looking out the window and mouthing the words. Two crooned songs later I pulled up at a motor lodge on a deserted strip of road. On the sepia-colored sign was a neon martini glass and the word "Cocktails" in a flowing script.

Angus leapt out of the car and opened the door to the cocktail lounge. Inside, through the gloomy dark, I could just make out booths with cracked red vinyl and tables made of dark pressed wood that was supposed to resemble mahogany. It looked like the set of a canceled TV show.

The waitress, a woman in her forties with a devastated face, sat smoking a cigarette on a stool at the bar. She wore a black miniskirt and beige panty hose with no shoes, and she was the only person there. We slid into a booth so small that my knees were touching Angus's. I shifted around and crossed my legs. Angus leaned back and ran his hands approvingly over the vinyl. "I think I'm going to have a martini," he said. "Would you like a martini?"

"Okay."

"Jeanine," he called to the waitress, who had not gotten up. "We'd like two martinis here."

"Vodka or gin," said Jeanine, stubbing out her cigarette with what appeared to be total exhaustion. She reached down past the ashtray to where her shoes—black flats—were sitting on the bar, then pulled them on with a grimace.

"Gin, of course," Angus said. "And a big glass of water for my friend here," he added, smiling at me. "You know, gin is the canonical martini. If I wanted a vodka martini I'd *say* a vodka martini. To distinguish it from the standard version, right?"

"Olives or a twist," said Jeanine.

"Olives!" he said. "Olives, definitely."

"Me too," I said.

Jeanine nodded and set to work behind the bar.

Angus Beam would not stop smiling. He leaned forward, putting both his freckled hands palms down on the table. His fingernails were ragged and chapped around the edges.

"What's so funny?" I said.

"Nothing."

"You're smiling like there's something funny."

"I'm smiling," he said, "because I'm happy."

To this I had nothing to say. Jeanine brought the drinks in small plastic glasses, two tiny dark olives, shriveled as raisins, speared on each toothpick.

"I didn't think you'd do this kind of thing," I said.

"What, go on a date? I just had the impulse. I'm an impulsive person."

"This is a date?"

"Well. Never mind, if that's not what you meant. Go on."

"I meant going to a cocktail lounge. Drinking martinis."

"Why would you think that?"

"I picture you and your friends in some kind of outdoor hut, drinking naturally refined alcohol that comes from, like, hemp or something."

His eyes widened. "They can do that?"

"Not as far as I know, but I'm not the expert here."

He winked and mouthed both olives off the toothpick at once. "Listen," he said, chewing, "I think our world is an ungodly mess. That we live in a society overwhelmed by its own poisonous excesses. That people who don't see the truth of this are blind or stupid or both. But a world in which a man can drink a martini with a beautiful woman on a sunny afternoon—well, that's a world with some redeeming qualities."

I rolled my eyes. "I guess I'll drink to that," I said. We

clinked glasses and I raised mine to my lips. As I tipped it back the toothpick fell forward and I splashed gin down my chin and the front of my shirt. I flushed deeply and dabbed myself with a napkin. Angus noticed, but pretended not to, and I liked him for it.

When I finally got some gin down it filled me with a kind of gorgeous, beneficial warmth, as if I'd been cold without knowing it for days. The room dimmed then, and yellow light flickered in some plastic sconces on the wall. From some crevice of the lounge, music began to play, another crooning torch song, this time by a woman whose voice I didn't recognize. It turned out to be Jeanine, sitting on her stool by the bar, her lips against a microphone connected to a karaoke machine. She stared at our booth and sang in a tuneless, gravelly voice:

> *I met a man in a hotel bar*
> *He was in from out of town*
> *He said I was cute*
> *I thought he was quirky*
> *He took me out for dinner*
> *And fed me tangerines*
> *He took me for all I had*
> *And left me in Albuquerque.*

At the end of the song she nodded and stood up, and we clapped. Into the microphone she murmured quietly, "The lyrics are my own."

We drank one round and ordered another. We were still the only patrons.

"So," I said. "Did you grow up in Albuquerque?"

He shot me an amused look. "No, I'm from Brooklyn," he said. "Flatbush Avenue."

"You're kidding."

"I am not."

"So how'd you wind up out here?"

"You say that as if there's something wrong with Albuquerque."

"There's nothing wrong with it. It's just the middle of nowhere, that's all."

"I happen to like nowhere," he said. "Besides, I found work here."

"Which is?"

"I'm a plumber. I work for Plumbarama."

"You fix toilets?" I looked at his fingers grasping the stem of his glass, at the dirt underneath the fingernails, and thought about that odor that surrounded him constantly: the smell of chemicals and ammonia and water.

"Toilets, sometimes, yes. Also sinks, bathtubs, washing machines, drainage systems, septic tanks. Nothing functions without plumbing. Nothing goes forward without leaving waste behind. Plumbing is the circulatory system of the civilized world. It allows us to forget our dirt, our shit and stink. It allows us to pretend. Wash our hands of it, as it were."

"As it were."

"But everything in this world has its price, even cleanliness. We can't continue to pump our waste into the waterways without figuring out how to recirculate and clean it. We can't allow First World nations to monopolize gluttonous quantities of water while Third World countries suffer for lack of it. If we don't deal with plumbing, then we aren't confronting the basic reality of our own presence here."

This made a certain kind of sense, I thought, although it might've been due to the gin. "You think about this stuff a lot, don't you?" I said.

"I guess so. I have time, while I'm unclogging somebody's sink, to consider the larger implications."

"So how does being a plumber fit in with all your group activities?"

"It's all connected." He opened his wallet and withdrew a folded piece of paper, an intricate, hand-drawn diagram, rather beautiful, of pipes and arrows overlaid in a complex geometry. There were tanks and tubes and valves and other mechanical forms that I couldn't begin to identify, each labeled with neat, tiny letters going down the alphabet.

"What is it?"

"It's the future of plumbing," he said, and his eyes held mine in a brief, electric moment before he went on. "Citywide composting toilets. Gray-water usage and flow constrictor fittings and pipes made of recycled plastic. A quasi-steady state system that will restore logic to the human component of the hydrologic cycle. In twenty years, when the Beam model is fully implemented, our current plumbing equipment will seem as grotesque and outdated as the shit-filled streets of the Middle Ages."

"Wow," I said.

He nodded and put the paper away. Round three followed with reassuring speed. Jeanine sang a couple more numbers. Angus talked about the ideology of plumbing and ran his hands through his red hair until it was poking out all over. I felt the gin coursing through my veins. At some point—who knows when?—he stood up and threw some loose bills on the table, grabbed my hand, and pulled me to my feet. We waved goodbye to Jeanine and then we were standing in the parking lot of the motor lodge, next to a red pickup truck, kissing like crazy.

Things were soft and warm and endless. The moon shone somewhere behind my right eye. I leaned back against the body of the truck and pulled him toward me until his hips ground against mine. I felt a crucial need to be naked. In the shadowy air of room 102, comforter thrown to the carpeted floor, thin sheets slippery against my skin, I ran my hands over his warm shoulder muscles and down to the small of his back; he touched me everywhere. We had sex, passed out, woke up, had sex again.

When I woke up the second time it was only midnight. This seemed implausible, even shocking, but I guessed that when you start drinking in the afternoon, you open up a lot of extra time in the evening. I peered through the blinds at the parking lot, my stomach quivering and uneasy. A low, lumbering shape I hoped was a raccoon was nosing around the trash can by the ice machine. Music was playing distantly. Angus Beam lay with his cheek pressed into the pillow, his face crumpled and red, snoring lightly, one freckled arm flung over the side of the bed, the fingers grazing the floor. His skin glowed in the dim light like a Renaissance nude's. His smell was on my skin.

I was in the car before it occurred to me that I was still drunk and shouldn't be driving. The city streets were wide and empty, though, the white lines like arrows directing me home, and I floated above it all, directing the car from a great and mighty distance, like a ship in space. I was home and in bed in what seemed like no time at all, and fell into unsettling, science-fiction dreams stippled with images so bright they almost woke me up. In one, my father came back to us, older, silver-haired, and confessed that he hadn't died at all; in another, the sun turned from yellow to red, an apocalyptic event signaling environmental catastrophe, and cascaded down toward the earth where, just before impact, it became the red hair of Angus Beam.

My bladder woke me at four-fifteen. I went to the kitchen to down some more water and was leaning against the counter drinking when I heard noises outside, and for a second I just waited, my stomach trembling. Sidling up to the living-room window, I could see a figure in the driveway beneath the jaundiced rays cast by a streetlight. My brother was standing there in the dark, bent under the open hood of the Caprice.

Five

"Hi," I said.

Wylie jumped about a foot in the air and dropped the dipstick, which clattered loudly against the asphalt.

"Lynnie," he said, "what the hell are you doing here?"

"I was about to ask you the same question."

"I'm checking the oil." He picked up the dipstick and held its tip in front of his face, scowling at it. The oil mark was just barely visible in the wan light. "Have you been driving my car?"

"Maybe," I said.

He shook his head and turned again to the engine. His dark-blue T-shirt said CAMP KIKOWAWA 1992 on the back. Underneath the worn cotton his scrawny shoulders stuck up in points, and his dark hair hung down in a skinny, knotted braid. I was sure I weighed more than he did.

"What are you doing at home?" he muttered to the car.

"I came back to visit," I said. "Where the hell have you been?"

"Bisbee," he said.

"I sent you an e-mail weeks ago telling you I'd be back. I've been looking for you."

"Bisbee, Arizona."

"What's in Bisbee, Arizona?"

This question met with a long, irritated pause, during which Wylie reinserted the dipstick, drew it out again, and examined it, scowling all the while. I leaned against the side of the car and waited.

"Bisbee, Arizona," he finally said, "is what's in Bisbee."

"I never would've guessed. You're being kind of annoying, by the way."

"Well, you would know."

"Wylie."

"Lynn."

I crossed my arms. Wylie slid his scrawny body under the car and started tinkering around down there. I sat down in the driveway, my head still swimming a bit in the aftermath of drinks and sex and sleep, and looked up at the sky. The moon was fat and sagging. Far down the block a couple of dogs were barking at it testily from their yards.

Wylie's feet stuck out from beneath the car, the toes of his sneakers pointing and flexing as he shifted his weight. I could hear him grunting. Across the street Mrs. Sandoval's rock lawn gleamed in the moonlight. Near my right hand a cockroach sped across the asphalt, and I shuddered and stood up. Our house was dark, and my mother was in there sleeping.

"Wylie," I said to his grimy shoes, "Mom really wants to talk to you."

"I know."

"Why don't you sleep over?"

"I can't."

"Just stick around for breakfast. Fifteen minutes, so she can see you. A cup of coffee."

"I don't drink coffee," he said.

"Yeah, like that's the point."

A clanging, rusty sound came from under the car; then Wylie said, "Shit!" and scooted out with oil on his face. "See what you made me do?"

"Sorry," I said, and laughed.

He gave me a mighty scowl and stood up, then closed the hood of the car and started gathering up his tools.

"Wylie?"

"I can't talk to her."

"Why not?"

"Because she doesn't understand the kind of life I'm trying to live. She can't admit that I'm an adult making serious moral choices."

"Those are your actual reasons?"

"Plus she nags me all the time."

"You could stand it for fifteen minutes."

He thrust the tools angrily into a backpack and shouldered it. When I touched his arm, he flinched. His skin was darkly tanned, his face drawn, and his wrist was hardly thicker than mine.

"No, I couldn't," he said, then strode down the driveway, his back slouched under the weight of his backpack. He looked like a thirteen-year-old heading off to school. Above him, the sky had already begun to lighten in preparation for sunrise. Two condos down he turned around. "If you absolutely *have* to drive the car," he said, "take care of it."

"Okay," I said. He kept walking, and a minute later I heard the same angry dogs raise another, accelerated alarm—this time, I was pretty sure, about him.

The sun and my hangover together woke me at seven. For a while I just lay there on my back, looking up at the white ceiling and wondering if everything I remembered from the night before was a dream. Did Wylie really come back? Did I really drink martinis with a man I hardly knew while an aging waitress sang karaoke songs she wrote herself? Did I really have sex in a motel room, *more than once*?

"Oh, my God," I said out loud. I could feel the night's imprint on my body: the parched throat, the sensitive skin, a few memories in other places. Down the hall I could hear my mother moving around, the fizzle of the shower, and then some dish-clanging in the kitchen. I was surprised I usually slept through this racket.

I found her sitting at the table, tapping her spoon precisely at the dome of a soft-boiled egg.

"Good morning," I said. She looked tired and wan, I thought, her skin even whiter than her office blouse.

She looked up, dropped her spoon, and made "I'm having a heart attack" motions over her chest. "Isn't this a sign that the world's coming to an end?" she said. "You getting up before noon?"

I poured myself a cup of coffee and watched her scoop out neat spoonfuls of egg and slip them gracefully into her mouth. I'd forgotten how much she liked these rituals—place settings and cloth napkins and square meals. An egg cup next to a slice of toast and a glass of juice: it was like a breakfast commercial.

"So, guess who I saw last night."

"Someone who kept you out until quite late, that much I know."

"It was only midnight." I cleared my throat. "Wylie came by. Late last night or early this morning. I heard him in the driveway and went out to talk with him. He's doing all right. He mostly seemed preoccupied with oil in the car. He really loves that Caprice."

Relaying this news—even though Wylie came back on his own, and not due to my efforts—gave me a sense of accomplishment I hadn't felt in quite some time. I sat back and waited for the inevitable kudos. Instead, she took her breakfast things into the kitchen and rinsed them in the sink.

"He's been in Arizona," I added, "but now he's back."

When she finally looked at me, her face was taut with anger, and her voice came out a whisper. "I cannot believe you let him just stop by and then prance right off. I cannot believe you didn't wake me up, that you didn't strap him down with *rope*."

"Mom," I said.

"This is not a gas station."

"I know."

"It's not a place where you check the oil and leave after five minutes."

"I understood what you meant the first time."

"I am very disappointed in you," she said.

I sat there staring at my coffee cup. My throat hurt, my head hurt, the hair on my head hurt. I didn't know what to say.

She took her purse and left, just like Wylie had.

Alone, I tried to find comfort in my usual routine—TV watching, ice-cream eating, et cetera—but couldn't sit still. In Brooklyn I'd passed whole days without moving ten feet, but now I roamed around the far reaches of my mother's condo for less than half an hour before deciding I had to leave. I put on my sunglasses and headed out into the day.

Angus's hat was on the passenger side, neatly folded in half along its sweat-stained brim. I crammed the Sinatra tape inside it and threw them in the back, where I wouldn't have to think about either one.

On the streets of Albuquerque, young guys in lowriders with family names calligraphed on the back windows were cruising around, bass lines pounding from their stereos, staring harshly at drivers whose cars bore different family names. Skateboarding kids were taunting children on foot. I noticed huge, disheveled crows hanging out on all the power lines and stray dogs meandering down the dirt alleys, skulking against walls and crossing streets heavy with traffic. At an outdoor coffeehouse a homeless man was busing people's tables, whether they were done or not, then begging for change. Everybody I saw was suntanned and squinting.

My first stop was the university library. I wanted to look up the artist of my father's paintings—as I'd come to think of them, even though I couldn't remember him ever talking about them—and see whether there was any information about Eva Kent's life and work. At the computer I went through the usual rituals—my father's name, his book on the screen—before proceeding to my scholarly tasks. There was a reassuring familiarity to the stacks of torn scrap paper by the terminals, the useless stubby pencils, the Library of Congress classifications. I was in my element, or as close to an element as I had.

I rummaged through the sections on New Mexico artists of the later twentieth century, flipping through journals and small-press books and leaflets for any sign of her name.

Two hours of looking yielded exactly one item about Eva Kent, a 1978 magazine article about a show at the High Desert Gallery that contained none of her work. But scattered throughout the article were pictures taken at the opening-night reception: men in mutton-chop sideburns, women in dirndl skirts and turquoise squash-blossom necklaces. Everybody was smoking and looked drunk. One black-and-white photo showed two men laughing their heads off on either side of a lithograph; behind them, frowning slightly, was a woman. The caption read: "Ernesto Salceda, Bruce McGee, and Eva Kent."

She had parted her long, black hair down the middle—a habit she must have adopted years earlier, because the part had widened to reveal a stripe of scalp. She had a substantial, commanding nose and a wide, tight-lipped mouth. She looked like someone who'd never spent a day lying on a couch eating ice cream in her entire life. Also, there was one other thing: she was unquestionably, enormously pregnant, but she didn't carry herself like any pregnant woman I'd ever seen, at least anyone who was that far along. She didn't have her hands clasped beneath her belly or resting above it, wasn't sitting down or leaning back to compensate for the additional weight. Instead she was leaning forward, rather daintily, and frowning at the lithograph, ignoring the two men beside her, a cigarette burning in her right hand.

I sat for a while looking at the picture, turning possible events over in my mind. Eva Kent had a child, then painted the reverse pietà. As a portrait of motherhood, it was less than idealized, that picture of hers. From *The Wilderness Kiss* to *The Ball and Chain* wasn't exactly a sentimental journey, and I couldn't help wondering what had happened to her later. Since there were no other references to her after that opening in 1978, it occurred to me that maybe she'd stopped painting after having the child. I could do something with that, though it would be better, for what I had in mind, if something really bad had happened to her—a greater tragedy than the feminine mystique, that is. This was cynical, but no less true. Suzanne's surrealist had died young of his brain tumor, whose side effects supposedly accounted for the more egregious imagery in his work.

I thought back to the night Michael and I wrote the abstract for my dissertation. The artists I was researching showed in alternative spaces and staged performance art, embracing the female body in all its sexuality and powers. They celebrated the vaginal imagery in O'Keeffe's flowers and made a heroine out of Frida Kahlo. My project was supposed to reexamine this time period using the very modernist terms these women had worked so hard to defy. Michael thought it would make a big splash, but felt that I had to find the right kind of artists, and not performance artists, to elevate and promote.

"You need a Georgia," he'd said. "You need a cult of personality."

"Greeting cards in the making," I'd answered lazily, trying not to fall asleep. "Coffee mugs and calendars." We were in bed in his apartment, on a quiet Saturday evening, and Marianna was at a conference in Denmark. Those were the most peaceful nights I ever spent in New York: half-asleep and half-awake, books on the blankets, the noise of the city far away below us.

As I looked back on it, that conversation seemed a long way from staring at mediocre paintings in Albuquerque, and I asked myself how I'd gotten from one place to the other. I'd started studying women artists in college, once I'd gotten through the basics of art history and noticed how male-dominated it was. I thought I could understand their anger and defiance; by dealing boldly with their own bodies, they were taking control, asserting their presence. For a while I adopted an angry attitude myself, toward men and especially my father, whose quiet conventionality I saw as a patriarchal crime.

"I have cramps, Dad!" I'd make sure to tell him. "I'm *bleeding*." I wanted to make him uncomfortable, which was never hard. He'd offer me an aspirin and quickly exit the room. During these years we had few easy conversations, and only when I was starting grad school did I stop attacking him—too busy, I guess, defending myself against the onslaught of life in New York. We'd begun, then, to talk about other things, news, weather, anything, like ordinary adults; but he died before things could get fully normal again.

In the library I went downstairs and sat at a computer terminal, hesitating only a moment before I started to write.

The Missing Person

Dear Michael,

How's France? I have exciting news. I believe I have stumbled upon exactly the necessary material for my project. Thank you so much for pushing me into more active research. There is a set of paintings here that I believe to be quite extraordinary, and I feel with them the strong personal engagement you always said was required for the best scholarship. I have come across a female painter who deals with issues of the body with a remarkable mixture of formal skill and ideological heft. Her name is Eva Kent, and I'm researching her other work right now. I think you'll be pleased. Thoughts on how I should proceed?

Cheers,

Lynn

Whether I really thought the paintings were extraordinary was beside the point; I wanted Michael to think so. I knew him well enough to tell him what he needed to hear.

I made a photocopy of the picture and left the library. It was almost noon, and at the coffee shop across the street I ordered a chicken burrito with green chile and listened to the fresh-faced students at the table next to mine debate the various merits, as hangover remedies, of bacon and eggs, French fries, and Tabasco sauce. On the other side of me a pointy-faced girl in a peasant skirt was writing furiously in a cloth-bound journal.

Outside, traffic moved sluggishly from block to block and light to light. A woman with a baby strapped to her chest was jaywalking in between the cars, lightly brushing their hoods and trunks and fenders as she passed; it looked like some ritual benediction, her head canted to one side and a dreamy laxness in her gait. Traffic was slow but it had not in fact stopped, and people were honking. Still, she kept to her serene, peculiar route, and when she got to my side of the street I realized it was Irina.

I ran outside and caught her by her arm, and she said, "Sister of Wylie!"

"Hi," I said.

"I am so sorry to tell you I have forgotten your name," she said.

"That's okay. It's Lynn. I'm having lunch, would you like to join me?"

"But I couldn't impose."

"Please. It's my treat."

"I would like to, then."

Inside, she sat down at my table and immediately started nursing the baby, who pulled at her nipple with loud, aggravated sucking sounds. The hungover students, repulsed, cleared their trays in a hurry. I ordered a cheeseburger and a Coke, at her request, and brought them to the table.

"So, Irina. How's everything going? Have you seen Wylie?"

She shook her head and looked as if she were about to say more, but then became distracted by the cheeseburger. She ate faster than anybody I'd ever seen. Her round, pretty face shone with sweat and happiness, and she kept nodding rhythmically as she chewed. In between bites she licked the juice from all her fingers in turn. The baby also seemed happier, sucking quietly, one little hand curving around her exposed breast. Irina put her hand on the back of the baby's head. I finished the rest of my burrito and asked if she wanted dessert.

"Oh, no thank you! But I would happily eat one of those burritos."

So I watched her demolish a whole other plate of food, nodding and smiling at me all the while. Her appetite was both impressive and off-putting, like an Olympic event you weren't sure should actually be a sport. The baby went to sleep, and Irina tucked her breast back into her dress and kept eating. At the end of the burrito I held my breath, but she just picked up the Coke and leaned back, sipping on it with a contented air.

"Ever since I had my baby I can't stop eating," she said. "I think I am afraid she won't be nourished enough."

"She looks pretty happy," I said. In fact the baby's head was lolling out of the sling, heavy-lidded and drowsing, silvery strands of drool gathering at the corners of her mouth and fluttering gently as she breathed.

"Yes," Irina said, and belched. A few strands of her brown hair were stuck to her cheeks with sweat. "You know, when I was a little girl, I never knew there were things like this in the world, like cheeseburgers and burritos. No one ever told me that these things existed. But I think that somehow I knew. Because how else could I have come here, on a sunny day in June, to be sitting with you and eating such a wonderful lunch?"

I laughed. "That's a good question."

"I think so. Thank you for the food."

I told her she was welcome, and asked how she'd gotten to Albuquerque in the first place. I'd assumed she was a student, but then she told me her entire life story, slowly, while sipping her first Coke and then another. She'd grown up in Germany, then France, then Ireland. Her father was a doctor and her mother an artist, and they'd fled Prague in 1968, swearing they'd never go back. Which they didn't; but neither did they settle anywhere else, and instead they kept shuttling their growing family—Irina was the youngest by far of six and, she suspected, an accident—from country to country, language to language. They turned whatever city they were inhabiting into a little country of their own devising, speaking their own private language, with layers of jokes and family references that grew over the years into a kind of insular dialect. Irina's older siblings eventually rebelled. One married an Irish woman and settled in Dublin, refusing to speak even a word of Czech; his children were named Patrick and Siobhan. Another brother went back to the Czech Republic and swore that it was the only place he could ever live, though he'd never lived there before.

When Irina was eighteen, she planned on studying accounting at a local university. But one day she was sitting with her parents in London, where they now lived, and watching the BBC, a nature special called *Deserts of the World*.

The camera traveled to Africa, then to Asia, and finally to the American Southwest. It flew over the Chiricahua Mountains of Arizona like a bird. It blew, seemingly on the wind, to White Sands, New Mexico, over miles of glistening white dunes, shifting and forming, the sunset pink and explosive. "What . . . is . . . this . . . place?" Irina said to herself—and she whispered it to me across the table, slow and sibilant, hissing like a fanatic sharing a secret code. "And so I came here," she said.

"Because of something you saw on TV."

"Because I fell in love."

"With a place," I said, though I meant it as a question, whose answer might encompass her baby. But she just nodded, smiling widely. Her expression was exactly that of a freshly married woman who'd just described how she met her husband. It seemed both ridiculous and plausible to me that she could have moved across the world for the reasons she'd given. All these people—these friends of Wylie's, and Wylie himself—were motivated by such strange, off-kilter passions. They seemed to do things—leave home, draw plumbing diagrams, move to Albuquerque, New Mexico—just to feel the sway of those passions on their bodies, for the sake of surrendering to them. Irina's face was flushed, her smile generous. And then the baby woke up.

Psyche scrunched her face up and howled until we left the coffee shop and strolled through the streets, empty and hushed in the afternoon heat. I realized that we were heading in the general direction of Wylie's place. My take-charge mood apparently had been left behind at the library, and instead of barging in and asking everybody where Wylie was or how I could find him, I decided to stick with Irina for a while and see if I couldn't figure it out myself. She bent her head and sang a delicate little song to her baby in what I imagined was Czech. In the resplendent sunshine, with her falling hair and radiant cheeks, she looked like a sacred painting. I thought about the picture of Eva Kent in my pocket, her rigid posture and massive belly and burning cigarette—a motherhood that seemed totally unrelated to this one. I wondered how my father had ever come across her or her paintings in the first place, and what had happened to her baby.

Irina had a key. Inside, the shades were drawn and the air was still and close but actually fairly cool. In the kitchen, above the sink, was strung a little clothesline, with cloth diapers, cloth kitchen towels, and plastic bags washed and hung up to dry. It was seriously advanced recycling. Sledge, the skinny brown dog, was curled up in a corner, snoring.

"Thank you so much for my lunch," Irina said. "I think, if it is not too rude, I may go lie down a little while with the baby now. You can wait here for him if you would like."

"Wylie's coming here?"

"I mean Angus."

"I'm not waiting for *him*," I said quickly, and blushed horribly. Irina smiled and went into the back room off the kitchen as I stood there feeling stupid in every way.

There wasn't any furniture, so I sat on the floor. The apartment was very quiet. I could hear my own breathing, along with the dog's. Then he made a deep sighing noise that wasn't a sigh; a horrid stench overtook the room, and I hurried outside onto the landing, looking at the street full of falling-down student housing, lawns of sheer dirt, trash on porches, tape on windows. Lacking a cigarette or a magazine or anything to help pass the time, I pulled the photograph out of my pocket and examined Eva Kent's scalpy part and thick fingers. She wasn't wearing a wedding ring.

Then I heard whistling and someone calling my name. Angus came sauntering down the street, his red hair sticking up, his back straight, his shoulders broad and muscular, his grin showing all his teeth. He was wearing yet another decomposing shirt. The instant I saw him, I knew that we'd be sleeping together again; it was a foregone conclusion. "A woman has needs" was actually the very first thought that went through my mind. I sighed. It was getting to be a very weird summer.

He stopped at the base of the landing and squinted up at me. He was still grinning, and it seemed to be genuine. "I'm so happy to see you," he said. "I think you have my hat."

Six

After I told Angus that Irina was sleeping, he crouched down beside me and asked if I'd been drinking my water.

"I know enough to drink water," I said. My voice sounded surly to my own ears. "That was just a one-time thing."

"All right."

"It could happen to anybody."

"It happened to *you*," he pointed out, raising his red eyebrows. I frowned at him, and he shrugged.

Across the street, a couple of young guys came out from one of the dilapidated houses, one sitting down on their porch, the other leaning back into the shade cast by a large pine tree. They opened cans of beer and lit cigarettes, and the smell of smoke wafted across the street to where we were sitting. It seemed like pretty early in the day to be drinking, though I was hardly one to talk.

"And now I find you sitting out here," Angus said, "baking in the sun once again, without any sign of water, or even the protection that you yourself pointed out to me is so important. By which I mean a hat."

"First of all, I'm sitting in the shade. Second of all, the inside of that apartment reeks from your disgusting pet. And third of all, it's really none of your business."

"My disgusting pet?"

"That gassy dog."

"Oh, the dog," he said, and waved his hand dismissively. "That isn't a pet. He just lives with us. Pets are little slaves we maintain to convince ourselves that we can be kind to animals, while every other part of our lifestyle promotes the extinction of animal life. You know what's the most disgusting part of this pet mythology? Paying hundreds of dollars for a purebred while thousands of strays are killed every year in pounds. Anyway, Sledge can come and go as he pleases."

"But you feed the dog," I said, "and he's living in your apartment. Isn't he your pet in practice, if not in theory?"

He threw back his head and laughed generously, showing the diminishing spray of freckles down his pale neck. "You're sharp," he said, "and I like that. You stand outside of things, and observe them, and form rapid judgments. I like that too."

This didn't exactly strike me as a compliment. I felt tired then, and annoyed with myself. "It's just . . ." I said, my voice dwindling. He leaned closer to hear me, and I could feel, beneath the general heat of the air, the more specific warmth generated by the closeness of his skin to mine. "You know, I keep looking for Wylie, and he won't talk to me, and I don't know why. I'm sorry."

Angus stood up and pulled me to my feet. We stood there for a second, holding hands, mirrored, swaying a little. "Don't apologize for anything," he said.

Inside the apartment, Irina was up and nursing the baby again. Angus went to the kitchen and poured water into his Nalgene bottle, which he handed to me and stared until I drank. Then he nodded—pleased with himself, it seemed— and turned to Irina. "Who's coming today?"

"I'm not sure," she said. "Stan and Berto for sure. I don't know about Wylie."

The Missing Person

"No one ever knows about Wylie," Angus said, and winked at me. "Maybe he'll be at the thing tonight. Do you have the maps?"

"Yes, hold on." Irina reached into the sling, somewhere underneath her baby's butt, and pulled out a folded, creased piece of paper.

"What's going on?" I asked, and was conspicuously ignored. Sledge came over and sadly licked my ankle. I found a shallow dish in the kitchen and gave him some water, which he drank in great sloppy mouthfuls. Then I spent a while nosing through the cupboards, which were stocked with neatly labeled plastic containers: rice, dried beans, lentils, oatmeal. There was enough food to keep a group going for weeks, as long as they didn't mind eating the bomb-shelter diet. I remembered Wylie badgering our dad for more Nilla wafers when we were hiking, which in an attempt to guarantee good behavior were withheld until the last possible moment. I guessed he'd put Nilla wafers behind him by now.

I wandered into the bedroom, where Irina had been napping. At least this room held ordinary signs of habitation. A single cot draped with a sleeping bag sat against the back wall, underneath a window whose blinds were drawn. On the foot was a supply of cloth diapers, a jar of talcum powder, a box of baby wipes. The air smelled of baby: part dirty diaper, part No More Tears shampoo. I pulled up the blinds and looked into the backyard of another apartment complex, where a motorcycle was leaning on a rusty kickstand underneath a green archway that made it look like some kind of shrine; morning glories composed the arch, their blossoms twisted and closed, all the vines sagging in the afternoon heat, everything drooping and listless and dry. I turned from the window and opened the closet, which was empty. There were no pictures anywhere on the walls, no clothes thrown in the closet or on the floor, no tracts or manifestos, even. Aside from the traces of Irina and Psyche the apartment was desiccated, stripped of the invisible currents that people bring to a place they live. It was clear that Wylie didn't live here anymore—at least not in the way that I defined living.

Back in the living room, Angus and Irina were sitting cross-legged on the floor, examining maps and muttering like spies.

"Are they metal or plastic?"

"Metal."

"Pop-ups or shrub?"

"Pop-ups."

This went on for some time. I stood behind Angus and peered over his curved back at a diagram that showed a long pipe with a spring curling around it, housed in some larger casing. The parts weren't labeled, and I had no idea whether the thing was a carburetor or a bomb.

"What's the earliest we can go?" Angus said.

"Gerald would know."

"Who *is* Gerald, exactly?" I said.

"A friend of ours," Irina said. She was crouching on the floor with her bent knees splayed out to either side, the baby asleep on her chest, her face inexplicably radiant. I couldn't believe she was actually comfortable.

"Stan and Berto were supposed to be here already with his information," Angus said.

"Who are Stan and Berto?" I said.

"Friends of ours," Irina answered sweetly.

I sighed. "You guys have a lot of friends."

Without saying anything Angus reached behind his back and wrapped his hand around the bare skin of my right ankle. It was so quick that I actually gasped a little bit. I could feel his dry palm, even the calluses, and as he peered over his shoulder I met his light-blue eyes. Then he broke into another wide smile and said, "We're friendly people."

The Missing Person

The door opened and two guys walked in without knocking or even saying hello. They both looked familiar, so I must have seen them at the meeting. One looked like a wide receiver, with a muscular hairy chest he was flaunting under a tight white tank top. The other was short and older, a gaunt, gray-faced man whose shorts hung slackly on his skinny hips.

I stepped in front of Angus and Irina and stuck out my hand. "Hi, how's it going? I'm Lynn."

"Stan," said the wide receiver. "This is Berto."

"Yo," said Berto.

Stan set a backpack down on the floor and pulled out a plastic bag. "Supplies," he said.

These turned out to be peanut-butter-and-jelly sandwiches on white bread with the crusts cut off, which Stan offered around in a cursory manner before he and Berto devoured them. Aside from Psyche, Sledge, and me, everyone was huddled around the diagram, nodding.

"Gerald says earliest tee-off is ten-fifteen," Berto said. "Get it?"

"Right."

"I still think we need to have a name," Berto said. "I was talking about this to some other people at the meeting, and they agreed with me."

"Go work with them, then," Stan said, and when Berto scowled at him, he scowled back. "The name doesn't matter."

"Can't claim responsibility if we don't got a name."

"We don't need to claim responsibility."

"They'll think it's just a bunch of fucking kids."

"Maybe we are a bunch of fucking kids," Angus said.

"That's bullshit," Berto said angrily. "And not all of us are kids, man." He reached into the bag and took another sandwich, shaking his head.

"No name, no claims," Angus said decisively. "Nothing matters but the action itself."

"What about, like, Citizens for Environmental Action? CEA," Berto mused, waving his sandwich in the air.

"Berto, let the name go."

"You're right, it's kind of bland. Okay, what about Earth Now? Kind of like Earth First, but different."

"Tell me what you guys are planning," I said.

"Excuse us," Angus said. He stood up and pulled me by the elbow into the kitchen. My back was against the fridge, and his face loomed close to mine: his red hair, his pale skin, all those freckles. "Do you understand that I'm doing you a favor?" he whispered.

"No," I whispered back.

"Wylie will be here, okay? He'll be with us tonight. So just tag along with the crowd."

"I'm more of a loner, generally speaking."

"Try," he said.

He bent down and kissed me then, gentle and unhurried, for a period of several minutes. I put up zero resistance. For some reason, the word "consent" rose over and over in the back of my mind, but I saw it as more substance than word: something liquid pouring over me, hot and wet, capillaries opened, skin flushed. Behind my eyelids the world turned red.

Afterwards, the group went on making their plans, although they apparently were keeping them vague in my presence. I was still curious but didn't ask any questions. The sandwiches finished, Berto went into the kitchen and rinsed out the plastic bag, then hung it up to dry. Looking around, I counted the sleeping bags rolled against the walls—four, including the one on the cot—and realized they were all living here. Beyond the occasional backpack and Irina's baby supplies, none of them had any belongings to speak of. It was bizarre and impressive at the same time. Most people know that we shouldn't live as wastefully as we do, but could never change their lives as drastically as these guys had. Irina was right: they were living differently.

I cleared a space on the counter and listened. Berto continued to obsess over names and was repeatedly, uselessly shushed. Irina sang low-voiced songs to her baby and nodded in agreement, though rarely was it clear about what. In the dark room—most of the light came through the bedroom blinds I'd opened—time stretched itself out, slowly.

Stan and Angus were talking about water: the dearth of it around the globe, our reckless overindulgence in it as consumers, its diversion by financial interests. The government encouraged individual citizens to reduce their residential water use while giving tax breaks to corporations whose water use was massive in comparison. We were groundwater overdrafting, taking more out of our water account than we had. In China the water table was dropping by a meter a year. The Nile Valley was drying up. The Athabasca Glacier was receding. The Aral Sea was gone. The Ogallala Aquifer that extended through the West had been overpumped for decades. Half the world's wetlands had been destroyed in the last century. The Yangtze, Ganges, and Colorado rivers rarely flowed all the way to the sea because of upstream withdrawals. Pollution was decimating freshwater fish species, twenty percent of which were endangered or extinct, and causing at least five million human deaths a year from disease. The world was rife with appalling scarcity, and people unwilling to face it.

These two had an array of statistics, and a familiarity with geography, that far exceeded mine, as well as a kind of fervor I'd seldom encountered after sophomore year of college. When Stan said that people were guilty of cynical and craven acts, he glanced at me, and I almost flinched; but then he looked back at Angus and went on to say that they planted desert shrubbery while insisting on hour-long showers every day. Soon everything would be ruined—most things already were ruined—and it was all our own fault.

"The world is going down the drain," Angus said, and laughed. But as they talked on and on, Stan flexed his significant arm muscles as if he wanted to pummel some sense into each water delinquent, one at a time. He predicted there was going to be a war over water. He said there *ought* to be.

Who knows how long we sat there? The conversation was circular; Irina's songs never ended; the dog whimpered and chased something in his sleep. Then my brother walked into the apartment—panting, flushed, bent beneath the weight of a massive backpack, carrying two six-packs of beer under each of his scrawny arms—and everybody fell quiet.

Without acknowledging anyone, Wylie set the beer down on the floor and slipped out of the backpack, which hit the floor with a clank of metal. Pine needles and other leaflike matter nested in his hair. He was wearing the same camp T-shirt he had on the night before, and smelled bad even from where I sat.

"I brought beer," he said.

"Where'd you get all that, man?" Berto said.

"Stole it from some frat boys," Wylie said, grinning, "then ran like hell."

"Excellent!" Berto stood up to give him a high five, and the tension in the room visibly dissipated. Everybody started drinking, including Irina and me. After a terse hello, Wylie acted as if I weren't there at all. Every once in a while Angus came over and put his arm around me or touched my shoulder, and I watched for my brother's reaction, but there wasn't one.

"Hey, Wylie, what do you think about this list of names I've got?" Berto asked, and they immediately plunged into a deep discussion of semantics and philosophical resonance and educational or promotional value. Irina and Stan disappeared and eventually came back with a bag of apples, a round of cheese, and several loaves of bread. The food wasn't bagged, and I didn't ask where it had come from.

As I was eating, Angus brought me another beer. "You're biting your lip," he said.

"He's ignoring me."

"Maybe you make him uncomfortable."

"I haven't said anything!"

"Maybe that's the problem."

"Why's he so weird?" I said.

Angus laughed as if this was the funniest thing he'd ever heard.

"You're not very patient," he said. "I like that."

I sighed. "I'm starting to think you're not very discriminating."

"Hey," Wylie called from across the room. I expected him to be looking at me and Angus, but he wasn't. "It's time," he said.

It was already dark. The group fanned out on foot. I saw Wylie and Stan turn the corner, heading south. Angus loped off down the street in the opposite direction without saying anything, and I found myself in step with Irina and Psyche.

"Where are we going?" I asked. In the lit windows of the houses we passed people were on display. A woman laughed drunkenly at a dinner party, the table crowded with candles, guests slumped in their chairs, the chaos of emptied plates. A cat peered angrily into the darkness from the back of a sofa. A young couple sat on a front-porch swing, smoking cigarettes and watching their sprinkler fan back and forth across the lawn. From most homes, falling over the sidewalks was the blue light of television.

"We'll be there soon," Irina said. "Stay by me and I will tell you what to do."

We walked for half an hour through quiet residential streets, seeing no trace of the others. I suspected that Irina's job was to divert me from whatever task was at hand. From within the sling Psyche gurgled softly to herself, as if forming opinions on the journey. Irina was humming—whether to herself or to her baby I couldn't tell, or what she might be thinking about, if she thought at all. Maybe she just followed Angus wherever he went, enjoying her television-induced fantasy of the great American desert.

"Who's Psyche's father?" I said.

Irina answered with one of her sweet smiles, and I was annoyed. How many smiles and nonanswers could a person take in a single day? The baby gurgled again, louder and with an edge in her voice, as if sensing the approach of a sensitive subject.

"I mean it," I said. "Who is it?"

"It is nobody who you know."

"Do you have to be so coy?"

"I don't know," she said. She stopped and looked at me with what appeared to be real consternation. "What is 'coy'?"

"It's . . . like lying."

Psyche's gurgle crescendoed to a pissed-off wail. She beat her tiny fist against Irina's chest and her cheeks flushed and swelled with reproach, tears streaming down her face. People came to their windows to see who was crying. Irina hushed her, swaying her hips and whispering into her child's tiny ears. Finally Psyche sniffled and buried her head against her mother's neck.

"Don't call me a liar," Irina said into the sudden quiet, hoisting the sling higher on her hips. "It's unkind."

"Look, I'm sorry."

"I said it was nobody you know."

"And I said I was sorry."

She then picked up the pace, and I had to work hard to keep up with her. She didn't look at me at all. We were in a nicer neighborhood now—well-tended gardens, chile ristras and rock lawns, wind chimes above doors, the spicy smoke of piñon wood rising through the air from backyard barbecues. Psyche was asleep.

"This way," Irina said, her voice low. We were at a service entrance to a golf-course development that wasn't far, if my geography was right, from the cemetery where my father was buried. She slipped through a gap in the fence—surprisingly agile, I thought, for a woman carrying a baby—and then skulked around the perimeter of a vast expanse dotted with huge houses. I thought I could see other forms moving around, but they might have just been shadows. It was very quiet. The air wafting over acres of thick, green grass smelled cooler and wetter—like a giant swatch of Connecticut now stranded, far from home, in New Mexico. Had I come across this place in the Northeast, it would have seemed pleasant and generically suburban, but now, after hearing all the talk about water, I saw it as decadent and even outrageous, ghastly as a fur coat.

Someone whispered my name in the darkness, and I almost tripped on my brother, who was crouching against the trunk of an elm tree. "Get down," he hissed, and Irina and I kneeled down beside him. He kept glancing over his shoulder, craning his head to look down a nearby street and even up at the sky. I'd never seen him so twitchy. A car came through the gated entrance, its headlights bearing down as if on purpose on where we huddled together behind the tree. Wylie was pressed up against me, and I could smell the sour stench of his breath and his unwashed hair.

After the car turned the corner and disappeared, Wylie pulled out flashlights from his backpack and handed one to each of us. "You're looking for glinting metal in the ground. Irina, go over to this side of the fairway. They should be spaced about twenty feet apart, okay?"

"Yes, of course," she said, rolling the *r*, her voice dreamy and sweet. He reached again into his backpack and pulled out something wrapped in a towel that turned out to be a wrench. She took it and left immediately, keeping close to the fence.

"You're ready?" he asked, as if I were a stranger he'd been assigned to buddy with. I nodded. After despairing of catching even a glimpse of him, it was strange to be sitting so close, and I held my breath for fear any movement might startle him. He unwrapped another towel and handed me a wrench. "Come on," he said.

We jogged across the golf course, playing the flashlights here and there, though my eyes were fixed on his dark ponytail.

Then he stopped short and pointed to the ground. "Put the wrench around the nozzle. If possible, you want to pull out the riser it's mounted on too, and the spring around it. But if you can't, just the nozzle's okay. Then go twenty feet and look for another nozzle with your flashlight."

I looked down at the wrench in my hand. "Is that really going to work?"

"According to my study of the diagrams, it should work perfectly."

"Wylie, this is stupid. Petty vandalism? Their insurance will cover the repairs, and it'll all be back to normal in a couple of days. What's the point?"

He glowered at me in the dark. His thin shoulders rose and fell with the swift rhythm of his breath, and his chest heaved in and out, almost too fast to see. "If you're not here to do this," he said, "then you should leave."

He looked like he hated me. But he was my brother, and I missed him in the elemental way that you can only miss your family or your home. I bent down and started to struggle with the wrench, and Wylie ran off in the dark.

I had no idea what I was doing, and was able to accomplish nothing at all with the wrench. Every time it slipped uselessly on the nozzle, I shook my head in amazement. Somehow Wylie was able to extract sprinklers from the ground, keep a twenty-year-old car running, and live successfully in the mountains for days or weeks at a time. I had no idea how he'd come by all these skills. Neither of our parents was mechanically inclined. My father, the scientist, was rendered helpless by the sight of a clogged toilet or a blown tire; after inspecting such problems, he'd shrug vaguely and leave them to my mother, who would then call the appropriate professional.

After a couple of minutes I stood up, leaving the wrench on the grass. Then I saw Angus—even from a distance I could make out his red hair—running toward me in his military posture and knees-up gait. He grabbed my hands and pulled me into a spin that landed us with a thud on the ground.

"I can't get the thing off," I told him.

"I know. I've got a bolt cutter," he said. He set to work, his hands fast and sure. A short while later the metal nozzle crunched and a small spray of water spurted from it onto the grass. He handed me the sprinkler head, then ran off to the next person.

I trudged down the fairway looking for Wylie. Down the slope ahead of me, a sand trap lay cut across the grass like a ditch, almost silver in the moonlight. Up by the green my brother was crouched over a sprinkler with a bolt cutter. His backpack was very well supplied.

"I'm done with mine," I said. "Angus helped me."

"You only did one?" he said. He ripped the sprinkler loose, an expression distantly related to a smile twisting his mouth, and ran off to find another.

For a few minutes I walked around the golf course without seeing anyone, still holding my sprinkler head, then found everybody gathered on the bank of a pond. We threw our confiscated goods into the water, where they splashed and sank, and Irina beamed at me and said, "Isn't it wonderful?" There was a lot of manic, happy whispering. I would have liked to join but didn't feel entitled, due to my total incompetence.

Stan led us to an exit road on the far side of the development, and Angus said, "Let's all scatter and meet at the apartment." Irina gestured for me to walk with her, but I shook my head and said, "I'm going with Wylie." For a second my brother stood there on the sidewalk tensed on the balls of his feet. Then he just shrugged, and people started peeling off.

The moon shone on the reflective surfaces of signs warning of children playing, one-way traffic, resident parking only. Slouched under his backpack, Wylie soldiered on, his fists clenching and unclenching with the rhythm of his hurried steps. I kept waiting for the absolute perfect thing to say to appear in my mind, and the longer I waited, the more absolute and perfect that thing had to be. Meanwhile his silence was so conspicuous that I could practically see it surrounding him. When he was little, instead of refusing to eat food he didn't like, Wylie just stuck it into a corner of his mouth, sitting at the table like a deranged gerbil, his cheek bulging with brussels sprouts until my mother, half laughing, ordered him to spit it out.

He went inside a 7-Eleven and came out with a bottle of Wild Turkey in a paper bag.

"Could we stop for a second?" I said.

"Why?"

"Because my feet hurt and I'm tired."

He shrugged again. On the next block, a small, disconsolate playground occupied a patch of dirt. I sat down on the merry-go-round, and Wylie stood punching a tetherball around its pole. We passed the bottle back and forth. Then he pulled a joint out of his pocket and lit it, and we shared that too. I felt slightly better.

"So what's next?" I finally said.

"Are you sure you want to know?"

"Didn't I just ask?"

He thrust his hands into the pockets of his jeans. "We've got a whole summer's worth of stuff planned. Our launch program will roll out activities on a regular schedule. A city experiencing escalating chaos will have to ask itself if its priorities are in the right place."

"You think so?"

He sat down next to me, and the merry-go-round shuddered slightly under even his delicate weight. We started to spin, slow but definite, pushing off with the soles of our shoes.

"Lynnie," he said, his voice urgent and guileless, "what does it mean to have beliefs if you don't act on them? Doesn't every single moment of our lives come with a choice attached? You might say these are philosophical questions with no practical bearing, but what I'm trying to tell you is that philosophical questions are the only questions there are." He lay back against the spinning platform and spread out his skinny arms, the cloth beneath his armpits yellowed with sweat.

"Where are you living?" I said.

"I sleep wherever. Sometimes I camp. I scrounge food from dumpsters. I don't want to get mired down in trappings. I don't want to consume."

"Except for Wild Turkey."

"Flexibility," he said, "is the difference between ideology and dogma."

Across the street, a light went off and slipped us further into darkness. I couldn't see his face anymore, and but for the rank smell I might have doubted he was there. I let my feet drag in the dirt to stop the spinning. "Listen," I said. "Speaking of flexibility, I really wish you'd come home. Just for like an hour or something."

"I can't do that."

"Wylie, you're being so stupid," I said. "Of course you can."

We wandered slowly back to the apartment, talking about nothing in particular. Sirens rose and fell in the distance, and the wind flapped my hair across my face and into my mouth. By the time we arrived the party was in full swing, music playing, Irina slow-dancing with Angus, the baby cradled in between them. There was some Wild Turkey left, and also beer and gin. The dog, annoyed by all the commotion, got up and padded into the other room to sleep.

Seven

We all lay sprawled on sleeping bags, the sounds of breath and snores mingling in the quiet with the rising clatter of birds. Sledge woke me by licking my ankle and prodding his wet nose repeatedly against my foot. Irina was next to me, her head inadequately pillowed on Wylie's stomach, with Psyche pillowed in turn on her more ample body. Angus was nowhere to be seen. Sledge licked me again, this time on the cheek, and whined in my ear. I didn't know why he always picked me. I rolled over, got a dangerous close-up of Stan's hairy armpit, and rolled back again.

It was my second hangover in as many days, but either I hadn't drunk as much last night or I was getting used to the condition. I felt surprisingly fine. I opened the front door and followed the dog down the stairs to the gravel parking lot. The sun was bright yet mild, the street empty, and morning glories I hadn't noticed before bloomed full and blue. Sledge nosed around in the weeds and relieved himself on a prickly-looking shrub with orange flowers. Above me, the apartment door opened and Wylie stepped onto the landing, squinting. "Are you leaving?"

I shook my head. "Not unless you come with me."

He made a face. "You can't make me."

"I can try."

He walked down the stairs, glacier-slow, scowling all the

while. At the bottom he called to the dog, who ignored him, being otherwise occupied pawing the dirt and then sniffing it, over and over. Finally he lost interest and trotted to my side, sitting down on his back legs, his face attentive and alert, apparently awaiting further instructions.

"Man, he really likes you."

"It's unrequited." I climbed the stairs, and Sledge followed me. I made like I was going inside, and when he scampered in, I closed the door behind him. On the other side of the plywood I could hear his shocked and aggrieved complaints. Having outwitted him gave me an undignified but real sense of satisfaction. Then I went back down and faced Wylie. "Listen," I said. "You can come now or a week from now, but you do have to come home. I mean it, I'm not leaving until you do. I honestly don't care if you want to vandalize golf courses and eat food out of dumpsters, but you can't not talk to Mom. Seriously, you can't do that."

In the ensuing silence a jet plane cut across the sky, heading for the Air Force base, trailing a precise white line.

My brother turned his scowl to the ground, to the plane, and reluctantly back to me. "She doesn't understand."

"I don't care," I said, holding up the keys to the Caprice. "The car's parked on campus. Let's go."

We pulled up at the condo just as my mother was leaving for work. At the sound of the car maneuvering boatlike into the driveway she turned from locking the front door and froze.

After a single night in Wylie's apartment the small condo loomed like a four-star resort: elegantly furnished, indulgently large, with washed windows and manicured grounds. For a second I felt a glimmer of revulsion, an almost physical sensation akin to nausea, or a sneeze, and shook my head at my new sympathies. I was turning into the eco-freak Patty Hearst.

Wylie got out of the car and faced her, saying nothing. She looked like she wanted to scratch his eyes out; he looked like he was waiting for her to do it. I felt ignored and beside the point, which almost came as a relief.

"You look terrible," she said to Wylie.

"So do you," he said.

I could see him looking her up and down, passing judgment on everything from her office job to the big brown purse weighing down her right shoulder. Back in Brooklyn, on the receiving end of all those late-night messages, I thought that Wylie had patterned himself on our father, with his scientific terminology and pseudo-academic pursuits. But now, seeing the two of them together, it occurred to me that he was much more like our mother, with the same rigid insistence on getting his way, the same tendency to withhold his emotions from the world. She unlocked the door and held it open.

"You're coming in this house, right now, and you're not leaving until I say so."

Wylie glanced at me and snorted, and I said, "Please."

As he passed her, she wrinkled her nose and told him in a level, furious voice that he looked disgusting and smelled like a farmhand, and that she shuddered to think by what behavior he had come by such a smell. She said she hadn't raised him to live in a ditch and disappear for months at a time, and asked whether by doing these things he hoped to send her to an early grave. "Is that your goal?" she kept saying. She elaborated on this theme for the next half hour, while Wylie stood in the living room, head bowed, in the posture of a martyr. Finally, as the barrage showed no sign of letting up, he started for the white couch, and she said, crisply, "If you think you're going to set your filthy behind on my clean furniture, then you think wrong."

She called Francie at the office to explain she'd be late due to "unforeseen circumstances," and then turned on the shower and stood outside the bathroom tapping her foot until Wylie stepped inside.

While he was showering she made scrambled eggs, fried bacon, brewed coffee, and put bread in the toaster—each gesture, from stirring the eggs to putting juice on the table, executed with the oppressive accuracy of the truly angry. Not knowing what else to do, I set the table, which was getting to be my main contribution to the household.

When Wylie came into the kitchen his hair was flowing loosely down below his shoulders, still wet and gleaming red-brown in the morning sun. He was wearing a pair of khaki shorts and a plaid short-sleeved shirt I recognized—my heart turning over in my chest—as my father's, and he smelled like strawberry shampoo. Our mother nodded at a chair, and he sat down, in what seemed like the first step in some ritual indoctrination. I kept waiting for her to bring out the clippers and shave his head, like at boot camp, but instead she brought out a spatula and served eggs. Wylie and I ate enveloped in stiff silence, throughout which she would not stop staring at him, even as she sipped mechanically at a cup of coffee. I shifted in my seat. She stared and stared.

If Wylie noticed it, he gave no sign. He tucked his long hair delicately behind his ears and ate two servings of bacon and eggs. The silence didn't seem to bother him even a bit. He put away five pieces of toast, an entire sliced tomato, and three glasses of juice.

When he finished, my mother ordered us to do the dishes, then wiped her lips with a napkin and gathered up her purse and keys.

"I have to go to work now, because that's what responsible people do," she said. "You will be here tonight when I get home at five." She waited for Wylie to answer, but he didn't. "Lynnie," she added, and I nodded to make it clear I understood.

The Missing Person

. . .

The silence lasted while I did the dishes and Wylie dried them and put everything away. I was looking forward to hitting the couch and checking on my old friends in celebrity television, with maybe a side trip to the Weather Channel. But Wylie'd started jittering—tapping his toes, just like our mother, and glancing out the window every fifteen seconds—and I felt compelled to pick up where her staring had left off.

He looked at me, annoyed. "Are you going to do this all day?"

"You heard Mom. If you leave, my life won't be worth living."

"Lynn, leave me alone. Where I'm going, you can't follow."

"And where is that?"

"To the bathroom."

"So you're not leaving, right? Promise me."

Wylie sighed, and I stared at him until he nodded.

"Okay," he said, "promise."

I let him go. I stretched out on the couch, feeling drowsy— still tired from the night before—and when I woke up there was a coin of drool on the couch cushion and a woman on television extolling the long-lasting clean of a brand-new detergent. The house seemed ominously quiet.

I jumped up, checked the bathroom and the bedroom where I'd been staying, then doubled back to the living room and kitchen. It wasn't like there were a lot of places he could hide, but I kept circling through the condo, purposeless and rushed, the way you do in dreams. The Caprice still sat in the driveway, its ivory paint glowing dully in the yellow light of the afternoon. I hopped up and down on the baking asphalt and then headed around back, where my mother maintained a small patch of lawn, and on a shady strip of ground along the side of the house I found Wylie, still moderately clean, snoring in the dirt.

One arm was flung over his side in a gesture of total exhaustion. He looked as if he'd literally fallen down asleep. For a couple minutes I sat in the weeds and studied him: the veins roping down his tanned legs, the slack fabric of my father's too-big shirt against his chest, his nicks and bruises and scars. With shorter hair and glasses, I thought, he'd look eerily like the pictures I'd seen of my father as a young man. Did my mother see this too, every time she looked at him? I didn't know how she could stand it. Seeing him now, exposed and asleep and alive, was almost more than I could handle.

I reached out and flicked my index finger against the thickly callused sole of his right foot, which he moved. I flicked the other foot and he moved that one too, then moaned softly. I flicked his arm and said, "Hey. Wake up." He nestled his cheek deeper into the dirt, apparently too comfortable to budge. "Let's play cards," I said. "Or Monopoly. I'm bored."

After some more flicking and a couple of well-placed pokes, he opened his bleary eyes. The circles beneath them had faded to a vaguer blue. "What are you, six years old?"

"I bet I can still beat you at hearts."

"In your dreams," he said.

"My years away from the game have only sharpened my thirst for victory," I told him.

He sat up. He'd tied his hair back again, and although it was still shiny and thick, he'd managed to rub some dirt and weeds into it during his nap. He was looking like his old self again. "Youth and ability are on my side," he said. "Let's go."

We spent the afternoon playing cards and drinking orange juice in the quiet living room, listening to so-called edgy pop music on the radio. I had the feeling that our truce would hold as long as I didn't mention guerrilla tactics, mother's wishes, alternative lifestyles, or weird friends. As a result conversation was limited. We stuck to the game and, in a hobby that dated back to childhood, the construction of elaborate snacks from whatever we could find in the kitchen. After a multi-course meal involving peanut butter, chips and salsa, bananas, ice cream, and popcorn dusted with Parmesan cheese, another round of napping ensued.

Our mother came home at the dot of five, and she didn't come alone. Two seconds after I heard her pull into the driveway, a second car parked alongside the curb. David Michaelson stepped out into the street wearing another Western-style shirt and blue jeans held up with an elephantine silver buckle that would have been useful for attracting the attention of search-and-rescue planes overhead. Two young men then emerged, each a variation on the theme of David Michaelson: beefy, with dark curly hair and thick chests, but slimmer and clean-shaven. They had to be Donny and Darren, the sports stars.

"Oh, God," I said.

Wylie didn't even look up from his most recent snack, an open-face sandwich layered with tuna fish, cheddar cheese, shredded carrots, and olives. "And you wonder why I don't like to come home."

The Michaelsons helped unload countless grocery bags from our mother's car and conveyed them up to the front door, as Wylie and I braced ourselves in the living room.

Our mother came inside first and greeted us with a brisk smile. "Children," she said.

We were having a dinner party. Our mother established head-quarters in the kitchen and ordered everyone about: arranging for the unstocking of groceries, the placement of appetizers, the ordering of cocktails.

"Lynn," David said. "Wylie. What can I offer you both to drink? I believe we've got a full bar."

I looked at Wylie, who sat with his head bowed, licking tuna juice off his thumb. "I'll have some wine," I said. "I'm sure Wylie wants a beer."

"Alrighty then!" David slapped a large hand on my shoulder and went back into the kitchen, crossing paths with his sons, who sat down and slouched back in their chairs, so far that their muscular legs were almost parallel with their heads. Their faces were pale. I knew they both spent a lot of time playing hockey, but couldn't remember which was Donny and which was Darren.

"So," one of them said. "Long time no see." He was wearing shorts and a pair of flip-flops with little fishes stuck on the plastic stems between his toes.

I gave them what I hoped was a polite smile. "Since we used to live next door, I guess," I said.

"Yep," the other one said. "Long time."

When their father came back with the drinks, I drank half of mine and asked them how school was going. One of them launched into a complicated story about a fierce rivalry with another team, a saga of violence and retribution that had been going on all season. This led to a greatest-hits list of reminiscences, with highlights about practical jokes and personal vendettas. "So then we go, right?" Donny or Darren said. "And he body-checks me? And gets thrown out of the game?"

"That landed Donny in the hospital," David said to me. He was sipping from a glass of red wine, and the bottom of his mustache was wet. "He had to have sixteen stitches. This kid was violent."

"And that's when Darren hatched his nefarious plan."

"What was that?" Wylie asked.

Michaelson Sr. sat down on the arm of the couch, next to me, with his legs crossed and his arm stretched along the back. The last time I'd seen him, over enchiladas, he was counseling an intervention for Wylie, but he didn't seem about to confront him now.

"My plan involved a frog," Darren said. "Actually, several frogs."

"Where we live—you guys remember—we had a lot of frogs in our backyard," Donny explained. "We captured them, and put 'em in a shoebox and then stuck 'em in his shoes, so when he took off his skates, right . . ." He had to stop, since he was choking on his own laughter.

"He squishes these little frogs with his feet!"

"Oh, man! You should've seen the expression on his face!"

All three Michaelsons were paralyzed now, clutching their stomachs and listing from side to side, their laughter coming in breathless hoots.

"And the smell!" Darren said.

"Wow," I said. "That's really gross."

The brothers bobbed their heads up and down in asthmatic hilarity.

"Yeah," Donny finally got out. "Gross!"

"So, you're saying you killed them in advance?" I said.

"Well, yeah, obviously. Otherwise they would've jumped out of the shoes."

"How'd you kill the frogs?" Wylie said. I glanced at him, but his tone and face were set and calm.

"We, um, squished them."

"But carefully, you know, so that they'd still be squishy in the shoes." Darren wiped a tear from his eye and shook with a few final tremors.

David Michaelson looked at Wylie. "Now, I realize it might not be too politically or animalistically correct," he said, "but you've got to admit it's pretty funny."

"You had to see the guy," Darren said, "running around the locker room with frog parts stuck to his feet, yelling 'What the fuck! What the fuck!'"

"I thought I was gonna die it was so funny," Donny added.

"They were probably toads," Wylie said.

"Is that a fact?" David said.

"Where you live it was more likely to have been toads," Wylie said. "Wide and fat, with warty skin? Their habitat's around the Northeast Heights. Some of them are desert toads. Down by the Rio Grande there are a lot of bullfrogs, but up where you are there's less water, so, yeah, I think you actually killed a lot of toads."

"Toads, huh?" Darren said. He thrust his hands in his pockets.

"Ah, well," David said, "boys will be boys."

"And toads will be toads," Darren said. Donny elbowed him in the ribs and said, "'What the fuck! What the fuck!'" and they both cracked up again.

Our mother came out into the room, smiling another brisk and terrible smile. "Who'd like another drink?" she said.

"I would," Wylie and I said at the same time.

I followed her back to the kitchen, where things were simmering in multiple pots. The oven was on and onions were turning golden in a sauté pan. Everything smelled excellent, and it occurred to me that she was capable of much better cooking than anything she'd served me so far this summer. In the other room I could hear the Michaelsons launching into yet another story guaranteed to please Wylie, probably involving the torture of puppies or the wanton discarding of recyclable materials.

"I think it's going well, don't you?" my mother said.

I poured myself another hefty glass of wine. "Are you out of your mind?"

"No, I don't believe I am. And I'll thank you not to speak to me in that fashion."

"Sorry," I said. "But seriously, Mom, what were you thinking? Can't we just have one night, the three of us? I finally get Wylie to come home, and this is what you do?"

"David is part of my life now, and you children have to accept that."

"So's David's wife, and you didn't invite her."

She kept her back to me, tasting something with her finger.

I considered repeating myself, in case she hadn't heard me, then thought better of it and headed back to the living room, where a troublesome silence had taken over.

Wylie was sitting with his head practically between his knees, clutching himself for dear life.

David looked up at me with an expression of concern, placed a hand on Wylie's back, and said, "He's not feeling very well, I don't think."

I saw a shudder run down my brother's spine.

"I'm fine," Wylie muttered from between his knees.

"Maybe you should lie down or something," Donny said.

"I think dinner's almost ready," I offered helpfully.

"I'm fine," Wylie said again, and uncurled his head. "Just a little nauseous."

"It's probably all those snacks," I said.

"No," he said, "it isn't."

We sat there sipping disconsolately from our drinks until my mother announced that dinner was served. There were linen napkins on the table and the good china we once used only at Christmas. For a second the world slipped, loosened around its edges, and I was standing in the past: the smell and heat of candles, the white tablecloth with green trim, my father's face flushed as he lifted his chin and laughed at something Wylie or I said. All of this—this present day—seemed imaginary and flimsy compared to that memory; it shocked me to think that he was dead and the rest of us, here in my mother's house, were still alive. Then I sat down.

"Let us pray," David said. His sons bowed their heads, as did my mother. Wylie and I looked at each other across the table.

"Dear God," David went on. His voice was relaxed and familiar, as if God were a neighbor with whom he was accustomed to discussing baseball or the weather. "When we sit down in a lovely home with a lovely meal prepared by a lovely woman, in the company of family and friends, we remember to be grateful to you, Lord, and take it as a sign of your continuing and blessed grace which you bestow upon us every day, and we thank you for it. Amen."

"Amen," said everybody except me and Wylie.

Across the table, Darren winked at me and said, "Good grub, good meat—thanks, God, let's eat."

We were served a fine and complicated meal involving pork tenderloin and braised vegetables and sauces and sides, and I would have eaten a lot had I not spent the entire day emptying the kitchen cupboards. Instead I drank several more glasses of red wine and picked at my food. Fortunately, the Michaelsons were there to pick up the slack, and their appetites were substantial. Wylie, to my amazement, continued to eat without stopping, methodically clearing one helping and serving himself another, as if he were a camel or some other animal capable of storing enough food to last through the lean weeks to come. Seated at the head of the table, our mother poured wine and proposed toasts: to summer, to children reunited with their parents, to old neighbors, et cetera. From the other end of the table David toasted her back, the wet hem of his mustache glinting in the candlelight. Outside, the red sun glowered low in the sky, the horizon soupy and green, the world colored like an infection. We ate.

The first half hour passed without incident. Our mother

told stories about the travel industry, describing the outrageously false claims made by fleabag hotels charging luxury prices and the insufferable demands of cheapskate clients who wanted to tour the world for the price of a bus ticket to El Paso. Even Wylie laughed. David asked me how my studies were going, and his boys leaned forward to hear my answer.

"I'm working on my dissertation, I guess."

"You must be smart," said Donny.

"Of course she's smart," David said. "You know, Lynn, I love art. Whenever I'm in a foreign city, the first place I go is the museum."

"Really," I said. I assumed my mother had told him to say this.

"Lynn's loved paintings since she was a little kid," Wylie said. "She used to just stand there and stare at them, like she was sleepwalking or something. You could talk to her and she wouldn't even hear you."

"You loved *paintings* when you were a kid?" Darren said.

"When I was a kid," Donny said, "I loved baseball and, I don't know, making fun of girls."

"Some things never change," Darren said philosophically, then elbowed his brother, and they both laughed.

David wiped his mustache delicately with his napkin and patted his belly as though complimenting it on a job well done.

Meanwhile Donny, Darren, and Wylie all used pieces of bread to clear their plates of any last vestiges and sat back with an air of regretful finality.

Donny grinned at Wylie across the table. "For a skinny guy, you can put a lot away."

"It's probably his first square meal in weeks," our mother said.

"If I don't eat real regular, I get irritable and off-balance," Donny volunteered.

"Now that makes sense," she said, looking at Wylie.

"I feel good now," Wylie told her quietly.

"I'm sure glad to hear it," David said. "You were giving your mother quite a scare."

"Was I?" Wylie said.

"Now, son, you know you were. Running around with all those—" here he paused, and smoothed his mustache with his right index finger—"antisocial types."

I watched Wylie smile at this, first gently and then widely.

"Those antisocial types," he said quietly, "are good people doing important work, and they're my best friends."

"Those people are spoiled brats and trust-fund babies. I'll bet you dollars to donuts that they're living off their parents while they run around thinking they're righteous because they spike trees."

"You don't know that they spike trees," I said. "You don't know anything about them."

"You'd be surprised what I know," David told me. "I know it's not all fun and games and some big party like you kids think it is." His lips were sputtering beneath his mustache. "I know that there are serious issues at stake."

"Like hell you do," I said. I was drunk.

At the end of the table, my mother covered her face with her hands. "Why are you defending those people?"

"Why shouldn't she defend them?" Wylie said.

"Now, listen, young lady," David said. "I'm as environmentally sensitive as the next person—"

"Sure you are, when the next person's a toad killer," Wylie said.

"What's that mean?" Donny said, and Darren shifted in his seat.

"Toad killer," Wylie said slowly. He was still smiling, his jaw clenched, and the words issued from between his teeth in a whisper. He stood up. In the flickering candlelight his smile shimmered with rage. "As in one who kills toads just for the fun of it."

"Sit down," our mother said. He ignored her. Across from me, Darren wiped a finger over his plate and licked off some final morsel. His father rose heavily to his feet and held up his palms in what I guessed he thought was a soothing gesture. But it had the opposite effect, and Wylie whirled on our mother and said, "You don't understand anything." I said his name, and he looked at me and shook his head, then ran out of the house in his clean, bare, callused feet.

I was the only one who went outside, calling his name again, twice. I knew he heard me, but he didn't turn around, running silently down the street and disappearing around the corner.

Inside, my mother was shaking her head, David had his arm around her, and the sons were doing dishes. I couldn't stand to stay in there. I went back outside and sat on the trunk of the Caprice. Lights around me blinked on and off: distant headlights showing through the gaps between houses, people drawing the curtains on a window down the street.

Later, much later, I fell asleep with the nagging feeling that there was something I could have done but didn't, might have prevented but let slip—a slim thought that kept getting away from me, like something glimpsed out of the corner of my eye, but when I turned my head, it was gone.

Eight

July came, summer bursting into full bloom, the long heat of arid days and the brown edge of wilt around plants. The city announced a water shortage and promoted discounts on rock-garden materials and low-flush toilets. On the Fourth, my mother and David invited me along to watch fireworks explode over the muddy dregs of the Rio Grande, but I declined. Instead I sat in a lawn chair in her tiny backyard listening to the manic end of a bipolar swing: the quiet, crickety hush that usually blanketed my mother's neighborhood gave way to the whistle of bottle rockets, the screech of tires, the occasional backfire, hoots and hollers of people driving by. Children calling out the names of other children. A vodka and tonic sweated peacefully in my hand.

Of all the seasons, summer felt the most like childhood. I was thinking about vacations when Wylie and I were little, the four of us piling into the car for road trips to Colorado, my dad's family in Chicago, or, once, the Grand Canyon. My father loved maps, and every night in the motel room he'd unfold one and draw a blue line over the road we'd traveled that day. One time, in a small town on the outskirts of Denver, I woke up in the middle of the night in a strange motel room, dizzy, entranced, sick with fever. My brother was breathing noisily next to me—he was a mouth breather—but he looked like a stranger, and so did my parents in their bed. Laid out on the desk was an unfolded map tracing our path from Albuquerque, heading north, but the world was a puzzle, the geography foreign: I didn't recognize the route we'd taken or the location of home. My father rolled over and asked what I was doing.

"I'm trying to do my homework," I told him, "but I don't *understand* it." He pressed a large palm flat against my forehead and then scooped me up. Shivering in my nightgown, I fought against him because it hurt my skin to be touched, and a minute later I threw up in his lap. He was three years older than I was now.

"And so what," I said out loud, to myself, in the dark. I finished my drink. In a lull of quiet between illegal fireworks I heard the crunching sound of someone walking around the side of the condo. I stood up and found myself on the receiving end of a bear hug given by Angus Beam, my cheek smashed against his bare shoulder, my feet momentarily off the ground. I'd forgotten the odor of his body—part close skin, part distant chemical—and the dense spray of orange-brown freckles across his grinning face.

"Happy patriotic holiday," he said, releasing me. "Need anything plumbed?"

"Actually, there *is* a strange smell coming from the garbage disposal. Like a nasty, rotten kind of smell. Can you help with that?"

"I know just the thing," he said. "Get me a lemon and two glasses of ice."

"You're kidding."

He went into the kitchen without answering. I brought him the supplies, and he cut the lemon in half with a Leatherman he pulled out of his back pocket.

"Watch," he said. He poured a glass of ice down the disposal, switched it on—a ferocious, grinding sound—and turned on the cold water. He ground up half the lemon, too, then wiped his hands. "You're all set."

I stuck my nose over the sink, and the smell was gone. "Hey, it worked," I said. "What's the other glass of ice for?"

"I was hoping you'd make me a drink with it."

His eyes shone. He was the only person around who ever seemed truly happy to see me. We poured vodka, tonic, ice, and lemon juice into his water bottle and went for a walk, holding hands like a couple of civilized people.

The sky was fizzing. Small green rockets popped and showered in the air, and every once in a while a big white explosion was followed by a single bang, like a bomb going off, whose sound hit me right in the chest and made me shudder. At these moments Angus squeezed my hand. We drifted through the streets, not talking much. The smell of innumerable barbecues sailed out on the night air. Cars swerved recklessly through the streets and ran red lights, their stereos pumping. Everybody seemed to be drunk. On the enclosed front porch of an adobe bungalow, the windows of the house itself dark, a dog was shaking piteously and howling in fear. I told Angus about Wylie defining "toad killer" in his argument with my mother's boyfriend—I stumbled over the word, but couldn't think what else to call him, really—and he practically keeled over laughing. He was wearing jean cutoffs, and when he slapped his leg his hand left a white imprint on his skin.

"Those people sound horrible," he said when he finally straightened up. "How do you stand living in that boxy little place with the boxy little backyard and those horrible people? Why don't you leave?"

The idea had never occurred to me, though I wasn't about to admit it. "I don't know," I said. "My mom—"

"Your mom thinks I'm the devil."

"I didn't know you two had met."

"We haven't," Angus said, grabbing my hand again.

We kept walking, in silence now, until we came to the gate of a small, run-down cemetery with crooked graves whose colorful fake flowers competed against an army of weeds. We went inside and looked around, examining all the old Spanish names. Angus was quiet, and I knew he'd decided this was a romantic and memorable context for a kiss. I didn't think this kind of seriousness suited him as well as laughter did, and didn't feel like being the target of his courtship, so I got it all over with by kissing him.

We stood there kissing under the moon. I touched the nape of his neck, where delicate hairs lay slick with sweat. His skin radiated heat against the palm of my hand, and his arms came around my waist to pull me closer. There was a flash of red behind my eyes.

"Let's go to a motel," I told him.

"We could just stay here. It'll be gorgeous and unique."

I stepped back, although I maintained a gentle grip on his hands. "It'll be more gorgeous in a motel. Also, comfortable."

"Come on." He was grinning again, and running a hand through his hair, now all helter-skelter points. "Let's make love in the face of death. Let's feel alive."

"I'm leaving," I said. "Are you coming?"

He crossed his tanned arms. "I love the way you make unreasonable demands."

"You've got a real knack for compliments," I said.

I loved the sterile anonymity of the motel, its small bathtub and plywood dresser. We could be anywhere, I said to myself. We *are* anywhere. An hour later, Angus in the shower, I left a message on my mother's answering machine.

"It's me. Lynn. Listen, I'm going to be away for a few days but I don't want you to worry. I'll be fine. So will Wylie—I mean, I think he will, not that I'm with him right now or anything. Okay, see you. Bye."

Angus went out for a six-pack of beer and a pizza, and we sprawled on the bed watching CNN. Every once in a while he'd run the palm of his hand from my neck down my back, then start over again from the bottom. I fell asleep to the weather forecast, blue currents and red arrows crossing a map of the world.

I woke up to see Angus returning to the room from somewhere. He stood beside the bed jiggling keys, his white coveralls gleaming in the shadows.

"Where did you go?" I said. "How long have you been gone?"

"I have to work today," he said. "Want to come with me?"

"You really work?"

This seemed to offend him, and he stood up straighter, fussily adjusting the fit of his coveralls. "I told you, I'm a plumber. Today I've got an out-of-town job. We can go for a drive. It'll be fun."

"I don't have the Caprice, remember? We walked here."

"I went and got the van," he said.

"The *what*?"

He opened the curtains, unleashing massive sunlight through which, squinting, I could make out what looked like an enormous eggplant parked in front of the room. When my eyes adjusted I saw it was a dull purple van with PLUMBARAMA written in white letters on its side. Small drips of white paint burst around the letters, symbolizing either the excitement of plumbing or the reality of bursting pipes, I wasn't sure which.

I got dressed, and short minutes later we were cruising on the highway with Angus singing along to "My Way" from the Sinatra tape he must've recovered, along with his hat, from Wylie's car. He had a surprisingly pleasant voice, trained and lilting, and could hit the high notes without any apparent strain. The city spread into the desert, miles of development, chain restaurants and movie complexes and subdivisions, before petering out. On either side the land lay brown and skeletal, starved of grass or trees, under the enormous sky and the relentless sun.

Fifteen minutes later we passed a billboard with a background of lush, verdant lawns and the profile of a man in white clothes swinging a golf club: FUTURE SITE OF SHANGRI-LA. I laughed out loud.

"What?" Angus said, interrupting his performance of "Night and Day."

"They're building Shangri-la out here," I said. "Did you know?"

"Oh, I know all about it," he said, flushing red down to his neck. "Developing this land into a golf course is insane. It's a profanation."

"It definitely seems like an odd choice of location."

"Albuquerque's going to run out of water within twenty years. No water. *None.* The whole city shouldn't even be here, but what are they going to do about it? Build another golf course. And do you have any *idea* how much water a golf course uses? Do you think they're going to forgo the grass and use native plants?"

I guessed these weren't rhetorical questions. "I doubt it," I said.

"They're leasing the land from a pueblo, and you can't blame *them.* Of course they need to make money—but do they have to make it from this?"

"I don't know."

"It burns me up," he said, his face so red that it might well have burst into flame.

Five minutes later he took an exit that led past a gas station and then turned into a parking lot full of cars in front of a windowless gray building, flat and square as a storage compartment. The small neon sign outside read SUNRISE CASINO, with spikes of sunrays poking up from the o, but the sign was turned off and didn't glow in the late-morning glare. Inside, it still looked like a storage compartment, without decorations or pictures or even a carpet, a place stripped down to the barest of uses. Country music was playing, dim and static, on a bad sound system. Against the walls stood slot machines where people of diverse race and age sat smoking and pulling levers, the smoke hanging thick as cobwebs in the air over the blackjack and roulette tables in the center of the room. With his white overalls and healthy glow Angus looked alien here, and I expected we'd draw some unfriendly stares. But as he strode by purposefully, nodding to people here and there, they nodded casually back. He'd been here before.

I followed him down a green hallway with linoleum floors to a closed door whose black sign said MANAGER. Angus turned, sudden and intent, and kissed me, then knocked and opened the door.

"Gerald Lobachevski, man of many hats," he said, stepping inside. "This is Lynn Fleming, woman of my life."

Reclining in a chair behind the plywood desk was the middle-aged Native American man I'd seen at Wylie's place that first night—the same thick glasses and braided hair and turquoise jewelry. He gave the distinct impression, looking at me, of being unimpressed. I found myself reaching up to tuck my hair behind my ears.

"Wylie's sister," he finally said.

The Missing Person

I sighed. "Yes," I admitted.

"You look like him."

I had nothing to say to this. Angus sat down on the corner of the desk, next to a stapler and a beige rotary telephone. The office had gray cement walls and no windows.

"Scrawny. Same color hair. How'd you get involved with this guy?" Gerald cocked his head in Angus's direction.

"Gerald," Angus said.

"I was looking for Wylie," I said.

"Did you find him?"

"Yeah, I found him."

"But now you're hanging around with this guy here."

"I guess so."

"Well," Angus said, "show me what you need done."

"Do you gamble?" Gerald said to me, ignoring him.

"Excuse me?"

"Blackjack, slots, craps, roulette."

"Not really," I said.

Gerald reached into a desk drawer, pulled out several rolls of quarters, and held them out to me. "Give it a whirl," he said, "while I put this fellow to work."

I felt dismissed. "Thanks," I said.

Back in the gaming room, I watched people playing the slots. A woman in a red sweatsuit got up from her seat and wagged her chin in my direction. "I'm going to the ladies'," she told me. "You can have it."

I played for a while, and there was a rhythm to the clicking of the machine and the movements of the levers, a consonance and ringing, that I imagined was as addictive as the thought of winning or losing. Apples, oranges, cherries, apples, oranges, cherries. The wild card slot. I couldn't ever get a match, and lost all of Gerald's money in a matter of minutes. Since it was going back to him anyway, I wasn't too concerned. The people around me worked on their games as if in a trance, hunched over machines or tables, hardly speaking, every so often sipping from vat-sized cups of Coke. A wailing country song halted mid-lament, and "Night and Day" came on.

It was noon, and I hadn't eaten, but there was no food at the casino. Outside, the heat was malicious and extreme, and the wind blew a blinding dust into my face as I trudged up the road to the gas station. The girl behind the register looked no older than thirteen, and she handled each transaction with superb speed, her fingers flying as she counted back the change for lottery tickets and cigarettes. There were wizened burritos baking under the light of a heating element, and some crusty yellow popcorn that didn't look much better. I settled for a bag of pretzels and a soda, then sat down on the shaded curb outside.

It occurred to me that Angus could easily drive off and leave me here, that in fact I knew very little about him, that I didn't have enough money to call a cab, that there weren't any cabs around here anyway.

Trucks barreled down the road, their grilles and fenders shining in the sun.

A truck pulling a horse trailer parked at the pumps in front of me, and a stocky, dark-haired driver looked me up and down before heading inside. From the trailer came sounds of chewing and sneezing, so I went around the back to look. At least ten goats were packed tight in there, and they stared back at me and bleated their complaints.

The door to the shop opened, and the driver stuck his head out. "What you want there, lady?"

"Nothing," I said. "Just curious."

I took this as a sign to head back to the casino, the blown grit pelting my bare legs. I could see Angus, unmistakable in his white coveralls, standing on the naked brown land behind the building talking to Gerald, who kept gesturing toward the south. Angus was nodding, his hands on his hips, and when he saw me he grinned. Gerald, on the other hand, turned around and looked significantly less happy to see me.

"Hello," I said. "What's going on back here?"

"Just finishing up," Angus said. His coveralls were spotless.

"I don't know a lot about plumbing," I said, "but you're not even dirty."

"Easy jobs today," Gerald said. For the first time, he smiled, and his whole face changed; behind his thick glasses, his brown eyes looked suddenly warm. "A few leaky faucets is all."

"Even so," I said.

"I'm like a tightrope walker," Angus said, " and the coveralls are my net. I have them just in case, but I never fall."

"Hah. He's a kidder, this guy," Gerald said to me. "I've seen him plenty grimy, don't you worry."

"So did you win us a million dollars?"

"I lost everything," I said. "I had to sell the van."

"Glad to hear it," Angus said. He put one arm around my shoulder and extended the other to Gerald, who shook it. "We'll be off."

We walked back through the casino, Angus carrying a toolbox this time, waving to all and sundry. Most people ignored him but a few, including the woman who'd given up her slot machine for me, glanced up and smiled. She had returned to the same machine, and there was a bucket full of quarters in her lap, probably all the money I'd put into it. She saw me looking at the bucket and winked.

As we got into the van, I was still trying to figure out what Angus had been doing there. "How long have you known Gerald, anyway?" I said.

He shrugged. "Nobody really *knows* Gerald Lobachevski," he said. "I just work for him every once in a while."

"What kind of name is Lobachevski, anyway?"

Angus started the van. "His father was some Russian anthropologist—pretty famous, supposedly. Came to New Mexico to do research at a pueblo and had a little romance. He wound up leaving again before Gerald was born. I don't think Gerald ever even met the man, but he likes having the name. He likes to be different from everybody else."

I was going to ask more questions, but became distracted when I realized that instead of turning back toward town, Angus was driving north.

"Aren't we going back?" I said.

"Now why would we do that?" he said, and winked. Then he turned up the music, which was no longer Sinatra but something classical I didn't recognize.

"Because we're in the middle of nowhere?"

"I wish that were true," he said. "But it's not."

The landscape changed from brown to red, with green pine trees unfurling their branches. We were in the mountains now, and I rolled down the windows to let in the cool air. There were no houses, no towns, no nothing. It looked like nowhere to me.

He turned onto a dirt road and the van shuddered in its ruts. I looked at his freckled profile. He was leaning his head on his left hand, his elbow propped against the window, and looked calmer than I'd ever seen him.

He parked deep in the woods, the trees thick and tall, and what sunlight reached the ground beneath them was filtered thin. Angus got out, came around to my side, and opened the door. For some reason he was carrying his box of tools and for a second, looming there in his absurdly clean outfit, he looked like an undeniable threat.

"Aren't you getting out?"

"I don't know," I said. "Are you going to molest me or something?"

"Excuse me," Angus said. "I don't mean to be rude, but I believe you've already molested *me*. More than once. Could you get out now, please?"

"It's just that I associate being alone in the woods with, like, horror movies."

"That's both sad and ridiculous," he said.

I climbed out and followed him through the woods into a small clearing, where he set the toolbox down. My sandals were full of pine needles and dirt. Birds were chatting away in the trees. There was something weird about the place, and it took me a second to realize what it was. "It's cool up here," I said. "Much, much cooler."

"I thought you'd like that." He unzipped his coveralls and took them off, revealing the usual ripped shorts and tattered T-shirt. He folded the coveralls lengthwise and laid them on the ground. "Have a seat," he said. The coveralls were still warm.

He sat down by the toolbox and opened it up. "I asked Gerald to go to the store for us while you were gambling his money away," he said. He pulled out and laid on the ground a succession of items: a cluster of grapes, a block of cheese, sliced sandwich bread, a tomato, a can of tuna fish, a whole pineapple, a rotisserie chicken, a bottle of wine with a screwoff cap. It was a big box.

I started to laugh.

"Best I could do," Angus said. He took his Leatherman out of his pocket and started cutting up the pineapple on the lid of the box. The spiny skin fell to the ground in spirals. The sky was a flat, clean blue, and the sun was making everything glisten. He kissed me and held my hand, his own hands sticky with pineapple. I lay down on the coveralls and wrapped my fingers around the belt loops of his cutoff shorts. He smelled like water and ammonia and pineapple.

"I don't know why we're here," I said.

"You really are out of touch with nature," he said. "Not to mention the concept of hanging out."

"No, I mean, I feel like I'm probably not your usual kind of person. I picture you with an earth-mother type who doesn't shave her legs and hews her own wood. I couldn't survive a day by myself in the outdoors. I don't even know what hewing means, come to think of it."

He looked at me, then touched my face, and his expression almost made me laugh; but then I was past it, on the other side of laughing.

"I don't know anybody like you," he said.

I almost choked in exasperation. New York, I wanted to say, was full of people exactly like me. With Michael, for example, I'd always known I was a type, part of a crop, one in a long line of art-history girls with the same education and wisecracks and shoes. If he could see me now, on my back in the woods with a plumber and a pineapple, he'd raise an eyebrow and smirk. In my mind I told him to go to hell, and returned my attention to the moment at hand. "I'm not an unusual person" is what I finally said. "You, on the other hand, are definitely an unusual person."

Angus put his sticky hand on my bare ankle. "You smell good."

"Sure, compared to the other people you know," I said.

He kissed me, and I kissed him back. I didn't know how long we spent there, and didn't care. After lunch we took a nap, then went for a walk. When we got back to the van it was dusk.

I fell asleep in the van heading back to Albuquerque. When I woke up, my mouth was dry and cottony from hanging open the whole time, and I smacked my lips together, dazed. Angus was driving with one hand on the wheel and his hat pulled down over his eyes. We drove past eighteen-wheelers barreling along the interstate, past hordes of motorcycles and people hauling boats back from whatever excuse for a lake they'd managed to find around here.

Angus bought gas when we hit town, peeling some bills off a wad of cash in the glove compartment, and when he got back in the van he asked where I wanted to go.

I looked at the money; it was a ball the size of a grapefruit, seemingly composed of large bills. "I know we can't keep staying in motels," I said, "but the thought of going back to that apartment with everybody else doesn't really appeal to me."

"A motel it is," Angus said.

We drove back to another brown room, with brown wall-paper and a brown flowered bedspread. I took a long, hot shower. When I came out, he was asleep face-down on top of the bedspread, his arms spread wide to either side. I turned on the TV and watched a silent version of a sitcom from my childhood, Angus snoring gently, but I felt restless. I picked up his keys with the vague idea of going out to get us something to eat. The parking lot smelled strongly of baking asphalt and exhaust. I got in the van and glanced in the back at milk crates stuffed wildly with tools, which Angus, apparently, had emptied out of the toolbox for our picnic. There were wrenches and hoses and a plumber's snake and some other tools I didn't recognize. Which is why it took me a moment to notice the gun. It was stuffed in a crate with no regard for safety, and I grabbed its long barrel and pulled it out.

Then I went back into the motel room and shook Angus awake. "Why do you have this?" I demanded.

He rolled over, his freckled face creased by the polyester bedspread. "What are you talking about?"

"A gun. You have a gun. You have wads of cash and a gun."

"This is New Mexico. Everybody has a gun."

"I don't have a gun."

"You do right now," he pointed out. "And I wish you wouldn't wave it around."

"Explain this to me."

"Fine," he said. He rolled to his side, quicksilver fast, and he had the gun out of my hand before I knew what was happening. He pointed it at the wall and shot, the gun making a surprisingly docile sound. I walked over to the wall and saw a BB embedded in the brown wallpaper, small and silver as an earring.

"I'm a peaceful person," Angus said, "but I spend a lot of time alone in the desert, and going alone into people's houses. Sometimes it helps to look less peaceful than I am."

"Oh," I said, rubbing my fingers over the bubble of the BB in the wall. When I turned around to apologize, he was asleep and snoring again, the gun dropped to the floor.

I lay down next to him and listened to the drone of traffic from the highway, the shuffling noises people made as they moved in and out of rooms. The occasional rustle of Angus moving. The rhythm of his breath.

Nine

Here's what I learned in the flat hot days of early July: Angus loved his work. He left each day in the purple van, whistling as he went, his coveralls shining whitely, like movie-star teeth. He came home grinning with exhaustion and scrubbed himself clean with the rough towels of whatever motel we were occupying. In the evenings he washed his coveralls with bleach at a laundromat and folded them carefully. He seemed to get paid well and in cash, with which he paid our room bills. I had no urge to go back to Wylie's, and Angus, apparently, didn't mind. He kept whatever he needed in the van, and if he went back to the apartment he didn't tell me about it. When we craved a change of scene we moved to some new dive, off the highway where the truckers stayed, or downtown, where our shiftless neighbors lounged all day on their balconies, drinking Tecate and watching the cars go by.

"When the water stops," Angus told me at night as we lay in the sheets holding hands, "everything stops. And when the toilet doesn't work, people can't even stay inside their homes. They stand outside wringing their hands, waiting for the van to come down the street. They never think about plumbing until it goes away, and then—" he laughed—"panic."

"So you like the panic, or calming the panic?" I said.

He laughed again. "Both."

I thought about going back to the condo, but couldn't bear

the idea of staying there. I did slink back once, when I knew my mother would be at work, and took the Caprice. Every couple of days I left her messages, also during the day, saying I was fine. The machine always played her cool recorded voice telling me to leave my name and the time of my call, and I assumed, since she never changed this recording, that she wasn't very upset by my disappearance. She was probably relieved, I thought, after the dinner party and my rudeness to and about David Michaelson, not to see me for a while. I didn't know where Wylie was, and judging by the way he'd bolted from the condo without turning around when I called his name, I didn't think he wanted to know where I was, either.

One day when Angus was off plumbing the depths, as he liked to say, of Albuquerque's soul, I shook myself free from the spell of cable television and went back to the UNM library to check my e-mail. There was a message from Michael saying exactly what I'd expected.

Dear Lynn,

Delighted to hear that you're having such a terrific time of it in New Mexico; I hope the state's much vaunted natural beauty continues to inspire. I always knew that given the right topic your talents as a scholar would rise to the fore. It almost makes up for your absence here in Paris.

I would suggest you collect all available biographical data on this painter of yours, and make the strongest possible case for the lineage and context of the work. Also, work on a detailed formal analysis of the two paintings and relate them to her contemporaries, both male and female. Your final two months of fellowship work should be extremely productive. I look forward to reading your work.

Cheers,
Michael

The Missing Person

This was quintessential Michael, cheerful and dismissive at the same time: the slightly patronizing remark about New Mexico's natural beauty implying, by omission, its lack of cultural substance. (My first six months in grad school, he'd flirted with me by asking, practically every time we met, whether I liked New York better than Arizona; then he would stand back, his lip slightly curled in anticipation, and wait for me to correct him.) The backhanded compliments suggesting both that he had faith in my talents and that I had yet to actually demonstrate them. The quick forgiveness of my standing him up making clear how little he was hurt by it. His reminder that I had only two more fellowship months left, and no more institutional support after that. And then cheers.

I gritted my teeth and set to work. I pictured the two desert paintings in my mother's house, turning the images over in my mind. There was a certain amount of suppressed violence in both paintings. In *The Wilderness Kiss,* no actual kiss was depicted, yet the painting was clearly sexual; its arrangement of bodies, with the woman's legs wide open, hinted that something wild was about to happen. The same was true of *The Ball and Chain,* in which the same woman lay collapsed and prostrate on what seemed to be her own son. They really didn't seem like paintings a secretary would buy on behalf of her boss, and it was even harder to imagine my father choosing them as an appropriate gift for his wife. Then again, it was the seventies, and maybe things were different then, even in Albuquerque. In any case, I needed to find more about the real Eva Kent, where that violence had come from and what I could make of it.

I spent the next few days searching for her in online sources, phone books, real-estate listings, school records. It was mind-numbing and time-consuming, but I liked it, even the paper-cut dreariness of it, for the form it gave to my days. I ran into problems, however. There were Kents in Santa Fe and Las Cruces and Albuquerque, and none of them were Eva. Nor did any of them know any Evas. I got hung up on, most of the Kents assuming I was a telemarketer choosing names at random and harassing them.

"Eva? I told you my name was Ed! Leave us alone!"

"Is this the collection agency again? I already said we don't got no money."

"I knew an Eva once. Eva Chan. Lovely Chinese girl. Married an army fellow, I believe, and moved to California."

In the evenings, flushed with my exertions, I met up with Angus and drank gin and tonics on the balcony of the motel or, if it was too hot, inside the room with the curtains drawn and the ice bucket sweating on the dresser. I insisted on dates and he agreed: we went dancing, to the movies, back to hear Jeanine sing her songs in the lounge. Afterwards we had sex and then I fell deeply asleep, velvet in relaxation, and never once remembered my dreams.

This went on for almost a week, after which two things happened. First of all, I found a connection to Eva Kent. And second, Angus brought Wylie and me back together again.

I was in the library looking through the annals of a Southwestern art association, rich with everything I hated about New Mexico: the parochial smallness of it, the manufacture of folk art into tourist kitsch, the white people declaiming about Navajo culture, the hippies raving about the mystical qualities of desert light. This was how an actual place turned unreal. I was getting more and more irritated, shaking my head and frowning and making little clucking sounds with my tongue. A young librarian kept passing by my table and I realized she probably thought I was deranged.

The Missing Person

The pages of the society's records were first yellow and typed, then purple and mimeographed, the smell of aged reproduction machines still clinging to them. There wasn't a single reference to Eva Kent. My mind was wandering, and I'd realize after a few minutes that I had read the same paragraph four or five times.

In the sunny dusty light I turned more pages and was rewarded, finally, by the fact that the keynote address at the society's annual meeting in 1978 was given by "local art dealer Harold Wallace," who spoke on "The Woman Artist: No Longer an Oxymoron," which I supposed was progressive of him. In a black-and-white photo printed six months later in the society's newsletter, he looked like a seventies playboy, with long, feathery dark hair, a leather jacket, and a big grin. There was a touch of Peter Fonda about him, and one of his eyebrows arched higher than the other, lending his smile a rakish effect. He had been instrumental, the newsletter claimed, in bringing fame to the artists he represented—but not Eva, I thought— and exhibited at the Gallery Gecko in Santa Fe.

I went downstairs and checked the phone book. Gallery Gecko was no more, but an address and phone number were given for Harold Wallace, who to my surprise answered on the fourth ring, sounding aged and slightly sleepy, nothing like Peter Fonda at all.

"Eva. Eva Kent," he said. "I'm not sure I remember her. Was she kind of a stout gal, blonde, came from hard-drinking German stock?"

"I'd guess she was on the thin side," I said. "Long, dark hair parted in the middle? She made a pair of paintings, *Desert I* and *Desert II*, that belong to my family. I'm interested in learning more about her." I was calling from a sun-blasted phone booth outside the library, and the receiver was hot and slippery in my hand.

"Well, I'm not too sure," Harold Wallace said. "There were

a lot of those girl painters around in those days. Swarming around, if you know what I mean."

"Right," I said.

"We had some fun parties with all those girls. Ah, yes. Good times."

"Could you check your files or something?" I said. "It's really kind of important to me."

"Files," he said softly, as if he were about to drift off into either contemplation or a nap. "I've got some files somewhere."

"Maybe I could come by and take a look."

"Well, sure you can," he said. "Come by any time, sweetheart."

"How about now?"

"Persistent little thing, aren't you?"

"I'll be there in an hour," I said, and hung up before he had a chance to refuse.

I sped north in the Caprice along the parched interstate, which was adorned with the shreds of blown-out tires and flowered crosses marking the scenes of car-related deaths. I passed another billboard advertising the imminent construction of Shangri-la; in this one a man and a woman, their hair blond, their jewelry gold, sat drinking white wine at a bar overlooking a golf course as expansive as a sea.

Harold Wallace lived in a well-kept adobe townhouse close to the center of Santa Fe, on a street where sunflowers and gladioli bloomed brightly next to desert plants in large pots. Every home wore a decorative ristra, a blue-tile accent, or a Kokopelli door knocker. When I rang the bell I heard him long before he got to the door, a slow rustling, and so I expected someone much more decrepit than the handsome old guy who ultimately appeared. He was wearing a long white shirt over loose-fitting gray trousers and a necklace composed of small, chunky silver beads. With thin gray hair falling to his shoulders, his skin splattered with liver spots and the occasional mole, he looked like an aging actor or a very successful guru. I was wearing shorts and a T-shirt, and for the first time since leaving New York I felt underdressed.

"Well, I realize I don't even know your name," he said.

The house had been decorated in tones of off-white and white, the scheme relieved by an occasional flash of beige. "Call me Harold," he'd said, leading me to an off-white couch in a sunken living room and offering me a drink. When I requested water, he left the room and came back with a Mexican blue glass tumbler crowded with ice, lemon slices, and a matching blue straw. He kept looking, without even trying to hide it, at my breasts, and I let him, figuring it might help. I sat with the glass in one hand and my notebook in the other. Reclining opposite me in a wicker armchair, Harold flicked his thin hair over his shoulders, a weirdly girlish gesture, and asked in a broadly patronizing tone what he could do to help me with my "school project."

"It's my dissertation, actually," I said, straightening up and setting my glass on a bamboo coaster. "I'm intrigued by a pair of paintings that were purchased by my father, and that have your name listed on the backing. *Desert I* and *Desert II*, they're called, as I said on the phone, with subtitles in brackets, painted in the late 1970s."

"And you said the name of the girl was—"

"Eva Kent."

"Well, as I said, I don't remember every painting I ever sold or gave away, especially not from those years. You're too young to remember, of course, but the seventies out here in Santa Fe—well, you know. It was a good time to be alive and a man on this planet. A little too good, maybe. Sometimes things went a little bit over the top, over the edge, if you know what I mean."

"Not really."

"Well, maybe your father did. Sometimes paintings changed hands—well, you can see what I mean."

I tried to picture my father flirting with girl painters, or at all, and I couldn't even come close to imagining it. Forced to attend neighborhood parties, he'd retreat to the edges, smiling awkwardly, making the hostess and other women uncomfortable; they'd go over and start conversations on subjects he cared nothing about, sports or community activities or municipal taxes, and he'd nod and smile politely without saying anything in return. Half a drink later, all talk would wither on the vine.

"I doubt that about him," I said. "He was kind of a straight arrow."

"Well, you would know," Harold said skeptically. He spent some time staring blankly at a spot over my left shoulder. His eyes were an electric shade of blue, rare and attractive, marred by bloodshot streaks. I let a moment pass, thinking he was formulating some reminiscence; but he was just sunk in silence.

"I think she had a child," I went on. "In 1979. If you don't remember the paintings, perhaps you remember the child."

"The late seventies," Harold Wallace said, "were not a time for children. It may be difficult for you to imagine now, in this age of prudery, but back then it was all fun and sex and singles and swingers. When people had children, they left the scene." He shook his head and smiled at the rug as if at an old friend.

"You said you had some files? I'd love to have a look, if you wouldn't mind. Maybe I could find something to jog your memory."

"Oh, yes," he said slowly, still looking at the rug. "I do have a few files. You're welcome to look through them if you like, my dear, but you're not likely to find much. I traded a lot of my paintings for—how shall I put it?—black-market goods and services, if you know what I mean. We all did, as I was saying before. Things you wouldn't necessarily want on your books."

The Missing Person

I sighed and stood up, the image of my father as a seventies swinger still floating through my mind. I pictured him in his glasses and his receding hairline, his shirt opened halfway down his chest, a drink in one hand and a girl in the other. It almost made me laugh out loud. "Well, thanks for your time," I said.

Looking up, Harold seemed sad to see me go. "Are you sure you wouldn't like a drink?" he said.

"I'm sure." I scanned the living room. There were no traces of any other person, no family photos, nothing.

"Tell you what," he said. "I'll take a look through those files, and if I find anything I'll give you a call."

"I'd be very grateful," I said. His expression suggested he was wondering how grateful, exactly, so I gave him my mother's number and fled.

At the Route 66 Motel, I flung open the door and kissed Angus full on the mouth. He kissed me back, then gently moved me aside to get at a bag that was lying open on the floor. I saw a flash of metal and leather before he zipped it up. He was wearing work boots, but not the white coveralls.

"What are you doing?"

He didn't say anything.

The room was empty of all our clutter. My own clothes lay neatly washed and folded on the bed, inside a plastic bag from the grocery store. I felt suddenly sick. "You're leaving," I said.

Angus put on his hat and pulled the brim down low on his forehead. His mouth was set in a strange flat line—strange because he smiled so much—and the creases around his eyes sank deeper into the skin than usual. I felt a horrid tingle in my blood, the onset of panic, and I sat down on the bed. He knelt on the carpet in front of me. My skin hurt; it was as if my body was grieving.

"I want to come with you," I told him.

"Lynn Marie Fleming," he said, "you are an obstinate person."

"Can I come or not?"

"You don't really want to. It could be dangerous. It could be, well, *sublegal*. It isn't really your scene."

"I'm so sick of people talking about scenes." I sounded like a child, even to myself, and I straightened up and looked into his pale eyes. "Tell me the truth. Do you not want me to come because you want to protect me, or because you're sick of me?"

There was a flash of freckled skin, and I was lying on my back on the bed, with Angus on top of me, his heart beating, slow and definite, against my chest. I could never figure out how he managed to move so fast.

"You know the answer," he said.

"I'll drive the Caprice."

"Well," he said, "we could use another car."

At Wylie's apartment, Irina smiled and waved enthusiastically, though I was standing only a few feet away, and I waved back, surprised by how pleased I was to see all of them, not just my brother, even Stan and Berto. They already felt like some kind of family. They were standing around the bare room, waiting, I realized, for Angus to show up. Wylie was slouching against the kitchen counter, and when he saw me he grimaced and said, "What are you doing here?"

"Don't worry. I won't mess anything up."

He looked unconvinced. Angus walked up to him and whispered into his ear, their two heads close together: one hatted, the other bare and dark; one smile, one frown. After a minute Wylie shrugged and said, "I hope you're right."

Angus turned and clapped his hands. "It's time," he said.

Ten

Sometimes I forgot that my father was gone. It was as if he were on vacation or out of town, and in the back of my mind, that trickster of a spot, I had no doubt he'd be back. Then I'd remember that his absence was permanent, and couldn't decide which was worse: the forgetting or the remembering, the loss of knowledge or its sudden return. He was fifty-one when he died, an absurdly young age, seriously ridiculous; an age that would force you to wonder what was wrong with his heart, potentially my own and others' of my acquaintance, not to mention hearts in general, which seemed like flawed mechanisms all around.

Also there was the question of what I hated most. On one side was the fact that I was forgetting what he looked like. I knew he was angular and dark-haired, with hair bristling from his ears and nose; when I was little, I sometimes saw him in the bathroom, tweezing them out and swearing with pain, which made me feel both amused and sorry for him. But the way his eyes flicked rapidly from side to side when he talked, his rare laughter (highly prized by Wylie and me, because it was harder to get him to laugh than our mother) when we did something either funny or ridiculous, his tendency to fall asleep in front of the television and snore—at times I found myself recovering these things, and understood that I'd been losing them, that the reality of my father was receding and in its place were photographs, hardening.

On the other side was the fact that my brother looked a lot like him: the same dark hair, sharp shoulders, and slouch. Seeing Wylie bent over a map next to Angus was, however slightly, like seeing my father again, and I didn't enjoy it at all. And the more I saw him, the more acutely I felt that slingshot process of remembering my own forgetting, the push and pull I'd stayed in New York to avoid. I thought of my mother's voice on the telephone saying "Come home, you can't have to work all the time," and my own voice saying "I can't get away." We must have had this conversation fifty times since my father died.

And yet, I thought, looking at my brother, I'd been missing him, too. Missing people all around.

I stared over his shoulder at the map, even though he shot me a look of utter annoyance. I shrugged and said, "Don't let me distract you."

What they had was a map of the city, on which Wylie was highlighting, with a Day-Glo pink marker, a section of streets. I wondered if they had another sprinkler-related prank planned. I'd never met anyone who hated grass as much as they did.

"Up and down this whole street," he was saying, "is water waste central."

"Yeah, it's hideous," Stan agreed. "That is some ugly stuff."

"I hear you, man," Berto said glumly. He was eating corn nuts out of a plastic bag and, every once in a while, wiping his hands on his shorts. Sledge was lying there next to him, tenderly licking the fabric where this wiping occurred.

Irina sat nursing Psyche, a benevolent look on her face, as she motioned me over. "Isn't it all highly exciting?" she said.

"I'm not sure," I said. "What's going on?"

"Our committee is executing the second strike of the summer. Action number two."

"Something to do with pools, I take it."

From across the room I saw Wylie look up, and knew that he was waiting to hear my reaction.

"That's right," Irina said. Psyche pulled away from her breast, sucking her own lips and muttering to herself, and Irina covered her chest and smoothed the few strands of hair on the baby's head. "It is of course highly sad to have pools of water in the center of the desert. It is a wrong. So we are going to drain them."

"What, the public pools? In this heat? That won't make you guys very popular," I said. As soon as the first words were out of my mouth, I could feel unfriendliness building in the room. Only Angus continued studying the map, whistling under his breath.

"Not the city pools," Wylie said, standing up and stepping toward me. "Private pools. In this neighborhood practically every damn house has a pool. Think of the amount of water that is, and how little it gets used. It's a criminal overallocation of valuable resources."

"You said it, man," Berto said.

I pictured the pools of Albuquerque spread out in the brilliant sunshine, their turquoise surfaces ringed by gladioli and umbrellas, all of it pretty as a Hockney painting. "What are you going to do with the water?" I asked.

"Dump it into the aquifer!" Stan said.

"Can't do that," Wylie said. "We'll have to dump it onto their lawns. And if it kills all the nonnative plants, it serves them right. We should kill all that East Coast grass."

"Isn't it a little bit mean?" I said. He glared at me. "Because it's mostly kids who use pools." He was still glaring. "And kids like to swim when it's hot and everything," I finished lamely.

"If you want to talk about kids," he said, "picture the thousands who die of dysentery each year in India due to lack of clean water while little Johnny in Rio Rancho practices the front crawl with his private swim coach. Save your sympathy for the right people, Lynn. Chemically processing vast quantities of chlorinated water in the middle of an arid ecosystem is an absurd, destructive act. By confronting them with the untenability of this position, we can effectively illustrate the necessity of change."

"Confronting kids?" I said.

My brother shrugged. "Presumably their parents will notice as well."

"Totally, man," Berto said.

"Those pools are ugly," Stan said. "They are like an abomination upon the land."

"Plus imagine the looks on their faces when they see they're empty," Angus said, and winked at me.

I could tell Wylie wanted to continue lecturing me, but Angus waved him over. "We do need to talk about the drainage."

"Would you mind holding the baby?" Irina said. "I will be right back." She deposited Psyche in my arms and went into the bathroom. Sound asleep, the baby lay motionless in my lap. Her head was heavy and inert, like a miniature bowling ball. She was snoring, and her tiny hands were curled in delicate fists. I sat there and studied her. After a few minutes, her weight started to cut off the circulation in my legs—not exactly painful, but not pleasant, either.

"Look, Lynn," Wylie said, obviously bothered that he hadn't convinced me of their righteousness. "Once people come out and see what we've done, they'll *have* to ask themselves why." He was standing against the counter now, arms crossed.

They'll be asking themselves who vandalized their pool, I thought, but didn't say so out loud.

"I've been thinking about these issues for a long time, and I've decided that the revolution has to move out of the wilderness and into the city. It's no good sitting in a tree when the vast majority of people don't go anywhere near that tree. It's no good selling them calendars with glossy pictures of the landscape to help them decorate the breakfast nooks and entertainment centers of their oversized suburban homes. You've got to attack people where they live."

His eyes glowed in the apartment's dim light. Stan and Berto were nodding appreciatively, and Angus was looking at him and smiling.

There was a kind of logic to his argument, albeit only a certain kind. I couldn't summon a ready defense of swimming pools, suburban sprawl, and waste. I wondered what the hell Irina was doing in the bathroom that took so long. "Listen," I said to the room at large, "my legs are numb."

Angus laughed. He took the baby from my lap—expertly, without waking her—and laid her down on his own. Holding one of Psyche's feet in his hands, he peered into her sleeping face with a naked tenderness that made me feel somehow ashamed. She woke up and looked at him without dismay.

"A little chaos never hurt anybody," he said softly, moving Psyche's foot in a slow, lazy circle, as she watched him, expectant and oddly grown-up, like a patient with a physical therapist. Irina emerged from the bathroom, and I decided to use it too. When I stood up, my legs were on fire with the return of blood.

Wylie said, "It's not chaos. It's a calculated gesture."

"Sure," Angus said, "that's what I meant."

I was surprised to find the bathroom clean and smelling faintly of orange, with signs of Psyche everywhere: a bottle of organic baby shampoo, a spotless tub, a folded stack of un-bleached cotton towels. Some water usage was okay, apparently, at least where babies were involved. Lifting the toilet cover, though, I saw that flushing was only an occasional affair. When I returned to the living room Irina and Wylie were conferring and Psyche was standing in Angus's lap, his hands around her chubby body. She punched him in the face and laughed. He stuck out his tongue and waggled his ears, rolling her gently from side to side, as if his lap were an ocean and his motions the waves.

We didn't leave the apartment until well past midnight. Irina's job, she told me, was to stand watch in front of the houses. If anybody showed up she'd distract them, explaining that she was trying to calm her crying baby by walking her around the neighborhood.

"What if the baby isn't crying?" I said.

"It is often not so difficult to arrange," she said.

I drove the Caprice, Irina holding Psyche beside me, Berto staring glumly out the window in the backseat. My passengers smelled ripe and organic, like farm animals or produce just starting to rot. I was getting used to it, but rolled my windows down nonetheless. Angus, Wylie, and Stan were ahead of us in the Plumbarama van, and I followed them through traffic, feeling like a spy. There was a weird lightness in my head, neither adrenaline nor dizziness, just the loose, hazy excitement that comes from throwing good sense to the winds. Letting go of things—fear, logic, laziness, whatever—I turned on the radio, and a pop song bounced into the car. Irina swayed along with the beat, Psyche gazing dreamily up at her from her sling.

"You don't have a car seat for her?" I said.

"No," Irina answered without stopping her swaying.

The nighttime city was painted in lurid hues. The neon of stores, the lights of intersections, the custom paint jobs and trembling basses of cruising cars. Then ahead of me the purple van signaled a right-hand turn and we left all those colors behind. In a residential neighborhood the streets turned hushed and pastel: brown houses, pink flowers, the buttery glow of streetlights. Even the air itself seemed a lighter shade. I switched off the radio. The wind carried the smell of watered gardens into the car.

Psyche cooed and garbled a private language, delivering her own speech on the status of babies in car rides after dark. "Guala, guala," she said, or words to that effect.

"There's no gorillas here," Irina said. "Don't be silly."

"That we know of," Berto said from the back.

The van kept signaling, making lefts and rights through streets that all looked the same to me: row after row of the Albuquerque houses I remembered so clearly, with their flat roofs and windows trimmed in white or turquoise blue. I could picture each one inside, its hardwood floors and tile accents and the phone niche built into the hallway, with a shelf for the phone book carved out beneath it. "What are they doing?" I said.

"You can let us out if you want," Berto said. In the rearview mirror I could see his glum, jowly face. "We'll go the rest of the way on foot. If you're, like, having doubts."

"Berto," Irina said.

"I'm just saying, man, she doesn't have to come."

"I want to be here." And as I said it, I realized it was true. I wanted to know if they could get away with it, what would happen after, what conceivable difference any of it could make.

"We don't even know her," Berto blurted from the back. "Remember that last chick Angus brought along, Tiffany, when we were trying to break into the computer-chip plant that time? She was freakin' crazy, man, running around screaming her head off about how we should free the planet, free the animals from the zoo, free the children from the schools. And Wylie was all 'Shut that woman up!'"

"Berto," Irina said.

"But Angus just laughed, 'cause he thought it was funny, right, like everything's funny? Me and Wylie had to drag her away in the end, man."

"This is different," Irina said.

"How is it different?" Berto said. He saw me in the rearview mirror and looked away. "Nothing against you, like, specifically or anything."

"It's different," Irina said sweetly, "because this is Lynn."

Gratitude surged through me, and I turned to her and smiled. Psyche garbled her agreement. I caught Berto's eye again, and held it. "I'm Wylie's sister," I told him.

The van finally pulled to the curb on a street canopied by a tall line of elms and serene with wealth. Porch lights glowed on the faces of tall, gabled houses, reflecting off large, gleaming vehicles parked in the driveways and casting faint circles on lush green lawns. I parked a few feet back and cut the engine. It was almost one in the morning, and I wondered if everybody else had taken naps. Angus, Wylie, and Stan were scurrying across someone's front yard, keeping to the shadows, carrying a small blue machine I guessed was a pump. Berto scrambled out the back and set off after them, and soon they were climbing a fence at the side of the house, clanging the pump against it, a terrible noise. Down the street, a dog issued a warning howl.

"This is going to end badly," I said.

"Everything will be fine," Irina said. She got out of the car and stood beneath the trees, her two hands clasped beneath the base of the sling, and I joined her. In the driveway was a small, sporty Miata.

"Why this house, anyway?" I asked her. I could hear the sound of splashing, Berto cursing, Wylie hissing at him to shut up.

"All these families have two cars at the minimum," she explained. "Usually one is a large SUV."

"What if that's parked in the garage and everybody's home?"

Irina frowned. "I am thinking this has been part of Wylie's research. Also the lights." She reached into the sling and pulled out a piece of graph paper, a chart filled with scratchy handwriting I recognized as Wylie's. Here he'd listed addresses, the presence of cars and their makes, the times lights went on and off.

"When the house lights follow the same pattern every day, that is when you know they're on a timer," Irina said. "And that no one is in the home."

"Clever," I said.

She beamed at me. "Yes!"

Then, from the backyard, I suddenly heard water rushing like a river. Glancing at my watch, I couldn't understand why Irina wasn't more nervous. Berto emerged from the shadows and fetched something from the back of the van, then dashed off again. It seemed like hours later when Angus and Wylie reappeared, carrying the pump between them, grinning like maniacs.

"Man," Wylie said, "I wish we had more than one pump."

"Only so much I could do," Angus said.

Berto stuck a sign—this was what he'd pulled out of the van, an unfolded piece of cardboard taped to a little wooden cross—into the front lawn: DESERT, it said, in black marker.

Everybody was happy now. We drove on in a convoy to another house, where Irina and I set up at our posts again, the Caprice and the van parked in a cul-de-sac just around the corner. I was almost starting to enjoy myself when the problems started. I was listening to the loud suctioning of the pump—relieved that the houses were spread far apart—when there was a sudden crash, followed by whispers and soft laughter that clearly came from Angus. Berto came running around for some tool in the car, and I asked him what had happened.

"Something got stuck in the pump, man," he said. "I don't know why these assholes just let their kids leave toys in the pool."

"Yeah, that's really inconsiderate," I muttered as he ran back. They were making an unbelievable amount of noise, and I wasn't surprised when the lights in the house next door came on. "We need to get out of here," I said, pacing around the car, trying to figure out how long it would take for everybody to pile into the vehicles and clear out of here. "Can you make the baby cry or something?"

"I am trying," Irina said.

All she was doing, from what I could tell, was jiggling Psyche up and down. I paced over to her and shook the base of the sling. "What are you doing? Pinch her or something. Pinch her!"

Irina swiveled around, her back to me, and scowled over her shoulder. "She will cry in a minute. You keep away from her."

"Sorry," I said, feeling myself flush. "I'm panicking."

Next door a middle-aged man in gray sweatpants and an NMSU T-shirt came out, squinting into the dark street. He looked to me like he was trying hard not to act frightened. I imagined his wife inside, goading him to see what the trouble was.

Irina didn't bat an eye but ran right up to him, Psyche cutting loose with an angry screech.

"Excuse me, sir," Irina said breathlessly, "I am having troubles. Can you help me please?"

He took one look at her pretty face and her crying baby and his expression softened.

I ran around the other side of the house into the backyard, hissing to Wylie that people were waking up. Angus was holding a long hose, from which enormous quantities of water were gushing out onto the lawn. The air stank of chlorine.

"We're almost done," Wylie said.

"We don't have time."

"Go back and start the car."

"Hurry *up,*" I said.

"The pump only goes so fast," Angus said, not even bothering to whisper. He looked completely unconcerned. I could hear Psyche in the front, sobbing now, and Irina's voice rising alongside hers. I hoped she was a good liar. Then I heard the neighbor say, loudly, "Maybe we should call the police," as Irina protested—"No! Please, no police, I beg you!"—and I turned to Wylie again.

"I'm leaving," I said, "in the car. And unless you want to get arrested, you'll come too. Time's up," I said, "*now.*"

Everybody scurried into the cul-de-sac. Irina said to the neighbor, "No, the police cannot help us," and her voice was as vexed and fretful as any wife's; then she spun around, hurried down the sidewalk, and ducked into the shadows beside me.

Somehow I drove—suspended in a kind of adrenaline calm—and fifteen minutes later pulled into an empty stripmall parking lot, with Wylie, Irina, and the baby in the backseat. The car reeked of chlorine and wet clothes. Psyche had stopped crying, and everything was silent.

My heartbeat was loud in my ears, but I let out a long breath—it felt like the first I'd taken in a long time—and then I started to laugh. "That was crazy," I said. I glanced at Wylie, expecting to see him laughing too, but he was fidgeting and looking back and forth from Irina to me, his eyebrows twisted in thought.

"Okay," he finally said, "let's go back."

"What? Wylie, come on."

"I'm serious. Let's keep going. We can do a country-club pool, maybe. We'll break into the poolhouse and use their drainage system. It might take me a couple of minutes to figure it out, but it'll drain faster than with the submersible pump, so that's an advantage." He was almost panting. "Listen, I understand it's a suboptimal situation, but flexibility's the key to our success."

"Wylie," I said, "no way."

Irina, in the back, kept silent.

"There is absolutely no reason we can't do this," Wylie said. Instead of slouching, he was straight and serious now, making eye contact with each of us. "We can be in and out in five minutes, tops. Once I get it draining, we can leave. Really, we can do it."

"No, we can't," I said. His expression told me that if I didn't put it in his terms, he'd never speak to me again. "Wylie, the plan's inherently flawed. We don't know what their system's like or even where it is. And instead of three other men you've got me, Irina, and a six-month-old baby. For a much larger pool. It'd be so much better to regroup and revise our tactics rather than risk everything for this."

"She is actually seven months," Irina corrected.

"Sorry," I said.

"It's okay, I am not offended."

Wylie was looking down at the seat and smoothing the duct tape over a tear in the upholstery.

"There will be plenty of other opportunities," I said. "But for tonight I say we retrench and, well, analyze the suboptimal nature of events. Then we can, you know, figure out how to do it better next time."

We sat in the dark, the Caprice's engine idling like a smoker's cough, while Wylie thought it over. When he met my eyes again I was almost sure—not a hundred percent, but nonetheless—I saw a flash of gratitude.

"It could be that continuing tonight isn't the most efficient use of our resources," he said.

I smiled. "I think you're right."

The Missing Person

. . .

Psyche cried relentlessly as we drove back to the apartment, which made conversation impossible. Wylie was slumped sideways against the door, and I could see him turning over the night's events in his mind, evaluating and analyzing and formulating alternatives for the future. You could say this much about him: he was always thinking. Irina, her round face ducked close to the sling, shushed and sang to the baby, but to no avail. Above us, clouds skittered across the face of the moon.

For some reason, I thought of Harold Wallace drinking alone in his well-manicured, beige-and-white house, and then about my mother, wondering where she was and what she was doing.

It was almost three o'clock when we got to Wylie's place. Irina disappeared into the back room with Psyche, who was still crying. Angus, Stan, and Berto were lying on the floor drinking beer by candlelight, looking sleepy and stoned. Angus smiled and gestured for me to come over, but I shook my head. Something about him was bothering me, starting with the way he'd laughed when things went wrong, as if none of this really mattered to him; it didn't mean that much to me, either, but it did to the others, and he was, after all, one of them. He stared at me hard for a second, then shrugged and turned his attention to Wylie, who was pacing in a tight circle.

"That," my brother said, "was a disaster."

Stan nodded his head. "It *was* fairly hideous."

"You got that right, man," Berto said. "Maybe we should go back to the stuff everybody else is doing? Like the demonstrations and all that shit."

"Fuck demonstrations," Angus said, keeping his eyes on Wylie.

"No need for harsh language, man," Berto said.

"Hey, if you want to start a letter-writing campaign, go right ahead," Angus said, smiling at him.

"Unforgivably disastrous," Wylie said, still pacing, and now clenching his hands into fists. "Completely fragmented. We've got to do a major overhaul of our planning process. This can't happen again. It's a waste of time and resources."

"Listen, it was only an experiment," Angus said. "We tried, and it didn't work out. Next time we'll do better."

Stan and Berto looked back and forth, expectantly, between Angus and Wylie. I had a feeling they'd been witness to these debates before.

"You said we could be in and out in five minutes!" my brother snapped. "You said we could drain half the neighborhood in one night! But we only got through one, Angus. You're the water-systems expert, you were supposed to deal with the logistics, and we only did one pool!"

"So it's my fault?" Angus still didn't look upset. He was just lying there, every once in a while drinking from his beer bottle. In the glow of the candles his hair looked darker than usual, its red turning to rust.

"I depended on your expertise," Wylie said, "and it was a mistake." He slowly lowered himself to the dusty floor and crossed his legs. "I won't make that mistake again."

"Hey, buddy," Angus said. "It wasn't that bad."

"Don't call me that," Wylie said. "I'm not your buddy."

"You sure as hell are, buddy."

Angus was still smiling, which annoyed me, but my brother was seething. Watching the both of them, knowing they'd be up all night arguing, I sighed. "I'm going back to Mom's," I said then. "I feel bad. I haven't seen her in ages. I don't even know how she's doing."

"She's fine," Wylie said.

"Oh, how would you know?"

"Do you think I don't go by to check on her?" His dark eyes were flashing. He was just as mad at me as he was at Angus, as he was at the rest of the world.

"I don't know what to think about you, Wylie," I said. "And you don't exactly help me figure it out."

He tapped his fingers on the floor and nodded in a tight staccato. "That must be tough for you," he said.

I left them all behind, their floor squatting and arguments and plans, the baby still mewling in the bedroom. My mother didn't wake up when I came in, and in her little guest room I crawled between soft clean sheets. I'd thought that it would feel like coming home. Nowhere else in the world promised that sensation—not Brooklyn, not cheap motel rooms or my brother's apartment, certainly not Paris or the Upper West Side—but my last thoughts before sleep were uneasy. I wished I knew where else on earth I should have gone.

Eleven

David Michaelson served me coffee. When I stumbled into the kitchen and saw him in a red-striped bathrobe, smiling at me, I realized I'd almost forgotten he existed.

My mother was sitting at the table with her coffee, her short hair unmussed by sleep. "Look what the cat dragged in," she said in an even tone.

"I've been with Wylie," I said, as if this excused everything, and took the cup from David's large hand. After the relentless grunge of recent days my mother's place seemed unbearably clean and orderly; I practically had to squint to look at it. Even the utensils sparkled alarmingly.

"How is old Wylie?" David set his own cup down on the table, sat down opposite me, and met my gaze without any sign of awkwardness. "I felt real bad about the way things ended last time. There's no reason we can't have a civil discussion about environmental issues. No reason at all."

"David," my mother said.

He smiled at her, pleasantly, then turned back to me, gesticulating in a lawyerly manner, his elbows on the table. "But if people just storm out every time there's a disagreement, well, civility doesn't stand a chance, now does it?" His reasonableness was making me queasy, or maybe it was the triangle of curly chest hair his bathrobe exposed when he leaned forward. I focused instead on my coffee, which was simultaneously bitter and enjoyable. It felt good to wake up and drink coffee in a normal cup, in a normal kitchen, with no hangover at all.

"David," my mother said again.

"Well, *does* it stand a chance?"

"You'll be late."

Lifting his meaty wrist, David checked his watch and nodded.

"You're right," he said, "as always," and then he winked at me. I squinted back. He left the table, lumbered out of the kitchen, and disappeared. My mother finished her final sip of coffee and stood up. "I'd better get ready too. By the way, someone called for you this morning before you were up. I didn't even know you were here, of course."

"Who?"

"Angus. Wylie's friend. If that's what he is."

"Angus called here?" Saying his name in front of her felt weird.

"At seven. He said he'd be out of town for a few days but that you shouldn't worry. He said he'd be working." Her emphasis on "working" made clear how little she believed this statement.

"He's a plumber," I said.

"I see."

"Have you ever even met him?"

"No," she said. She cleared the dishes and I followed her into the kitchen. "But Wylie used to talk about him all the time. Back when he actually talked. So you like him, do you?"

"Not exactly. It's more like—I can't seem to leave him alone." She turned to face me, and the look in her eyes was unexpectedly mild.

"Well, that's how it is sometimes," she said.

David Michaelson reappeared in a gray double-breasted suit and cowboy boots, presenting himself to us with open arms. "I'm in court today," he told me. "Gotta look shiny and new."

"Good," I said faintly.

He pecked my mother on the cheek—like a dutiful husband—winked at me again, then left. My mother changed into her sensible travel-agent clothes and left, too. I felt tremendously happy to be alone.

After roaming through the house for a while I came to her bedroom. She hadn't neglected to make the bed, and even the pillows beneath the covers were arranged to geometric perfection. I thought about passing out on the floor of Wylie's unfurnished apartment, with my brother sprawled beside me. It seemed highly unlikely that we were her actual children. But on the bureau, next to her small jewelry box, were pictures of Wylie and me in the grip of goofy, soft-cheeked adolescence, complete with rolled eyes and acne. And there, visiting family in Chicago, were all four of us, skyscrapers looming behind us, the wind lifting our hair.

Finding the red-striped bathrobe hanging inside her closet, I wondered how often David stayed over, and what he told his wife when he did. In my last snooping spree I hadn't noticed any conspicuous male clothing, and none was apparent now. There wasn't even an extra toothbrush in the bathroom; but maybe he toted one with him, or maybe my mother shared hers. Some things were impossible for a person to contemplate and still want to live.

I went out in the Caprice, determined to see the house I still thought of as home, and drove through endless residential neighborhoods toward the bare mountains. The dead air of mid-July rendered the city flat and even. I listened to country music and tapped my fingers on the vinyl steering wheel.

The Missing Person

Though two years had gone by since I'd seen the house, and though I'd lived through those years and recorded their passing, I was nonetheless shocked to find that the place did not look the same. It had been repainted a cotton-candy pink, first of all, and the people who lived there now had fixed to its exterior several gigantic plastic butterflies who were mounting an attack in a zigzag pattern, seemingly aimed at my old bedroom window. On the front door hung a wreath made of braided wheat and blue-checked Indian corn. I felt sure that somewhere in the vicinity, lurking, there were garden gnomes. The driveway, freshly asphalted, spread dark crumbles across the bordering expanse of our old lawn.

The last time I'd been here was a week after the funeral. A couple of days later my mother explained, briskly and undebatably, that she saw no sense in waiting and would be packing everything up and moving. I'd said fine, there was nothing I wanted anyway, and she smiled tightly and said she doubted this was true. Seeing the house now made me realize how much work it must have been for her and Wylie, and how drastic her resolve to break with the past. I wondered if this was when Wylie had decided to empty his apartment of its possessions, when he saw all of ours in moving boxes.

Instead of walking to the front door with the wreath I went next door to the Michaelsons'. At least their house still looked the same; shrubs formed a geometric ring in front of their door, and a basketball hoop hung above the driveway. Their yard, formerly a lawn, was now hard-packed dirt, which I guessed Wylie would've approved of. I rang the doorbell.

It was Donny, I was almost positive, who opened the door, wearing long surf shorts dotted with miniature surfers, each catching his own personal wave. Barefoot and shirtless, he was holding a tall glass of milk that had given him a faint white mustache. "Hey," he said. "Come to check out the old neighborhood, huh?"

"I guess so."

"I always wondered how come you guys never come by."

"You did?"

"Well, not, like, literally always or anything."

I looked at him. "You're Donny, right?"

"Yeah, you can remember 'cause I'm taller."

"Right," I said, not bothering to point out that Darren wasn't there for comparison's sake. "Can I come in?"

He glanced quickly behind him, then stepped back from the door. "Um, okay. Can you wait in here for a sec?" he said, and disappeared into a long, dark hallway, where I heard him murmuring to someone whose voice was too soft to make out.

The living room looked like the home of much younger children, with a baseball mitt on the couch and a soccer ball in the corner. An open box of Pop-Tarts was sitting next to some comic books on the coffee table.

Donny strode back in.

"Yup, the old 'hood. Let's go into the backyard, okay?" he said, leading me out through the sliding patio doors to the back. "The people who live next door to us now are super nice. They're real religious. They've got a sweet garden back there, too."

I looked over the fence at the yard where Wylie and I used to play. On summer nights we sometimes slept back there in a tent. Now it was divided into neat rows of squash and tomatoes. The Michaelsons' yard, by contrast, had been let slide. The lawn had faded into dirt splotched with a few patches of yellow grass, and the only sign of life was a battered picnic table under the shade of a pine tree, where Donny and I sat down.

"Remember when we were little, and you and Wylie always played those weird games in your backyard? You pretended you were savages or something."

I didn't remember, but nodded anyway.

"Darren and I watched you sometimes. We thought you were total freaks," he said, shaking his head in a fit of nostalgia. "No offense or anything. Hey, can I get you a glass of milk? Or a soda?"

"I'd take some water."

"You got it," he said. He padded inside, and I went back to the fence, hoping to look into our old house through the rear windows, but the glass threw back sheets of glare. I remembered one cookout we had, when Wylie got overexcited and poured a bottle of barbecue sauce right on top of his head; my father reached over with a paper napkin to wipe off his face, and none of us could stop laughing. The paper napkins kept sticking to Wylie and the more my father wiped the worse it got, until they both had to give up and take showers.

From the Michaelsons' house came the sound of shattering glass, followed by "Shit!" Donny said something else, but I couldn't hear what. I went inside and saw him standing with a broom at the far side of the kitchen, sweeping up some shards.

"I'm a total klutz," he said apologetically. "I'll be just a sec with your water."

I could hear a woman moaning down the hall, in a bedroom that, in our house, had belonged to Wylie. The door was open, and while Donny took care of the dustbin I walked inside.

Although I couldn't summon any specific memory of her from childhood, I knew it was Daphne Michaelson. She was sitting in an armchair reading *Vogue*, moaning softly to herself as she turned the pages. Her finger- and toenails were painted a brilliant shade of red, her brown hair fell in stylish waves to her shoulders, and her pale skin was dusted to an elegant beige. She was wearing a pink dress and brown slingback pumps, and she looked like a million dollars.

"Oh, excuse me," I said. She crossed her legs and smiled at me, stopping her moaning, and wagged her right foot up and down in its pump. "I used to live next door?"

"I have a permanent wave," she said, in a not unfriendly tone, but then turned back to the magazine.

Except for the armchair, the room was mostly bare of furniture. Lining one wall, floor to ceiling, were wooden bookshelves that looked homemade, filled completely with hundreds upon hundreds of *Vogue* magazines, their thick white spines neatly tapped into place.

"Do you remember me?" I said. "My brother, Wylie, and I used to live next door. With our parents. Arthur and Marie Fleming."

The names, even my mother's, provoked zero reaction from David's wife. She flipped a slick page with her index finger and shook her head. "They told me not to get a permanent wave," she said, "but where hair's concerned I know what I'm doing. I've been a student of hair since I was eleven years old."

Feeling hot breath on the back of my neck, I jumped. Donny was standing behind me, holding a glass of ice water, his cheeks flushed. He jerked his head sideways, to indicate that I should leave the room, and fast, then closed the door after me. Following him back through the house to the backyard, I tried to remember what his mother was like when we were young, but couldn't come up with a single thing. For all I knew, she could've been in that room reading *Vogue* the entire time; she'd clearly had the subscription long enough, anyway.

Donny handed me my glass of water and we sat at the picnic table, feet scraping the dirt, while I drank in silence.

"So, Lynnie," he said. "What are you doing tonight?"

"What?"

"Me and my friends are going to catch a movie, probably, if you wanted to come along."

I stood up. "Oh, jeez. I promised my mom I'd have dinner with her. Thanks for the water, though."

"Okay, maybe another time then. Hey, do you like miniature golf?"

"I really should get going, Donny."

He accompanied me around front to the Caprice, opening and closing the door in a gentlemanly fashion, and waved as I pulled away.

I turned the radio up high and took the highway to my mother's, driving extra-fast. I couldn't stop thinking about Daphne Michaelson flipping through *Vogue* and checking out runway fashions from a world she, so far as I could tell, had never encountered. And what on earth did she do during the school year, with both sons away, one for months on end, and her husband at work all day and then—a thought that tasted bad in my mouth—at some other woman's condo? Her plight seemed to me terrible. Then, from some distant part of my brain, I managed to retrieve a childhood memory: a backyard party at our house one summer night, a flock of people from the neighborhood, adults with cocktail glasses, kids with sparklers and hamburgers. The two Michaelson boys, toddlers, exhibiting athletic prowess even then, leaping over each other gymnastically, landing on their heads and bounding back up. My mother inside in the kitchen, talking with the other wives. My father at the grill, spatula in hand, frowning at the browning pieces of meat. And Daphne Michaelson by herself in the yard, quiet, exquisitely made up, swaying slightly in a flowered dress.

My mother and I got home at around the same time. Before she could say anything, I proposed that we have dinner together, "unless you have other plans," and she smiled awkwardly and said that sounded fine. I offered to make something, with the caveat that my cuisine extended only to items unwrapped and placed in the microwave. She smiled and said she'd be happy to cook. There was a kind of elaborate diplomacy between us. Actually, I thought, we could have used some form of simultaneous translation to help us communicate, as if we were foreign dignitaries.

"Lynn, could you set the table?" *Since you've accomplished nothing else useful this summer.*

"Sure, Mom." *That's not fair. I did bring Wylie home, and you made a mess of that.*

"Do you like Italian dressing?" *At this point I don't even know what you like, or even, frankly, care.*

"Anything's fine with me." *The feeling's mutual.*

I asked how her day was, and the trials and tribulations of travel-agency life kept us going through most of dinner. A couple who wanted to vacation on cruise ships presented her with a budget of five hundred dollars; another family required a money-back guarantee they wouldn't come down with food poisoning on a trip to Machu Picchu. Adventure without risk, luxury at economy cost, entertainment without the stress of activities, structure without schedules, and, always, free cocktails: these were the standard demands. Over coffee she asked how my research was going. When I said I'd hit upon an interesting topic for my dissertation, she frowned and said she thought that was already well under way. Probably I'd told her so myself. I explained that this impression was widespread but false.

"It's those paintings from the old house," I said. "The ones by Eva Kent? I'm going to incorporate them into my work."

She looked blank.

"On modernist values in feminist painters of the later twentieth century."

Now she looked blank but impressed.

"I have a strong feeling about those paintings," I went on.

"Goodness, those things," my mother said.

"I've been wondering where Dad found them," I said.

"I told you, I thought probably his secretary. You remember her, don't you, Mrs. Davidoff? She had terrible bunions. She always asked after you children."

"I can't really picture Mrs. Davidoff buying those paintings."

"Well, maybe not. She was a little severe. Of course I think her feet were giving her an enormous amount of pain. She had surgery eventually, a bunionectomy."

This gave me pause. "That can't be a real operation."

My mother looked offended. "Of course it is."

"Never mind," I said. "So do you think Dad could've bought them at a gallery? Or did he know any artists?"

"Your father didn't know anybody except the people he worked with, and us," she said. "You know that. He didn't have what you'd call a wide social circle."

"So where did he get them?"

"Well, sometimes they have those kiosks at the mall," she suggested.

I tried to picture Eva peddling her strange nudes outside a food court, and my father interrupting his shopping to speak with her, holding the painting by its frame and nodding his head in appreciation of the couple in *Desert I: The Wilderness Kiss*. Neither part of this was imaginable. When I was in middle school he almost always came home late from work, and would heat up his dinner in the microwave as I sat at the table and told him about my day. He'd eat straight out of the container, apparently indifferent to what it was, and I often thought I could've covered cardboard or mud patties or Styrofoam packing peanuts with tomato sauce and he wouldn't have noticed.

"I still think it's possible Bev Davidoff got it somewhere," my mother went on. "Secretaries used to do that kind of thing. There's no big mystery about it, Lynn. It was just a gift."

"But two paintings—a pair?"

"Maybe it was a sale," she said drily. "Frankly, I'm surprised you're even interested. You never seemed to care about New Mexican art before."

"I know," I said. "Listen, I saw Daphne Michaelson today."

My mother wrinkled her nose in a gesture I took for distaste and wrapped her hands around her coffee cup. "Did you," she said. "Where?"

I stared at her. Did she think that Daphne Michaelson was out grocery shopping or hiking in the foothills? Did she have any idea what condition the woman was in? "I went to their house. Well, I went to look at our old house, and while I was there I stopped by the Michaelsons' to say hello. David wasn't there but Donny was, and so was she."

"I see. So what does it look like? The house."

"It's covered in giant butterflies."

"Fake ones, I hope."

"They look tacky."

"The people who bought the house seemed very nice," my mother said in a pious tone. "A young couple with children."

"How long has she been crazy?" I said. "I don't remember anything strange from when we lived there."

"It's not nice to call people crazy." My mother stood up and began clearing the dishes. "Donny's a nice boy, isn't he? And Darren is, too. When he's away at school he calls David every Sunday night at seven o'clock sharp."

"So you've told me," I said. I followed her into the kitchen, carrying the sugar bowl and the rest of the plates.

"I always wondered why Wylie wasn't better friends with those boys. I know they're a bit younger, but it's not that big an age gap."

"You're kidding, right?"

"No, I'm not. They're perfectly sweet."

"They kill frogs for sport."

"Toads, aren't they? And he didn't know that until the other night," she said, dismissing it with a wave of her hand. Then she filled a sink with water and started doing dishes. I grabbed a towel and took over the drying. For a few minutes we worked together in a harmony I had a hard time puncturing. The condo's air-conditioning pumped audibly for a moment, then subsided. Outside, crickets sang their shrill, unmelodic song.

"You never answered my question," I finally said.

"What question was that?"

"About Mrs. Michaelson. How long she's been like that." I started putting plates and cups in the cupboard, lining them up in careful rows.

"I'm not sure," she said after a while. "I do know that her condition doesn't seem to be worsening. If she takes her medication and avoids stress, she's fine. David briefly had her in some kind of, you know, residence, but he couldn't stand seeing her in there. So he brought her home."

"How much does she understand of what's going on?"

"You know, Lynn, I've never asked her," my mother said, glancing away and—I suspected—rolling her eyes. She turned off the faucet and drained the sink, then paused for a moment with a sponge in her hand. "Up until ten years or so ago she was really quite lucid. When you kids were young we had no idea. You could talk to her, and she was odd—but within reason, you know."

"So to speak," I said.

She ignored me and set to wiping the sink and the surface of the stove, which, I didn't point out to her, was not dirty in the first place. "But then something happened, with the medication or something. I'm really not sure. Apparently your brain can adjust so the medication's no longer effective. Anyway, she got worse." She stood in the sparkling kitchen, looking for something else to clean. When she couldn't find anything, she put her hands on her hips and nodded, once.

"David will never leave her," I said. "Doesn't that bother you?"

"Of course it bothers me," she said, her voice rough. "It bothers me that you come home for the summer and do your best to ignore me from the minute you get here. It bothers me that my son lives in the same city I do and I'm lucky to see him every two months. A great many things bother me, Lynn, but I try to keep going as best I can."

This silenced me. A film of tears trembled in her eyes. Then the phone rang, and she stepped away from me to answer it.

"It's for you," she said.

Although I'd left him without regret the night before, I found myself hoping that it was Angus, calling from out of town or, better still, from some motel down the street. If he'd come to the door right then, I would've run out to the van within ten seconds. But it wasn't him on the phone; it was Harold Wallace.

"You told me to call if I thought of anything else," he said. "Well, I just thought of something else."

Twelve

I followed Harold Wallace into a back room. His blue eyes were crisscrossed violently with blood, but his hair was neatly gathered in a ponytail, he was again wearing expensive, loose-fitting clothes, and overall he seemed more alert than the last time. On the phone he'd been annoyingly mysterious, refusing to explain what he'd remembered until I arrived on his doorstep, and this morning he'd offered me coffee, tea, and even a plate of bizcochitos before I suggested, politely, that we just get down to business.

"Well, here we are. My office. The nerve center of the entire operation," he said. If this was true, then the operation was in a lot of trouble. The small bedroom—underneath a stack of books and loose papers, barely visible, was a single bed—had been buried beneath years' worth of bureaucratic detritus. Several filing cabinets stood half-open, their drawers stuffed beyond capacity with manila folders. Framed paintings and prints were leaning against every available surface.

"It's a system I devised myself," he said. "I know it looks strange, but it works for me."

"How long have you been retired?"

"Oh, I'm not really retired. I still sell work from home. Yes, I've still got the eye, if you know what I mean." He eyed my chest. I caught his bloodshot gaze and shook my head, and he shrugged and turned away, his smile hinting that it was mostly done out of habit anyway.

"So you remembered something," I said.

"After you left, I got to thinking about what you said about the child, and I remembered a girl who got pregnant and kind of disappeared. She was a wild one, that girl. Anyway, a few years later, she sent me a photograph of herself. A look-what-you're-missing-out-on sort of thing, if you—"

"I know what you mean," I said.

"So I just have to go through these files and look for it. Maybe you'd like to sit down? This could take a while."

I cleared a spot for myself on the bed and sat down to watch as he withdrew files, examined them, muttered to himself, then moved on to the next handful. Of course he could have done this before I came over, or left me alone to wade through the files myself. But he either meant for me to witness all his hard work or simply wanted company; watching him rifle through stacks of dog-eared manila folders, every once in a while glancing at me over his shoulder, I suspected it was the latter. Humming as he worked, Harold seemed perfectly happy to devote the entire morning to the search.

Actually, I felt more or less the same way. The night before, when I'd gotten off the phone, my mother was in her bedroom with the door closed, and I slunk off to my room feeling guilty and agitated. If she was going to run around with a married man whose wife was mentally ill, then she had to expect people to comment on it from time to time. That's what I told myself, but still I'd stayed awake for hours, thinking that I'd made my mother cry.

I thought about my father too, wondering if Harold could possibly be right about him knowing Eva Kent. Maybe he was driving back from the labs in Los Alamos one day, stopped for lunch, and got lost—people always do in Santa Fe. Say he went into the Gallery Gecko to ask directions, and there she was, sitting beneath one of her paintings and luring potential buyers with her brittle talk and strange, striking looks. She was the kind of woman who talked people into things, and my stammering scientist father was an easy mark who found himself glued to the tile floor in the small gallery's close, hot air. Eva told him her name and demanded to know his. "Arthur?" she said, smiling ferociously. "So do people call you Art?" At this point, my scenario ground to a halt. It was impossible to imagine my father falling into step with Eva, in whatever form it might've happened. Then again, I never would have imagined my mother with David, either, and this made anything seem possible. All parents, I thought, are mysteries to their children.

"How's it going over there?" I asked Harold.

He was sunk in thought over an open file, its manila wings vibrating in his trembling hands. "Here," he said, and handed it to me.

Inside, there was a photograph of Eva Kent standing on a beach somewhere, smiling, in a swimsuit and a sarong. The date on the white border read 1982. There was no child with her. Her body was heading toward middle age, spreading and sagging slightly. Her hair had been cut and layered, and its dark strands, waving in the breeze, were sticking up above her head like antennae. There was a kind of wild excess to her smile, as if she were uncomfortable, or drunk, or mentally unbalanced. Her arms and legs looked badly sunburned.

Also in the file were several pieces of paper. One was a yellowed strip of newsprint, a local paper's review of a group show, with a ballpoint star next to: "One artist of particular promise is Eva Kent, a fiery oil painter with a sure sense of composition and style. Her violent technique contrasts meaningfully with her cool-eyed appraisal of the relations between male and female." Beneath this was a letter from a gallery in New York, written to Harold, expressing interest in Eva's work, requesting slides and dangling the prospect of a solo exhibition. I flushed with satisfaction: I wasn't alone in feeling that jolt of electricity when confronted with her work.

The last item was a letter written on a sheet torn from a notebook, the writing slanted and blocky, almost childlike:

Dear Harold,
Here I am in California. I am feeling a hundred times bet-
ter. I know you will take care of things.
                                        XOXOXOXOXO
                                                Eva

"What kind of things did you take care of?" I said.

"Oh, Jesus, who knows what that crazy lady was talking about." Harold took the folder back, shut it, and sat down next to me on the narrow bed, puffing a little. "I've been thinking back to those days," he said. "Eva Kent. The memories come flooding back when you look at this stuff. She *was* one of the better girl painters, all right. And you know, it was a great time for men when women decided they needed sex if they really wanted to be free."

"I'm not sure that's exactly what they decided."

"It was definitely what some people thought, believe you me," he said, and smiled. "We'd go up to Madrid and take over some run-down houses up there and stay all night. Eva'd be right there in the mix, always with a different man. She was aggressive, liked to do the choosing and the talking, and it worked well for her, especially with shy, quiet types. You said your dad was a straight arrow, right? Well, maybe that's how he got the paintings. What do you think?"

I chose not to answer, thinking of my father—who was

nothing if not the quiet, shy type—partying with painters in an abandoned mining town on the Turquoise Trail. This made me smile. Harold smiled too, though I didn't know at what.

"The paintings my father got are really very good," I said. "So what was the rest of her work like?"

"Which ones are those? Oh, yes, the desert ones. Well, I'm not entirely sure what happened to the other ones."

"What do you mean you're not sure? Didn't you keep records? Isn't that what this room's for?"

Harold gazed at me, the file fluttering gently in his hands. "The seventies," he finally said, "weren't a time of meticulous filing."

I sighed. "What happened to her child? I mean, she did have one, right? I found a picture taken when she was pregnant."

"Yes," he said, "I remember. After she had the kid, things really weren't the same for old Eva."

"What do you mean?"

"She got that thing that women get," he said.

"You'll have to be more specific, Harold."

"After they have kids. You know, they get tired and emotional. As the British say."

"Do you mean postpartum depression?" I stood up, turning the concept over in my mind. "How bad was it?" Bad as a brain tumor, I was thinking, or a love affair with Diego Rivera?

"I don't exactly know," Harold said, shifting around uncomfortably on the bed. "She was definitely on the wacky side there for a while."

"Who was the father?" I said.

Harold shrugged. "Could've been anybody, you know. Anybody at all."

"What happened to the child?"

"I have no idea," he said.

"Are you sure? Isn't there anybody you could ask? And

what about her other paintings? Somebody must know what happened to them, don't you think?"

Harold physically retreated from this volley of questions, leaning back against the wall with the folder pressed against his chest, as if shielding himself from my thirst for knowledge. "I'd have to give it some thought," he said.

"Okay." I stood there looking at him, waiting.

"It might take a couple days."

"Well, all right."

"You'd come back, wouldn't you?" he said. "I'm starting to enjoy our little chats."

"Can I hold on to this picture while you do?"

"I guess so."

"Think away, Harold," I said. "You've been a tremendous help." At the front door, I turned around and kissed him on his dry, old man's cheek, and he beamed.

On the interstate, just past the future site of the Shangri-la golf course, I took an exit and turned back to Santa Fe. There was something suspicious about Harold's display of going through the files, only to pull out the right one at the exact moment I asked about his progress. The way he'd nodded so quickly and said that the father could have been anybody, and kept insisting that my father and Eva might have known each other. He knew more, it seemed to me, than he was letting on. For the moment I set aside my thoughts about the dissertation, and how I could sell it to Michael, to focus on my father. I felt an almost physical sensation of curiosity, a prickling down my spine, at the idea that I was going to learn something new, that there was a side to him I'd never noticed while he was alive.

Harold's red SUV was still parked in front of his tidy

condo, ready to navigate the ruggedly potholed streets of Santa Fe. I nudged the Caprice behind another expedition-style vehicle—fortunately, all the cars were so large that it wasn't difficult to hide mine—and rolled down the window. A breeze guided the smell of pine trees into the car. I could hear the tinny notes of an ice cream truck trolling for kids along some nearby street, the half-broken melody sounding sinister and intent. It was just past noon.

Harold came out fifteen or twenty minutes later, wearing a dark-blue shirt over skintight black shorts that glistened in the sun. Over his shoulder he carried a large cloth bag that reminded me of Irina's baby sling. I trailed him through lunch-hour traffic, wondering where on earth he was going in that outfit. His first stop was a health-food store in a strip mall. I gave him a few minutes, then stepped inside. If he saw me, I planned to act surprised and engage him in polite conversation about the benefits of whole-grain foods. But he was standing at the counter with his back to me, talking to a clerk about bee pollen. The smell of incense hung heavy in the air. Lurking behind a stack of unsweetened cereals and herbal teas, I listened to his querulous, shaky voice.

"I need energy," he was saying to the clerk, a young woman with a long ponytail and glowing, rosy skin. "I feel so run-down, I can barely get up in the morning. You know what I mean?"

"It sounds as if you have systemic issues," she told him.

"What do I take for that?" Harold said.

She steered him in the direction of some vegetarian multivitamins, and I went back to the car. Several minutes later he came out bearing a large brown bag, presumably full of systemic cures.

Back on the road, we weaved and dodged and changed lanes and turned corners—I tried to keep right behind him, for fearing of losing him—until he parked at another strip mall, in front of a coffee shop specializing in "locally roasted" beans. Pulling to the curb, I unrolled the window and smelled the burnt, acrid scent of the roasting. There were some elderly people lined up outside, apparently desperate for a jolt of caffeine. But Harold took his cloth bag next door, into Blue Butterfly Yoga. All of a sudden, following an old man with systemic issues to a yoga class, I didn't feel like much of a scholar. I crossed my arms over the sticky vinyl of the steering wheel, telling myself I was an idiot. Then I saw a woman with long dark hair get out of a yellow convertible and go into the yoga studio. From the back I couldn't tell how old she was, but I had a passing, insane thought: What if Harold knew a lot more about Eva than he was saying? What if this was her?

Inside, harp music was playing, and pairs of shoes were stacked in a cubbyhole unit in the entryway, exuding an unpleasant aroma. Copies of the Blue Butterfly class schedules were piled on a table and I grabbed one and stuck it in the back pocket of my shorts. On the other side of a blue batik curtain I could hear violent slapping sounds, punctuated by the occasional grunt, as if people were getting paddywhacked back there. I stuck my head around the curtain and saw it was a martial-arts class and that the slaps were people being flung to the floor by their instructor, a tiny young woman with her hair in pigtails. When she noticed me, she smiled brightly—a two-hundred-pound man still groaning at her bare feet—and said, "Ashtanga's in the other studio."

I left my sandals with the others and snuck into the back of another room, where Harold's shiny black butt was now cradled gently on a folded blanket. He was sitting in the lotus position, his back to me. At the front of the room, a thin young man with short brown hair sat with his palms pressed and his eyes closed, humming. Wearing a see-through purple tank top and blue tights, he appeared to be in amazing shape; even the veins that ran along his biceps looked perfect in their contours.

The room was very warm. There were around ten people, including the woman with the long black hair, who was sitting next to Harold. I grabbed a folded blanket from a pile at the back and sat down in the lotus position. My knees cracked loudly, and a bald man turned around to stare. I could hear Harold chanting "Om," his voice reedy and weak. The instructor raised his stringy arms straight up, displaying twin thickets of armpit hair and some remarkably well-defined abdominal muscles. The woman with the long dark hair released a long, sexual-sounding groan, but Harold paid her no mind. Imitating the instructor's movement, I swayed to one side, held the position, then swayed to the other. I closed my eyes. It was remarkably easy to follow someone, I thought, and insert yourself into their day. I should do it more often.

A general shuffling sound made me open my eyes. Everyone else had moved to the sides of the room, where they lay flat on their backs with their legs hoisted up on the walls, and I scrambled to follow. This was a mistake. No way could I get my legs flat against the wall, not without snapping them in half. The instructor moved lightly through the room, touching shoulders, at one point placing a foot on someone's stomach to flatten it. He had very long toes. When he reached me, sitting there in the lotus with my head bowed and eyes closed, I could hear him pause momentarily before moving on.

The heat now seemed even more intense, and sweat was streaming down my back. The people around me had moved to the middle of the room, where they sprawled on their backs, their legs doubled backwards over their heads and their arms twisted together. I had no idea how they'd accomplished this feat, or for what purpose. Even Harold had managed to contort himself into a semblance of the appropriate position. His T-shirt had slipped up, revealing a broad expanse of his starkly white skin, and sweat was puddled around him. Some people were twisted so far around that they were now looking back in my direction, their cheeks flushed and eyes eerily unfocused, their breathing labored.

The perfect muscles of the instructor were folded in on themselves like origami. "Hold it," he was saying. "Hold it."

How he could speak from within the pretzeled confines of his body was beyond me. I couldn't even make out where his head was. My own legs, though I was trying to extend them over my back like the others, refused to go any higher than my ears, and my stomach was killing me.

"Feel the toxins of the day draining away. From your heart, your liver, your kidneys. From your tongue, your teeth, your throat. Feel everything letting go."

Throughout the room, the breathing eased and quieted. People were actually taking the opportunity to ruminate while remaining in their positions. My legs mutinied and crashed onto the floor with a slap that broke the mood. The woman I'd taken to be Eva Kent turned her head and stared at me. She couldn't have been older than I was.

"Close your eyes. Feel the worries of the day leaving your heart." The instructor's voice was light and pleasant, with a chime almost, like a musical instrument. "Your heart is a feather in your chest."

I tried picturing this, and couldn't. Then I felt a hand touching my knee, and when I looked up, the yoga instructor was kneeling by my side.

"Feel the toxins draining from your system in your sweat," he said in his chiming voice. Then he hissed in my ear, in a distinctly unpleasant tone, "This isn't a beginners' class. Didn't you consult the schedule?"

"I'm sorry," I said. "I just wanted to check it out."

"Inside your body purity is emerging," he said sweetly, still glowering at me, and then whispered, "Level one meets on Tuesdays. Today's Wednesday!"

"Sorry," I said again.

"This happens *all the time*," he said, no longer bothering to keep his voice down. "It drives me completely freaking insane."

I stood up. "I'm going now." Everybody in the room was looking at me, all in various stages of unfurling, like fronds in spring. I gave Harold what I hoped was a nonchalant, vaguely surprised "Oh, you're here too?" wave. He just sat up and stared at me.

"I don't know why I bother to make these schedules when nobody reads them," the instructor said. "This is *advanced* Ashtanga, for crying out loud. Put your blanket back. Don't leave here without putting your blanket back."

I did as I was told.

"Folded!" he said.

The drive back from Santa Fe passed quickly, borne on the tide of my absolute embarrassment—Harold's face looming always before me, along with the rest of the unfurling yogis. What the hell was I thinking? I wished very much that the whole day had never happened.

I hit town at five o'clock, when Albuquerque's offices were evacuated as if in a sudden panic. So far as I could tell, nobody in this town ever worked a minute later. Fleeing employees stalled the roads in every direction, one per car, heads lolling in boredom, staring straight ahead. I rolled down the windows and got a lungful of exhaust-redolent air. The two interstates that met in the city arched and crossed, bridges above air, in the center of the sky. Over everything in my view lay the pallor of dust. I exited and drove the back streets instead, recognizing in my desire to keep the car moving, even if the route ultimately proved far longer, a tendency of my father's. Wylie had it too. Waiting at a red light behind two other cars, I thought I saw the eggplant-colored Plumbarama van drive past in the opposite direction. I made a quick right, but by the time I got turned around the van was nowhere in sight. Probably I had just imagined it.

I cruised through residential neighborhoods, at a speed that felt more like walking than anything gasoline-powered. Dogs lay still and panting in the shade of trees. Cats were in hiding. In someone's yard two small children were playing a game that seemed to involve the simulation of vomiting. As I drove past, one of them lifted his arm and shook his fist at me.

Threatened by children, humiliated by yoga instructors, and sticking sweatily to the vinyl front seat, I finally pulled into my mother's driveway. Nobody was home. I tossed my sweaty clothes onto a pile and took a quick, cold shower. Then I found a beer in the back of the fridge and sat in the backyard, the sweet relief of alcohol slipping down my throat, the wafting suburban smells comforting me: the charcoal smoke of backyard grills, the first hints of citronella, the gasoline putter of lawnmowers and weed whackers. I was half-asleep by the time a car door slammed shut out front and my mother and David came around the back.

"Hey, it's Lynnie!" David said, holding out his hand. "We saw that fearsome contraption of your brother's in the driveway and guessed you were back."

I nodded. My mother, without meeting my eyes, gestured toward the back door. I held it open for her and she stepped inside, carrying a brown paper bag of groceries.

"You'll join us for dinner, I hope," David said.

The Missing Person

In the kitchen my mother was making short work of the groceries. Into the crisper flew the broccoli and green beans. Up into cupboards went the cereal. The breadbox, of course, was the destination of bread. Plastic bags, empty, folded, and creaseless, met their fate in the recycling bin she kept beneath the sink. David and I stood on opposite sides of the kitchen, watching her.

"Nobody puts away a load of groceries like your mother," he said fondly. Crouched down on the floor, rearranging some delinquent items on the lower shelf of the fridge, my mother blushed and glanced at him briefly, a swift, demure look that made me feel like an intruder. I was about to go back outside when she straightened up and held out a bottle of beer in my direction, still not looking at me. I opened it by covering it with the hem of my T-shirt and twisting, which David seemed to interpret as a sign of weakness.

"Let me do that for you," he said, holding out his large hand.

"That's okay. I've got it, thanks."

"If you're sure," he said. I was already drinking from the bottle. He smiled down at my mother.

"Excuse me for a second," I said. I walked down the hallway to my room, which in every respect contrasted poorly with the rest of the house: the bed was unmade, the floor littered with clothes that had a faint but unmistakably organic scent. I was becoming one of the great unwashed. Eva Kent's paintings sat on the dresser, their thick layers of paint as violent and mysterious as ever. I sat down on the bed. In a pine tree just outside the window, a bird—I didn't know what kind—cackled and squawked. The world was densely populated with things I did not know. There was a soft knock on the door, and my mother came in. She'd changed from her office clothes into shorts and a loose-fitting shirt, and looked comfortable but fatigued, very fine lines etched everywhere on her skin. "Everything all right?" she said.

"Mom," I said, "I just didn't have a very good day."

She sat down next to me, and I remembered how, when I was sixteen, I'd been forced by my parents' machinations to go on a date with Francie Garcia's son, Luis. I had a zit on my forehead the size of a quarter and felt monstrous and degraded by adolescence. The date, by mutual consent, was short. I slunk home afterward and found my mother waiting for me on the couch in the living room, with the television on. My father had already gone to bed, and I sat down next to her, furious, undignified, and told her I would never let her do that to me again. Then I leaned my forehead against her shoulder and cried. "If you wait long enough," she said, "this will all be over, and it will get better. I promise."

Now, in silence, we sat in her condo with her married boyfriend here and Wylie not here, and I wondered if this was what she'd meant by "better." Then she put her hand on the small of my back, still not saying anything, and I knew that this at least was true: in this house, on this day or any other, I would never be refused.

Thirteen

An uneasy peace is peaceful nonetheless. I was surprised at how happy I was, over the next few days, to play the good daughter, tidying up around the house and waiting for my mother to get home from work. I put all thoughts of Harold Wallace and his yogically contorted buttocks out of my mind. Several times we had dinner with David, the three of us marshaling enough energy for friendly conversation about topics of the day. We never talked about Wylie. David's manner toward me became less bombastic, more subdued, and he no longer cried out my name like a cheer every time he saw me. This came as a relief. My mother cooked a sequence of elaborate meals—from braised lamb shank to chicken satay—which she arranged on serving plates in displays worthy of food magazines. There were desserts and specially chosen wines. She emerged from the kitchen bearing fragrant dishes, blushing proudly at our praise.

I thought, None of this is so hard.

One sweltering Wednesday I even went down to her office so we could have lunch with Francie and Luis of the long-ago date. He and I ate enchiladas and watched our mothers beam at each other with pride. After a little while I understood what Francie had meant by saying she didn't think Luis would ever settle down: he was gay. All his teenage awkwardness had been replaced with an almost intimidating social ease. He was beautifully dressed and mannered, pulling out chairs for his mother and mine; drawing his mother out on the subject of her spectacular garden; making us all laugh. Francie put her hand over his and squeezed it as she bragged relentlessly about his accomplishments at work and exclaimed how lucky she was to have him around. It verged on disgusting. Then, halfway through the meal, she excused herself to visit the ladies' room, and I saw a trace of exhaustion emerge on his careful features. All this politeness and admiration and laughter was part of some agreement between them, some ongoing negotiation that made everything else, within limits, okay.

When Francie came back from the restroom, pink lipstick and blue eye shadow brilliantly reapplied, she asked what was new with Wylie these days.

My mother shook her head. "I've deferred to Lynnie," she said. "She's the only one who can talk to him."

Francie gave me a generous and approving smile. "It's so good you're back!"

"I guess so," I said.

"It's been like that ever since they were children," my mother went on. "Wylie would keep secrets that only Lynn could hear about. He'd creep into her bedroom at night and whisper them to her. Nobody else could know."

I looked at her. I remembered Wylie chattering, and me telling him to shut up and go to sleep, but whether there was any exchange of secrets I couldn't say. Luis smiled at me, sipping his iced tea.

"She even got Wylie to come back for dinner," my mother said. "I'm hoping by the end of the summer, he might even spend the night. It's like domesticating a wild animal. You have to take it a little bit at a time."

Francie and Luis laughed. The tone of my mother's voice

was confident and humorous and, it seemed to me, utterly false. Not to mention the improbability of Wylie coming home any time soon. She was either offering the most favorable interpretation of events or else hoping that by presenting an optimistic scenario she could somehow make it real.

The idyll of the good daughter lasted less than a week. What broke the peace was this: I drank at least a bottle of wine over dinner with my mother and David, preceded by a gin and tonic and followed by a healthy dose of Kahlua she'd produced from some hidden cupboard, after which I fell into a deep yet troubled sleep rife with pornographic dreams. Then I woke up at five in the morning, thirsty, restless, and wracked by the kind of loneliness that can't be cured by having a nice chat with your mother. I had to see Angus again.

It was so quiet in the condo that I could almost hear my mother and David breathing behind their closed door. Outside, the sky was packed with stars, but already lightening to purple in the east. There was a burnt tinge to the air, the distant smell of wilderness fires. I got into the Caprice and drove to Wylie's apartment, feeling alert and alone. There was no answer when I knocked, but when I tried the door it wasn't locked.

The place was empty and dark, and I stood in the middle of the room waiting for my eyes to adjust. Then something damp and rough brushed against my leg: the dog, licking me.

"Are you all alone here, Sledge?" I said. "For a bunch of animal lovers, these guys don't pay you much attention."

In answer, he worked his tongue down my calf.

"That's enough," I said.

There was a rustling sound, and a shadow appeared out of the back. Even in the dark I could tell the figure wasn't tall enough to be Angus. After more rustling and some muttering, a flashlight clicked on and I could see Irina, in a blue nightdress, standing there blinking, looking sleepy and confused.

"Irina, it's me," I said.

"Oh, my goodness. Is everything all right? Are they in prison?"

"Are who in prison?" I said.

"Oh, my goodness," she said again. "Never mind, then." She set the flashlight down on the kitchen counter, so that its pallid ray stretched across the room. Sledge whined once, as if for show, then lay down at my feet.

"I'm sorry to disturb you," I said. Even in the dark, I saw her face was creased with sleep and concern.

Suddenly the flashlight rolled off the counter and crashed onto the floor. Sledge jumped, and from the bedroom came the anguished sounds of Psyche waking up. I picked up the flashlight as Irina went back to get her, and played the light, in turn, on the dog, the bare floor, and the bedroom, where Irina stepped out cradling the baby in her arms, rocking back and forth and cooing soothingly.

I went to the window and pulled the sheet loose from the duct tape, letting the vague light of early morning into the room.

"Are you all right?" Irina said. I looked down at myself, at shorts and an old T-shirt I didn't remember putting on, feeling as if I'd only just then woken up. "Where is everybody?" I said.

"They're off working."

"Wylie too?"

"Sometimes he helps on Angus," she said.

"Out," I said. "He helps out."

"That's what I said," she said, smiling. "Would you enjoy some breakfast?"

Somehow, in an apartment with no power, she made a delicious meal. First, she put a clean baby blanket down on the floor and laid Psyche on top, the baby watching us drowsily, kicking her fat legs a few times before falling back asleep. Then she pulled a small camp stove from a milk crate and heated water over the propane flame, adding dried fruit and powdered milk and maple syrup to some kind of hot cereal, and finally brewed tea. We lingered over breakfast in the cool, gradually brightening apartment. Through the window early-morning sounds made their way into the apartment: trucks barreling distantly past on the highway, the twitter of birds. Psyche smacked her lips in her sleep, but her moon face was otherwise still. We were sitting on the floor, with steaming, maple-scented bowls between us.

"Why did you ask about prison?" I said.

"Oh, no reason."

"Most people don't bring up prison without some reason," I said. Irina shrugged, and the baby lifted her head and said, "Guala guala," still asleep. Irina smiled. "She is practically obsessing with gorillas."

"You were telling me about prison."

"Nobody's in prison," she said firmly, and hoisted Psyche onto her chest. She was sitting cross-legged, and for the first time I noticed that her legs were unshaven, brown with hair down to her ankles, and her toes had thick, curved nails. She reminded me of some fairy-tale creature, part human, part animal, who lives in the woods.

Then Psyche woke up and moved a tiny curled fist to her mother's breast. Irina unbuttoned her pajama top and looked up at me. "Does this bother you?"

I shook my head.

"I am glad of that," she said, starting to nurse the baby. "Some people we know, they do not like to see the baby."

"They don't like babies?" I said. "What's their problem?"

"It's because of VE. I'm not adhering."

"What's VE?"

"Voluntary extinction," she said. "No breeding. That's what they call me. The breeder. Not Wylie or Angus, but some of the others."

"Jesus H. Christ," I said slowly. "That's crazy."

Irina shrugged and cupped the back of Psyche's head in her hand. The baby was sucking dreamily, one hand resting gently against the exposed breast, her eyes closed. "It's actually the opposite of crazy," Irina said. "It is totally logical. The logical consequence of thoughtful people observing our world. If you think that humans are destroying the planet, Lynn, and the population is growing too fast, then it only makes sense not to procreate. Trying to slow things down is everyone's responsibility. VE begins at home."

In a way, I thought, this made sense. If you believed that overpopulation was an ecological crisis, why would you bring a child into the world? And if you believed that most people's lives were ruined by unnecessary materialism, then it made sense to share an empty apartment with a handful of like-minded people. And yet, I thought, looking at the baby cradled in Irina's arms, they were crazy, too. "Jesus H. Christ," I said.

"You keep saying that," Irina said sadly, "but I don't know why."

I smiled at her then. She seemed like the most innocent person I'd ever met. "Who's Psyche's father?" I asked again.

She smiled at me shyly, then blushed deep crimson. "It's no one you know."

"Are you sure?"

"You are afraid it's Angus," she said suddenly. "It is not. And it is not Wylie, either, in case you are wondering that."

Now it was my turn to blush. "Okay," I said.

Psyche had stopped nursing and was fast asleep.

"Do you know," I said, trying to sound casual, "when Angus is getting back?"

"Oh." Irina looked surprised. "I thought you had arranged the plan to meet him here. He's coming back today."

I felt strangely contented, hanging out in the bare apartment with Irina and her child. We could hear the building rise slowly into life, the banging of doors and the starting of cars, an early-morning argument downstairs.

Irina told me about meeting Wylie, and this version of her life story was less mythological than the one about being transported by a nature special. She had arrived in Albuquerque, a little over a year earlier, but she was homeless. Her dreams about a new life had slipped so far from her grasp that she couldn't remember how she'd come to hold them in the first place.

"I was also," she said, "having a little problem with the drugs."

"What kind of drugs?"

"Many kinds. The social worker said I had a diversified appetite."

I looked at the baby, who had rosy, healthy skin and an appetite confined, from what I'd seen, to Irina's milk.

"So. I was living out of the dumpsters. And I met these people, these boys, who were also living out of the dumpsters. We were always meeting at these same dumpsters. The ones behind the pizza restaurant by the school are good, and also behind the grocery store. But these young men are doing this by their choice. It was like a whole new idea to me, do you see? A whole new meaning of life. I thought, maybe I am not just a drug-addicted person. Maybe I can believe in something also."

There was a pause.

"I know what you're thinking," she said. "You are thinking, Jesus H. Christ. But this is what happened. And then Wylie, he helped me go away from the drugs, and he let me stay here whenever I wanted to, and the rest was easy. I have learned so much since I have met these people."

"Okay," I said. I stood up to stretch, and I was in the middle of a big one—arms above my head, stomach exposed—when Angus opened the door and saw me.

"Hello, stranger," he said, and his voice warmed me like the sun.

Then my brother, Stan, and Berto came through the door behind him, their skin and clothes smeared with dirt and sweat. Sledge went into a welcoming frenzy, leaping up on each of them and licking their faces and stinking bodies. I felt the same way the dog did. I was being released from my calm existence in my mother's condo, from the days of boredom and good behavior. I caught Wylie's eye and said hello as Angus and the others carried backpacks and milk crates into the apartment and dropped them on the floor.

"What are you doing here?" he said.

"Looking for you," I said, "like always."

"Yeah, right," he said, glancing at Angus.

I blushed for the second time that morning, strongly and with conviction. I'd really taken to shame, it seemed. Then I looked over at Irina; she smiled as if she understood, and I felt better. "Where have you guys been, anyway?"

"Bisbee," Wylie said.

"What the hell's in Bisbee? And please don't say 'Bisbee.'"

"It's just a place we like to go," Wylie said, and rested his skinny hand, for the briefest moment, on my shoulder.

The group convened, cross-legged, on the floor. It was daylight now, and through the open windows I could smell freshly laid asphalt from some distant driveway.

Angus clapped his hands.

"The time has come," he said, "for the next plan."

I was more curious than I would have expected to hear what new instance of extreme behavior they'd invented this time.

"No way, man," Berto said, to my surprise, his gray, hang-dog face even more ashen than usual. "The time has come for breakfast, man, if you know what I'm saying."

Angus put his hands on his hips. His clothing was in tatters: his jeans had holes, his white T-shirt had holes, even his socks had holes. Through the tears in the fabric his pale skin glowed. I wanted to go over and touch it.

"Is this how everybody feels?" he said.

Everybody nodded.

"I can cook breakfast if you bring me some supplies," Irina said from the counter, where she was perched with the baby in the sling.

"All right, then," Angus said. "The time has come for breakfast."

So the morning began all over again. Angus left and returned with a backpack crammed full of fruit and eggs and bread and sausages, which Irina cooked over the propane stove. People showered, more quickly than I'd thought possible, and some even rummaged around by their sleeping bags for clean clothes.

After eating, Stan and Berto fell asleep on the floor, their heads on their still-rolled sleeping bags, Sledge snoring along with them. My brother was standing in the bedroom doorway watching Irina and the baby, who were also sleeping. He'd grown a beard since I'd seen him and looked fatherly and devoted, and in the back of my throat I felt the sudden, harsh salt of tears.

Angus came up behind me and put his hands on my shoulders. "There's a roof," he whispered.

We climbed up a fire escape and found ourselves looking out over the drab rooftops of the student ghetto. It was still early in the morning, and the sun was gentle. Angus lit a joint, then handed it to me.

"Did you get this in Bisbee?" I said.

"What's that supposed to mean?"

"That's where Wylie said you went."

"Well, Bisbee's less an actual destination than a state of mind."

"If you say so," I said. I was trying to identify precisely when I got stoned, a moment that had always eluded me in the past and now seemed, for some reason, within my reach.

"How's the research coming along?" Angus said.

"Not so good," I said, not even wanting to think about it.

Angus sat down on the roof, leaning back on his elbows, and grinned at me. His cheeks and the bridge of his nose were pink from the sun. I sat down beside him, wondering where his hat was.

"You should leave the library and take to the streets," he said. "Put down your pen and join the cause."

"I mostly use a computer," I told him. "Not a pen."

"My point remains the same," he said, and exhaled smoke.

"I think you'd like some of the art I work with," I said. "I study a lot of revolutionary people, guerrillas who were trying to change society. Women putting their bodies on the line."

He raised his eyebrows and looked unconvinced, then rolled onto his side and put his hand on my thigh. "Like how?" he said.

"Picketing museums, doing outrageous performance art in public spaces, that kind of thing. This one woman wrote a poem, rolled the piece of paper up, then scrolled it from within her, you know, *body* and read it out loud to an audi- ence. And there were these others who dressed up like cheerleaders and each had a letter on her sweater—a C, a U, an N, a T—and they did cheers to, like, take back the word or whatever. They were very political."

Angus was smiling, with his eyes closed. "I like you," he said, "because your secret rebellious side is so badly concealed. That's why you hang out with me so much."

"I don't have a secret rebellious side."

"In fact it's not even a secret."

"It is too," I said.

"So you admit it."

"I don't even know what we're talking about," I said.

Angus laughed, and after a second I did too. I lay down next to him, my face to the sun, and put my hand on his leg. The sweet smell of pot rose and buzzed around my ears. Angus covered my hand with his. Then, long before I was ready to leave, he stood up and pulled me to my feet and said it was time to get going.

Back in the apartment the troops were rallying, sort of, sleepily and with some complaints. "Does this have to be done *today,* man?" Berto kept saying. Wylie sat in the corner with Irina, silent and deeply tanned and expressionless, holding the baby. Even the dog lay on its side, only one eye open, mustering a minimum of enthusiasm.

"This one's ready to go, so why wait?" Angus said. "The hard work's been done. The rest of the troops have been informed. It's a cakewalk."

"What is a cakewalk?" Irina asked.

"It's something easy," Angus said eventually. "Easy as pie."

"You know, I have tried to make pie," she said, "and it is not very easy."

"Irina," Wylie said. "Never mind."

"It is the crust part that can be hard."

"What are you guys going to do?" I asked him.

"It's the Sandias," Angus said.

The plan, he explained, was to remove the crest of the Sandias from the life of the city, to take it away, temporarily, so that people would remember that it was there. Most people forgot to even look at the mountains, as they went about their pitiful day-to-day lives. This was what he called them, "pitiful day-to-day lives," in a tone I hadn't heard before: sharp with not just excitement but disdain. I wondered if he thought my mother's life was pitiful, or mine. In fact, I decided, he probably did, but also thought that I could be saved from it or somehow redeemed.

"So, we'll divide," Angus was saying. "Kickoff time is midnight. Stan and Berto, you two take the roads. Wylie and Irina and I will take the tram."

"Who's going to secure the airspace?" I asked. There was a silence. "Just kidding," I added, but nobody laughed. "Where do I go?"

"Home," Wylie said.

"No."

"Yes."

We glared at each other, both of us cross-legged on the floor.

"Children," Angus said quietly, seeming amused. "Lynn, you'll come with me. We'll all meet back here at midnight. Class dismissed." He clapped his freckled hands, and the dog jumped.

Angus wanted me to while away the afternoon in a motel, but I had other plans. Cornering Wylie, I told him there was something I wanted him to do with me.

"Not go home," I said, before his scowl could harden. "Someplace else. Come on, I'll let you drive the Caprice."

"You'll *let* me drive my own car?" he said.
"Yes. I'm that generous."

I directed him through traffic without telling him where we were headed, though he figured it out soon enough.

"Nice butterflies," he said, looking at our old house. "You're on a big nostalgia trip, aren't you?"

I opened the car door. "I want you to meet somebody," I said. I got out, walked up to the Michaelsons' front door, and knocked, Wylie following slowly behind me.

Daphne herself opened the door, wearing a navy-blue business suit with white hose and matching blue pumps with little white leather bows. She looked beautiful, glassy and severe, like a Midtown skyscraper. For a second I thought I'd imagined the entire thing: her insanity, her room, her collection of *Vogue* magazines.

Then she said, "I knew you were coming." She stepped back from the door and walked away down the hall.

I followed her, and could hear Wylie behind me, although I didn't look at him. Daphne Michaelson led us into the same room, the magazines neatly lining the walls, and sat down in the same chair, arranging her skirt neatly over her knees. She smelled like Chanel No. 5. There was nowhere else to sit, so Wylie and I just stood there.

"What I'm about to tell you," she said, "cannot leave this room."

"Mrs. Michaelson, do you remember us? Wylie and Lynn Fleming, we used to live next door?"

She nodded. "You're here for the files. Everything is carefully maintained." She pointed to a box on the floor that held another stack of magazines, an issue of *Mademoiselle* on top. "Rose red, romantic red, red in the afternoon," she said, looking back and forth between me and Wylie with a gaze of such intensity that I had to will myself not to nod. She took a manicured finger and wiped the pad of it across her mouth, then held it up. "Ragtime red," she said.

I realized that she was naming lipstick colors. "Mrs. Michaelson," I said, "I think—"

"Listen," she said, "I tried to tell you earlier. It's a permanent wave."

Wylie said, "Mrs. Michaelson, are you taking your medication?"

She stood up. In her classic pumps she was as tall as he was. "Light is what makes every color," she said. "Especially red. I prefer a red with bluish undertones myself."

Wylie was looking away from her, at the door.

"Light can be both particle and wave," she said to me. "Did you know that?"

I couldn't get enough of looking at her. I was fascinated by her conviction, her craziness, her aging, manicured beauty, and I wanted to hear what she would say next. She could have been a performance-art piece, a portrait of a madwoman in an attic of fashion magazines; yet she wasn't acting. I could have stayed there all day, and I probably would have if Wylie hadn't physically dragged me—exerting a surprisingly strong grip around my shoulders—from the house.

On the sidewalk, in the painful, brilliant sun, Wylie punched the air and said, "Why did you show me that? Why?"

"Because," I said, "there's nobody else to show."

Fourteen

At midnight, there were more people in Wylie's apartment than I'd seen since that first, partylike meeting, and the same atmosphere was building. Some people were drunk or at least tipsy, and Berto greeted me with an uncharacteristic hug, his breath sweet with beer. From what he and Stan said, I knew Angus had been out drinking with them, but it didn't show. His posture was as straight as ever, and when I came in, alone— after our little excursion, I'd gone back to my mother's and Wylie had taken off somewhere on foot—he only winked. I sat down on the sleeping bags next to Sledge, who was gazing balefully around the room.

There were at least ten people I didn't recognize, all wearing hiking clothes; some had clipboards and milled around with what looked to me like a false air of efficiency. One of them cornered Wylie, just as a young woman with a long braid and a red T-shirt sat down next to me, smiling brightly.

"I haven't seen you before," she said. "Would you like to be on our mailing list?"

I looked at her. "Um, I'm just Wylie's sister," I said. She nodded, still beaming, and held out her hand.

"I'm Panther," she said.

"Okay," I said.

"I'm the media coordinator. Would you like to sign our petition?"

"Sure," I said. I scribbled my name without even bothering to read the sheet, distracted by Wylie, whose quiet conversation had turned into an argument.

"We've put a lot of work into this," he was saying, "and you won't even listen to my position paper?"

"Because that's not how you deal with the media," the other guy said, exasperated. "Because there are *proven* ways to conduct *effective* activism. Because antics like draining pools detract from those of us making *real* change."

Wylie got right in his face, the toad-killer look back in his eyes.

"What do you call *real*? Sitting in a tree again? Helping suburban moms master recycling techniques? Giving inspirational talks to schoolchildren about saving the cute little animals of the forest?"

"Damn," Panther said quietly, next to me.

"Nothing ever changes. Go sell some more greeting cards."

"Those were postcards," the other guy said, "and they raised money for overhead."

"Get out of here," Wylie said.

Stan and Berto were staring at the ground. Angus was watching, avidly and without distress, as if it were a gripping scene from a movie. Irina, standing in the bedroom doorway with Psyche in the ever-present sling, went over to Wylie and touched his arm. It was the first time I noticed the way she looked at him—as if he were a hero whose most sterling qualities she alone appreciated. She stood on tiptoe to whisper something in his ear, and he shook his head and folded his skinny arms.

"Let's go," the other guy said. "This is bullshit."

"But you were supposed to help us with the media, man," Berto said.

"Wylie doesn't think you need any help," he said. All the

strangers filed out behind him, with their clipboards and backpacks and water bottles, and some of them, I noticed, looked like they regretted leaving the party.

When they were gone Wylie pulled a folded piece of paper out of the back pocket of his dirty jeans. "I've written our position paper," he said very quietly.

"Go ahead," Angus said.

Wylie read like a kid giving a book report, forgetting to pause at commas and periods, assuming he'd used any to begin with. "We are creating a wilderness refuge. What is the nature of a wilderness refuge? We think of it as a place where animals are guaranteed a livable habitat, but this guarantee is all too limited in scope. It is the habitat itself that requires a refuge from the constantly encroaching structures of civilization. We must develop a form of resistance to these structures. We must be willing to imagine an alternate world." As he read, I closed my eyes and remembered those middle-of-the-night e-mails; their tone seemed different to me now, less ranting than lonely. I bet he wished I were still in New York, the conveniently silent recipient of his ideas.

"Do we save wilderness so that humans can enjoy it, aesthetically or otherwise? This way of thinking leads to shallow, insincere, and manipulative forms of conservation. Trees left uncut by the highway while behind them denuded, clear-cut land extends for miles. Farmed salmon dyed pink to mimic the flesh of wild fish that have been harvested to extinction. These pretenses allow us to believe that we are not destroying the world in which we live. But we do not save wilderness for our own sakes; we save it for its own. Because ethics are real, and once they are acknowledged they must be pursued to their logical ends."

I listened carefully to this speech. Earlier in the summer I'd seen Wylie and the rest as operating under the sway of irrational passions, but by now my feelings had changed. I even understood their dissatisfaction with the larger group. They were after something bigger than greeting cards and media coordination. Most activism seems crazy at the beginning; any position that imagines changing the status quo contains an element of the fantastic. I thought of what Irina had said, the first night I'd met her: "Just people who want to be living differently."

"Ordinarily such an act of creation has been the province of the federal government but we see no reason why this power should be held in the hands of civil servants rather than ordinary and enlightened citizens. We see no reason why 'refuge' should be a bureaucratic label rather than a political act. Therefore as of today we are making the mountains into a wilderness refuge. The place itself is a refugee from humans; the place itself, not one endangered species or tree or habitat. The fact that this act will be temporary makes it no less meaningful. The wilderness needs a refuge."

Heads bowed, coughing slightly, we waited to see if this was in fact the end of the paper.

"That's it," Wylie muttered.

Irina clapped madly and everyone else joined in, making Wylie blush. Blushing was epidemic among this crowd. The saying "his heart is in the right place" ran through my mind, as if I could picture it, visible through his chest, his young, still-beating heart.

Stan and Berto took off on bicycles, their muscled legs pumping. Wylie got the keys from me and drove the Caprice with Angus next to him up front and me and Irina in the back, with Psyche in the sling murmuring commentary. "Guala guala," she said to the window. I spoke her name, and she turned to me and said the same thing. She had some kind of rash across her face, but it didn't seem to bother her. Angus kept looking back over his freckled shoulder to check on me and smile, which I found nice at first and then kind of annoying. After a while I stared out the window at the rows of subdivisions, the bright hulks of shopping malls and cineplexes, the great arcs of overpasses. As we approached one, I saw two shadows moving beneath a light up there, a movement that for a second resolved itself: teenage boys staring down at traffic, holding rocks in their hands.

After twenty minutes or so, Wylie turned onto a road that was dark and wooded, lacking in neon and traffic. We passed a church with a bright white sign: THIS IS A C H C H. WHAT'S MISSING? U R. Psyche began to fuss, and Irina jiggled her on her knee and then nursed her until she quieted. Nobody was saying anything, and I couldn't tell whether it was because I was there or because they were preparing themselves for what was about to happen.

The road started winding up the crest of the mountain, signs for picnic spots and fire-danger warnings posted alongside the asphalt. We hadn't seen a single car since turning off. I wondered how Stan and Berto were supposed to ride their bikes all the way up here after drinking for hours, and began to doubt that the plan would come off. I felt sorry for Wylie, actually, all his philosophy and passion dissipated into this midnight drive. Then he pulled onto the shoulder and parked.

"Wylie and I are disabling the tram," Angus said after we all got out. "Stan and Berto are working on it from the bottom. On the way down we'll close the road. You guys are lookouts."

"Lookouts?" I said. "That's it?"

"Lynn," Irina said softly, smiling her pretty, calming smile. "It's okay."

"But it seems so sexist. Men do the big stuff, and women just stand around."

Angus winked at me. "Can you wrestle a steel cable? Or drag a log across a road?"

"No."

He shrugged. "Then you're the lookout."

I put my hands on my hips and watched as Angus and Wylie disappeared into the darkness.

Irina didn't seem to feel slighted in the least and sat down on the Caprice's massive hood while managing to keep the sling in place around her chest. Nothing fazed her, I realized, nothing would ever faze her, a fact that annoyed me very much. I set off walking after Angus and my brother. It was almost cold up here at the top of the mountain, and I crossed my arms against my chest. Pine branches were scraping against each other in the wind. I thought I heard an owl hoot, although given what I knew about owls, it could as easily have been a distant car horn. Beneath the trees it was very dark, but as I followed the trail that led to the tram, I heard a crash and scuffle that was almost certainly the sound of vandalism and moved in that direction.

The last time I'd ridden the tram was with my family, when I was a teenager, and an old college friend of my father's was visiting. The only time anyone from Albuquerque takes the tram is with out-of-town friends. Mr. Dennison was tall, thin, and youthful, with curly black hair and a bizarre penchant for Adidas shorts and Hawaiian shirts. But it wasn't his clothes that bothered me. I was convinced he was looking at me inappropriately. I was fifteen and had just figured out that men were capable of and even prone to such behavior. I slouched against the glass as the tram ascended and my father pointed out various features of the steeply inclined landscape, the hay-colored sprays of cactus and stark, strong blooms of century plants. My mother and Wylie stood on the other side of the car, both facing out the window: Wylie with his nose pressed up against the glass, leaving smudge marks, and my mother behind him, her hands on his shoulders. Mr. Dennison kept glancing over at me and smiling with a friendly zeal that I found highly suspicious. "This is spectacular!" he said to my father, still smiling at me. My father just nodded and kept on listing species of cactus; he'd memorized all their names when he moved to New Mexico and never missed a chance to demonstrate this feat of botanical knowledge. Once we got to the top I took off on a walk, abandoning everybody else, and soon was standing in the pine trees, alone—fists clenched in anger, disoriented, wanting to make some kind of gesture or point—and lost. I was filled with wordless rage toward my parents, and especially my father, for not noticing what was going on.

I wondered now what my father thought I was doing, tramping off like that. Maybe he saw it as just another blind, teenage rage—which in a way, I guessed, it was. Probably I was as strange to him as he was to me. Anyway, I would never know if it had even registered on him at all. I kept walking for a few minutes, feeling my way in the dark, thinking I was getting closer, until I realized that once again I was lost. I had no idea where Wylie or Angus or the tram might be. Then the owl hooted again, twice, insistently. It *was* a car horn.

I turned around and started back, climbing upward, and before long I saw the car's headlights flash on and off, showing me where to go. By the time I got there, everybody was standing around, looking superior and amused.

"Don't say a word," I warned them, and they didn't.

Wylie pulled into a rest area toward the bottom of the crest road and parked, Stan and Berto promptly emerging from the trees with their bicycles. Irina unclipped their front wheels and started stowing them away in the trunk, so I helped her as the men walked off into the forest. When we locked the car and followed, I could hear rustling and voices but couldn't see a thing. Then Irina pressed a flashlight into my hand. "I'm going to wait here in the car until you come back," she said.

"Where am I going?"

"They have something to show you," she said.

By the anemic light I could make out four silhouettes far ahead of us. I beamed it directly on Wylie, who looked back at me, startled and wide-eyed as a deer.

"Don't do that," he said.

I hurried toward them, but Wylie was gone—his disappearance nearly instant and complete. I stood still, breathing hard, beaming the flashlight around until it lit on Angus, who was leaning against a tree trunk, watching me stumble around.

"How are you with small spaces?" he said.

"Tell me what's going on."

He was next to me then, taking the flashlight out of my hand and inserting his own hot, dry palm instead. He pointed the beam at a boulder ten steps in front of us, and I could see a hole in the ground with fresh dirt at the edges. "Down," he said. "About six feet. Then you'll walk a few steps, then go down again. I'll be right behind you."

"You have got to be kidding."

He laughed. "Your lack of courage is very honest." Then he pushed me forward.

Just below the lip of the entrance I could feel a horizontal bar, the top rung of a ladder.

"Don't bother looking down," Angus said, switching off the flashlight. For some reason I closed my eyes, as if that would be more comforting than the darkness of the forest.

"Six steps," he said. "Then dirt."

He was right. At the bottom of the ladder I stepped away and he came down after me, then we went farther down and moved along a cramped dirt tunnel into a space large enough to stand up in. A propane lamp sat on the open seat of a folding chair, Stan and Berto on the ground next to it, giggling and drinking beer. The air was cool and oddly fresh, fragrant with earth.

It was a room of dirt. Lining the walls were plastic bottles, dried food in pouches, garbage bags, and a bulletin board with a diagram of the tunnel system and a small Chamber of Commerce poster. A red sun was setting over a brown, cracked landscape below cursive blue lettering: SPEND THE SUMMER IN BISBEE, ARIZONA.

Wylie came in from some other tunnel and stared as if challenging me to say something, which I didn't. I could tell that he was proud of what they'd done, and it was pretty amazing, their little fort.

"We've got enough food and water," he said, "for four of us to last two weeks."

"Would you really stay here that long?"

"As long as it takes."

"Takes to do what?"

"Make a point," Wylie said. Berto muttered, "Excuse me"—to me apparently—and picked up an empty plastic bottle, then ducked out of sight into one of the tunnels.

"You can stay if you want," Wylie went on, "but you'll have to bring your own supplies. You can take Irina and Psyche back in the Caprice, and be back before the walls go up."

"You're welcome to stay," Angus put in. "But we thought you should see the place before you made your decision."

"What walls?" I said.

"We're barricading the road," Wylie said. "To make the refuge. Weren't you listening to my position paper?"

I sat down on the ground next to Angus, who touched my knee gently, in a gesture of either encouragement or concern, I couldn't tell which.

Berto reappeared, sloshing his plastic jug. "We're going totally feral down here, man," he said.

"Except for the beer," I pointed out.

"Nobody ever said beer and ecology are incompatible," Angus said cheerfully.

"How do you—" I said.

"The bottles are for pissing," Wylie said, "obviously. There's a funnel setup girls can use. Women, I mean. There's plastic bags and toilet paper for the other business. It's two weeks, Lynnie. Not the rest of your life."

I couldn't remember the last time I'd heard him use my name. He was waiting for me to answer, and I wanted to prove to him—to all of them—that I could make it. That they could survive down here impressed me as much as the space itself. But the smell of dirt all around me turned from fresh to rancid, and I thought about worms in my hair and the stench of shit in plastic bags. I imagined the tunnels collapsing, and couldn't breathe. "I'm sorry," I said, "but there's no way."

My brother nodded, as if he'd known all along that this would be my response.

Angus stood up, and he didn't look particularly surprised, either. "I'll take you up," he said.

Berto and Stan didn't even wave.

It was two o'clock in the morning when I pulled into my mother's driveway. I was about to unlock the front door when David Michaelson opened it.

"Well, if it isn't the coal miner's daughter," he said, smiling broadly.

I didn't smile back. "Excuse me," I said, pushing past him.

My mother was sitting on the couch by the television in a light-blue bathrobe, a mug of what looked like warm milk cradled on her lap. "You're back," she said.

"What are you doing up?"

"I haven't been sleeping well," she said. Her tone was so extremely neutral as to make it even more laden with reproach. "We were watching a late movie."

On the TV, Frank Sinatra was sweating horribly in black and white, and I thought of his sweet sounds playing in Wylie's car, Angus beside me, singing along. But here, in *The Manchurian Candidate*, Frank was drunk. Raymond Shaw, the angular, government-programmed assassin, was also drunk, and waxing nostalgic. "I used to be lovable," he was telling Sinatra. "You wouldn't believe how lovable I used to be."

"This is a good movie," I said, and my mother nodded.

"The days were lovable, the nights were lovable, everybody was lovable," Raymond Shaw said bitterly. He was recalling an innocent and happy summer of his youth, a time that was sunny and irretrievable, and I thought I knew how he felt.

My mother patted the couch beside her. David was still lingering somewhere behind me, waiting, I guessed, to see what I'd do. "Have a seat," she said in the same weirdly neutral tone. "Tell me what you've been up to."

I shook my head, gesturing down at myself. There was no way I could sit down next to her, in her clean bathrobe, on that clean couch. "I'd better take a shower," I said, "I'm filthy."

"That you are!" David boomed. When I turned around, he was smiling widely at me. "You're filthier than an alley cat in a rainstorm."

"Is that a saying?" I said.

"It is now," he said, patting my shoulder. "You go wash up, dear."

I fled the room. In the shower I lathered, rinsed, and repeated, trying to get my hair clean. The smell of my mother's strawberry shampoo was like candy. I felt like I couldn't keep going back and forth between these two worlds—from tunnels to strawberry shampoo—without going crazy. I understood, now, why Wylie couldn't answer my mother's questions about what he was doing: because it was absurd to be feral in a condo; it was ludicrous; it was damning. Yet the condo itself was absurd, too, its cleanliness and decor almost wilfully oblivious to the real matters of the world. I rubbed conditioner that smelled like almonds into my scalp, and stood in the shower for a long, long time.

When I got out, my skin was loose and puckered, and my mother was standing in my room, going through the clothes on the floor, checking the pockets before dropping them into a laundry basket.

"What happened to the movie?"

"I know how it ends," she said. "Angela Lansbury's evil."

"I've always thought so," I said, and lay down on the bed. *The Wilderness Kiss* and *The Ball and Chain* stared at me from the dresser, their thick slabs of paint stark and shadowed in the light of the room, and I propped myself up on the pillows to look at them. The man in the first painting, I noticed, was thin and dark, Fleming-like. Why was I so convinced my father couldn't have known Eva? How well had I really known him, after all? The longer I stared at the paintings, the more certain I felt that there was some reason I'd found them. I wasn't given to wild imaginings or superstitious by nature, but it was as if they'd somehow demanded to be unpacked and examined.

My mother dropped what she'd found in my pockets on the dresser, then hoisted the laundry basket and left, turning the light off as she went. It seemed like only seconds later that she was back, shaking my arm, and thinking she had some question about the laundry—did I sort my whites from my colors, and how on earth had I gotten so *dirty?*—I shook my head and told her to go away. Instead she opened the blinds, and sunlight rioted into the room. It was morning.

"You've got to come watch the news," she said.

When I wandered into the living room, she and David were sitting on the couch in their bathrobes, now holding cups of coffee. It was like a perpetual pajama party around here. I wondered whether they watched this much television all the time. Standing in the doorway, yawning, I looked at the screen. A massive barricade made of tree trunks and barbed wire was stretched across the road to Sandia Crest, draped with posters: NO BARBECUES NO LITTER NO TRAIL EROSION and WHO WILL SPEAK FOR THE MOUNTAINS IF THE MOUNTAINS CANNOT SPEAK FOR THEMSELVES?

"As if mountains even wanted to speak," David said.

"Shut up," I told him.

"Sorry," he said, to my surprise, as my mother sat watching with her hands curled tightly around her mug, ignoring both of us.

A reporter explained that the tram had been vandalized and the roads blocked by a group of "radical environmentalists" who had faxed a statement to all the news channels. I knew this must have been Irina, whom I'd dropped off at a Kinko's near campus. The reporter read a few sentences from Wylie's position paper; then the shot widened to include Panther, whom he described as a "local activist and author." Clipboard in hand, she was wearing her hair in a high ponytail. "These actions may be misguided," she said breathlessly, "but the issue of wilderness protection is crucial." Then the camera cut away to a Forest Service ranger, who said only, "Steps are being taken to reopen this popular wilderness area to the public."

My mother sighed once, heavily, as the reporter nodded and signed off—"Live, from the road to Sandia Crest." Neither she nor David said much as they got ready for work. I assumed that my mother didn't ask me how much I knew about it only because she didn't want to know how much trouble Wylie was going to be in.

Alone in the condo after they left, I kept checking the news, but there didn't seem to be any developments. Around noon, I drove over to Wylie's apartment, where the door was locked and no one answered my knocks. I wondered where Irina and Psyche were. Back at my mother's, I called Worldwide Travel, and my mother told me that she and David were going out to a movie.

"You could come if you like," she said. "Might be a good distraction."

I decided I wasn't desperate enough for distraction to be a third wheel on a date with the two of them, and declined.

On the five o'clock news, they showed bulldozers loading the debris from the barricades and reported that the tram would be back in service by the morning. I drank all the beer left in my mother's fridge and ate microwave popcorn for dinner, then crawled into bed by nine.

A nightmare woke me sometime before dawn: I was being buried alive, underground, and though I knew Wylie and Angus and Berto and Stan were there, I couldn't find them in the collapsing walls of dirt. I kept waking up every hour or so until early morning. When I finally got up, I was alone again in the condo, and on TV a different reporter was announcing that the Forest Service had taken suspects into custody. Back in the studio, the anchorman shook his head, smiled wryly, and moved on to the weather, which was hot and dry and lacking in surprises.

I drove to Wylie's apartment, which was still empty, and then down to police headquarters.

At central booking two young clerks were busily chatting and ignoring my existence.

"So she's all 'What are *you* doing here?'" one said to the other, who was posed by a filing cabinet, holding a folder in her manicured hand.

"And I'm all 'I was invited.' And she's all 'By who?' And I say, 'Maybe you should ask your *boyfriend*.'"

"Excuse me," I said.

"And she's all 'He's not my boyfriend.' And I'm all 'That's not what I heard.'"

"That's totally what I would have said," the other girl said.

"Excuse me," I said again. "I'm looking for some friends of mine. I think they might be held here?"

Both girls stared at me as if I'd wandered by accident into their home.

"Wylie Fleming?" I said lamely. "Angus Beam?"

The storyteller broke into a vague smile and swiveled in her chair to her terminal, her long fingernails clicking loudly on the keys. "Not here," she said, then spun away to continue her story.

"They were arrested up on Sandia Crest," I said.

She glanced at me over her shoulder, surprised and a little annoyed that I was still there.

"Oh yeah, the stinkies," the other girl said.

This made me bristle. "They're just standing up for what they believe in."

"They reek," she said.

"I know," I admitted. "Look, are they here?"

They looked at me skeptically, and I knew how Wylie and his friends must have felt all the time: indignant and moral and misunderstood. I stared back at them, waiting.

"One of them's downstairs," the first girl finally said. "Tall guy, in a tank top."

"Can I see him?" I said.

While she went to check, I flipped through a worn, stained copy of *People* magazine that was sitting on the counter, an issue I remembered reading in Brooklyn, right after Michael invited me to Paris. Thinking of him now—his bracelet, his arms, the line of hair at the back of his neck—was like looking at something through the wrong end of a pair of binoculars: shrunken and small, as if seen from a great distance. Finally the clerk escorted me down a hallway and into a room filled with long tables. I sat down at one, and a guard brought Stan in. He was indeed wearing a tank top and did indeed reek. There were circles under his eyes and streaks of grime on his muscular arms, but he didn't seem the slightest bit unhappy. He sat across from me with his hands folded, like an obedient student.

"Do you need a lawyer?" I asked him.

"No, we've got a court-appointed guy."

"Who's in here with you?"

"It's me and Berto."

"What about Wylie and Angus?"

"They got away. It was part of our agreement."

"Kind of sucks for you," I said.

He shrugged. "Next time it'll be somebody else's turn to take the fall."

"Do you need anything?"

He looked at me. "They'll probably take off for a while. Lay low. You're not going to tell anybody anything, are you?"

I shook my head.

"I knew you were all right," he said.

It seemed like the nicest thing anybody had said to me in a very long time.

Fifteen

When I got back to my mother's the condo was silent except for the hum of the air conditioner and the muted cries of sun-dazed children playing in the yard next door. I went to my room and lay down on the bed, looking at Eva's paintings. On the dresser was the junk my mother had removed from my grimy clothes, and I sighed and made to throw it away. Loose change, a bottle cap, a matchbook, scraps of paper: the negligible archaeology of my summer. One slip of paper turned out to be the flyer from Blue Butterfly Yoga. Harold was probably in class right now, breathing deeply. I glanced at the schedule, to see whether he might in fact be there, and only then did I notice that the name of the skinny, uptight instructor was Lincoln Kent.

I sat down on the bed and puzzled this through. I'd had the sense that Harold was hiding something, and while Kent wasn't a particularly unusual name, the yoga instructor looked about the right age.

Moments later I was driving the now-familiar route to Santa Fe, the Shangri-la billboard still promising a lush green future, though a corner of it had begun to peel away, revealing the old ad beneath. I saw a car stopped on the shoulder, and a man peeing beside it, with nowhere to hide in the open landscape and no shyness about it, either.

Harold answered the door wearing a long linen tunic and matching beige pants. His eyes were bloodshot, and his red face was crisscrossed with wrinkles and broken capillaries.

"Advanced Ashtanga," Harold said agreeably, and stepped aside. "Would you like to come in?"

Standing in his white living room, I wasn't sure what to say next. A glass of white wine was sitting on the coffee table.

"Can I get you anything?" He didn't seem at all disturbed that I'd just shown up, unannounced, at his house. "Maybe a drink?"

"Okay," I said.

He rubbed his hands and nodded, looking pleased. Any drinking companion at all was probably fine by him. He went into the kitchen and came back with another glass of white wine. It was barely noon, but I shrugged and took a sip.

"Lincoln Kent," I said. "He's Eva's son, isn't he?"

"Well, aren't you the detective," Harold said.

I guessed he was being sarcastic, and chose to ignore it.

He sat down on the couch and gestured for me to do the same, giving me another up-and-down look. I had the distinct feeling that he approved of the sundress I was wearing. I rolled my eyes and sat down at the far end of the couch. "Why didn't you tell me?" I said. "And pretend not to remember Eva in the first place?"

"Because it isn't really any of your business," he said. "You call my house, then show up asking all kinds of questions. Some people like their privacy, and I don't know anything about you."

"I'm not doing anything terrible," I protested. "I'm just trying to learn something about an interesting painter. How bad can that be?"

"I don't know," Harold said. "How bad *can* it be?"

"Is Lincoln your son?" I asked.

Harold sighed and took a leisurely sip of wine before setting his glass down again. He was shaking his head slowly, though whether in denial or disbelief at my nosy questions it was hard to say.

I decided to ask another. "What happened to Eva Kent?" I took a long swallow of the wine he'd poured for me. It tasted expensive. I put the glass down and turned my knees toward him.

He leaned back and laid his arm across the back of the couch. "Well, Eva had that postpartum thing you were talking about. We all thought she'd snap out of it but she kept getting worse. I was giving her a solo show at the Gallery Gecko, a big deal. We got all excited about it—you know, hanging the paintings just right. Little Linc was maybe a year old."

He chuckled, fondly, and sipped his wine, on the verge of another reverie.

I suspected this was a pose designed to keep me in his living room for as long as possible; it seemed less lecherous than desperate, and I wondered just how alone he was. "So then what?" I said.

"Right. Anyway, after this depression thing Eva'd been painting these crazy pictures. She thought she could see into the future. Her work was always real sexual, but after the baby it got kind of distorted, and people started freaking out. The pictures of her and the baby—well, they didn't seem right. This only egged her on, of course. She liked controversy. Or at least the attention."

"What happened to those paintings? Did you sell any?"

"No, I didn't," Harold said. "Because the night before the opening, after we finished hanging the show, she left Linc at home and burned the whole gallery down with a can of gasoline and a book of matches. She hated herself, I think that's why, but of course nobody knows."

"Jesus H. Christ," I said. "So most of her work is gone?"

"I thought all of it was," Harold said. "And I'm not sure how your dad got hold of the ones you have. But it really was tragic. She had talent, and everybody knew it. You could just tell she was working on a whole different level, if you—"

"I know what you mean," I said sincerely.

"Anyway, they put her in some kind of home. First they'd tried letting her live on her own, but she stopped taking her drugs and ran away to California—which is when she sent me that picture you saw. Then they got her back and stuck her in a place in Albuquerque, and she never painted again. Not that I know of, anyway."

"And Lincoln?"

"Farmed out to various relatives and whatnot. Under the circumstances, I don't know how he grew up to be so normal. It must be all that yoga. I go to his classes all the time. I like to keep an eye on him. Sometimes we have lunch."

"Are you his father?" I said.

Harold snorted. "God only knows. Well, God, and Eva."

I stared at him in repulsion.

"Oh, come on," he said. "I'm just kidding. I'm not his father."

"Are you sure?"

"Yes, of course," he said, staring down at his white carpet for another long moment. "I was doing a lot of stuff those days," he finally said. "It was a time of experimentation, of pushing boundaries."

I nodded. "Yes, I know. I study that period. Experimentation with sexual politics, a push to be frank and honest about the body's functions and desires."

"That's not exactly what I meant," Harold said wrily. "More like drugs and drinking . . ." His voice trailed off as I kept looking at him; then he added, "You can imagine the effect of that kind of lifestyle."

I had no idea what he was talking about: forgetfulness, or promiscuity, or sloppy personal hygiene? Then I did. If you do a lot of drugs and drinking, you can't always follow through on the body's functions and desires. From the darkness of his blush and the fact that he could not meet my eyes I understood that he was telling the truth, and that all his sexual bragging had been just that, an exaggerated fiction.

"I know what you mean," I said gently, almost wanting to put a hand on his shoulder. But if Harold wasn't the father, I thought, then who was? I pictured Eva in my mind, and the vision was nightmarish: she was dribbling a can of gasoline around a room, deranged and leering, insane, while fire trucks howled outside. Putting my father in that picture with her was impossible, and yet I couldn't stop thinking about it, either. I felt a kind of energy building inside me, a force that swam through my blood like intuition. Fragments turned and spun in my head: the disorienting paintings; Eva's strange, grinning face; my father, who owned her only surviving work. I remembered the serious and distracted look he always had after a long day at the office, and now in my imagination this look took on a deeper, more romantic cast. All my memories were changing, shifting their forms. I saw an almost logical progression from past to present, from him to me, that was confirmed by the paintings propped against my dresser. The reason I'd felt that jolt of electricity, that lightning-bolt sense of recognition when I'd seen them, had to do the persistence of objects, the power of physical things, which were how the dead could communicate with the living.

In *The Ball and Chain* there were slashes of paint on the woman's body, all shades of red, thick as mayonnaise, raised and bumpy. Some reds had blue undertones, others yellow, some as dark as Daphne Michaelson's red lipstick. I thought of the way she'd named colors, as if reciting a code. Light is what makes every color, she'd said, and can be both particle and wave—these were such weird statements coming out of her mouth, and not likely something she'd read about in the pages of *Vogue*.

It made me wish I'd deciphered my father's book on the temporal dimension in physics, and I thought, then, of Daphne standing alone at the backyard party, watching my father at the grill, watching the other women from inside the house. It occurred to me that she was trying to tell me something about my parents. She was there, after all, and could've seen everything that went on between my father and Eva Kent, between my mother and her husband. She'd identified the slash of red across her own face with a purposeful tone that was difficult to ignore; it was as if she were invoking the slash of red on the face of the woman in *The Wilderness Kiss*. And that light can be both wave and particle—what did that have to do with lipstick? Maybe nothing. Or maybe she meant that a single person can have two natures—that the father I knew was also painted by Eva Kent.

"What institution is she in now?" I asked Harold.

"It's right by the yoga studio," he said. "Linc rented that studio so they'd be close. He's a good kid, visits her all the time. Enchanted Mesa, I think they call it. Don't know where they come up with these names. There's nothing enchanted about the place, I'll tell you."

"Probably not."

"I guess you'll be going," he said, "now that you know the story."

He walked me to the door, looking defeated and sad. Before I could think too much about it, I leaned over and kissed his wine-sweetened lips. He accepted the kiss with a kind of stunned grace. "Thanks for your help, Harold," I said. "I mean it."

"You're welcome," he said calmly. As I drove away I could

see him watching me and leaning, as if swooning, against his front door.

It was late afternoon when I got back to Albuquerque, the day windless and harsh. Children and dogs were splashing in pools, shirtless men bent over the hoods of their cars, joggers with skin tanned the color of chocolate milk. In a city park, under elm trees, an extended family was having a barbecue, heat from its coals funneling up through the air, and the bright trash of chip bags and soda bottles scattered around them. There was only one person I urgently needed to see.

At our old house the butterflies still climbed across the walls, short of their destination. I rang the doorbell at the Michaelsons' and waited for a full minute before Donny came to the door, looking as if he'd just woken up, the thick creases in his meaty cheeks reminding me, eerily, of scars.

"You again," he said. "Can't get enough of me, huh?"

"Right," I said. "Can I see your mom?"

"My mom? Why?"

It was a perfectly reasonable question, and I wasn't sure how to answer. Because I wanted to know exactly what she meant by "It's a permanent wave"? This didn't seem like the right thing to say. I smiled at him.

"She must get lonely, sitting in that room all the time," I said. "I thought she might like having visitors."

Donny frowned. "I don't think she really gets lonely."

"How do you know?" I said. "Have you ever asked her?"

"Uh, no."

"So you don't actually know."

"I guess not." He nodded slowly, then stepped back from the door and started down the hallway. Passing the kitchen, I saw Darren standing there; when he saw me, he waved, seemingly without surprise, and asked if I wanted a Popsicle. I shook my head no, and he shrugged good-naturedly. Donny knocked on the door of his mother's room and let me in.

"You don't have to stay," I said. "I'll just visit with her for a few minutes."

He nodded again, slowly and a bit sleepily, and left.

Daphne Michaelson was as beautiful and well-maintained as the last time I'd seen her. Her red nail polish looked professionally applied, and her hair shone. She didn't look at me. She was reading *Vogue* and nodding sagely at the pictures, as if they were revealing truths she'd long suspected about the world.

"Mrs. Michaelson," I said, "What's the permanent wave?"

She lifted her head and stared at me, a band of irritation rippling across her face at the interruption.

"Do you know who I am?" I said. She didn't acknowledge the question, so I tried a different tack. I looked down at the glossy photos in her lap, where thin and gorgeous women were cavorting in an African savanna, wearing clothes of primitive and dangerous glamour; their lips were black and their teeth pointed and white. "I think those, um, fur-trimmed toga things are pretty," I said. "Although I think it would be hard to walk around with all those claws and teeth, don't you?"

Daphne straightened her posture and smiled at me. "It's only fashion," she said in a confiding tone. "It isn't about the everyday world."

"I guess you're right," I said.

"I know I am."

"What did you mean about the permanent wave?"

She smiled at me gently, as if she felt sorry about how dense I was, and I sensed she was going to tell me something important, an answer she'd been waiting to deliver for years. What she said was, "It's a chemical process for altering the texture of hair."

Just then the door opened and David Michaelson came into the cool, dark room. Daphne went back to looking at her pictures, without acknowledging him in the least. I spent a second wishing hard that I was not here, or that he wasn't. He was wearing one of his cowboy shirts with black jeans and a brass belt buckle. He was not smiling.

"Excuse me, Lynn," he said. "May I see you outside for a moment?"

I walked out on insubstantial legs. He held the door for me, closed it behind us, and then gripped me by the upper arm, hard, and marched me out of the house and to my car. I felt like a juvenile delinquent with an angry high-school principal. The sun outside was so bright it made my eyes water, and I must have looked for all the world as if I were crying. David stood with his hands on his belted hips, examining my face in a measured, leisurely fashion, like the lawyer he was. He smelled like sweat and men's deodorant, that fake, pungent musk.

"Why are you always here?" he finally said.

"I think 'always here' is overstating the case a little."

"You've been here several times."

"I've dropped by once or twice to say hello," I said.

David snorted at this response, and I couldn't blame him for it, really. He shook his head and tried again. "Why do you keep coming over to my house?"

"I didn't think you'd mind," I said slowly, "since you're always coming over to mine."

He breathed in sharply, his mouth open, and I could see his small, even teeth. Glancing away, I saw Donny and Darren watching us through the living-room window. Darren had an orange Popsicle in his hand; Donny grinned at me and waved. I waved back.

"Is that what this is about?" David said. "You don't like my relationship with your mother, so you're coming over here as some sort of revenge?" The words "my relationship" sounded very strange coming from him. "Again, possibly you're over-stating the case a little," I said.

He sighed and looked off into the distance for a moment. I thought I saw a glimmer of wetness in his eyes, but it could have just been the glare. "My wife is a very sick woman," he said. "She doesn't live in the same world you and I do. But that doesn't mean she can't be upset by things. I don't like for her to be upset."

In the house next door, the house where my mother answered the phone on the day my father died, staring at the receiver afterwards for a long time, as though it had grown utterly foreign to her—as if the world itself had grown foreign—a woman opened the front door and walked down the driveway carrying a large plastic cup with its own plastic straw. She opened the door to her SUV and waved in our direction. "Beautiful day, David!"

"Sure is, Marlene," he called back.

I took advantage of this break in the conversation to walk around to the driver's side of the Caprice.

David looked at me over the hood, squinting.

"I care about your mother," he said, "and you should be better to her. You and your brother both."

I was stuck to the ground, paralyzed. What saved me was a blur of orange Popsicle in the window, which somehow reminded me of Angus: the smoothness of his warm skin, its ammonia smell, its sweet, abundant freckles. As soon as I saw him again I could forget all of this existed; I would be calm. Was that a definition of love: a force that can drug you with calm and help you forget all the sandpaper realities of the world? Why not? On the force of this question I was able to get in the car and drive away, leaving all the Michaelsons behind.

Sixteen

Almost as much as the condo or Wylie's apartment or the motel rooms I'd shared with Angus, the Caprice had become a kind of home. Feeling at ease on its cracked vinyl seats, surveying its dark-red dashboard and ivory paint, I'd come to think of it as mine. So when I left the Michaelsons' I spent a while just driving around the August-dead city, the flowers dry and nodding, the grass in lawns gone halfway to dirt. The white rocks in other yards looked skeletal in the sun, each one a bleached, miniature landscape worthy of O'Keeffe. At an Allsup's I stopped for gas and a bucket-sized soda, its sweet cold shooting straight to my brain. At the counter, a middle-aged couple was arguing about the nutritional value of the fried, crusty burritos that lay baking under the orange heat lamps, while the teenaged clerk batted her long, fake eyelashes in boredom.

At a pay phone in the back by the restrooms, I called information and asked if there was a listing for Plumbarama. There was, but the phone rang almost ten times before a man answered.

"Yeah," he said. It wasn't Angus.

"Is this Plumbarama?"

"Who wants to know?" he said.

His voice, growling and a little bit slurred, sounded

vaguely familiar, but I couldn't quite place it. "I'm sorry," I said. "I must have the wrong number."

There was a pause. "I'm sorry too, lady," he said, then hung up.

I stood there for a moment sipping from my enormous drink, the sugar singing in my blood, and then called back. This time, the phone rang for almost a full minute.

"Yeah," he said.

"Is this Gerald Lobachevski?"

"Who wants to know?" he said again.

Now I was sure it was him. In the background, I could even hear faint trills of slot machines and country music. "This is Lynn Fleming," I said. The only reaction was silence. A boy in a red uniform came toward me swiping a dirty mop over the dirty floor, and I flattened myself against the wall to let him by. "Wylie's sister," I added. "I'm looking for Angus?"

"He's not here," Gerald said.

"Where can I find him?"

"I don't know."

"Can you tell him I'm looking for him?" I said.

"No."

The conversation reminded me of the first time I met Angus, a memory that was dramatic and sensual in my mind: the dark, bare apartment, Angus bare-chested and heavy-lidded with sleep. The beginning of things. Angus then was every bit as unhelpful as Gerald was now; all he said was that Wylie had gone to the mountains, to grapple. Maybe Angus had some grappling of his own to do, or maybe his location couldn't be discussed over the phone.

"If you see him, tell him I have a plumbing job for him."

"I won't see him," Gerald said flatly, and hung up.

I left the Allsup's and kept on driving. Where do you look in a sprawling city for an eggplant-colored van? Nowhere in particular. I went back to the foothills, where Angus saved me from heat stroke, and drank the rest of my Coke and dozed a little in a shaded picnic area. I was half-convinced that he'd automatically know where to find me, because he had a knack for showing up at the right place at the right time, and half-convinced that I'd never be able to find him again, a possibility that crashed inside me with dread. Inside the park restroom was a scrawl that read, JODI S. WILL SUCK YOUR COCK FOR FREE, ASK AT ALLSUP'S ON CANDELARIA, which was where I'd just been. I thought of the bored young woman watching the burrito argument from beneath her long fake eyelashes, and wondered whom she'd antagonized and how.

No one was home at Wylie's. Turn your back on these people for more than ten minutes, I thought, and they completely disappear.

I tried to think this through, from Angus's point of view. Say he was looking, what did he know about where to find me? That I was uncomfortable at my mother's, that I drove around a lot, and occasionally rifled through books at the library. So I headed to UNM, to the fine-arts section, and spotted a redhead asleep in a carrel next to the books on Southwestern art of the latter twentieth century.

"Hey," I said, shaking him. "Hey." I wasn't even going to pretend I wasn't happy to see him. He woke up and pulled me onto his lap all in one second. Feeling his skin against mine was like coming home; it was like having questions only he could answer. He kissed me, his hands on the back of my neck. I moved around so I was straddling him. His hands moved down my sticky back, his mouth all over mine. We were jigsawed, meant to fit together, making a whole picture. He tapped on my shoulder, hard, and I leaned back to ask what he was doing. But it wasn't Angus who had tapped.

"Excuse me," a young woman said, "but you can't do that in here." A student worker with a cart of books to reshelve, she looked dismayed in the extreme.

I reached a hand up to wipe my mouth. My whole face was wet.

Angus said, "We were just leaving."

So it started again: long hours in a motel room, the Nalgene bottle full of gin, the sweet delirium of sex, the TV on low. Midnight found us lying together hip to hip, the sheets disheveled, and Angus said, "We've got a real rapport."

"If that's what you want to call it," I said.

"We don't have to call it anything."

"True enough," I agreed, and fell asleep, breathing the smell of his skin.

Angus woke up laughing, which I'd never seen anybody do. He sat up and put his arms and legs around me from behind, my back to his chest, still laughing.

"What's so funny?"

"I was dreaming," he said in my ear. "I was dreaming *this*."

It was another hour or two before we left the room. Angus suggested we go past Wylie's and check in there; they needed to plan their next move, he said, now that the mountain project was over.

"No plumbing today?"

"I'm on a hiatus," he said vaguely, and started the car.

"You know, I called Plumbarama yesterday, looking for you, but they wouldn't pass on a message."

"You did what?"

"Called Plumbarama. I didn't know how else to get in touch with you, short of calling all the motels in town."

He was staring at me. "How'd you get the number?"

"It's listed."

"What did you say when you called?" He looked worried, for the first time that I'd ever seen.

"Why do you list the number if you don't want people to call?"

"Unlisted costs extra," he said, leaning his forehead against the steering wheel. "Nobody ever calls."

"Maybe you should look into advertising," I said.

"What did you say?"

"I said I was looking for you. I said I needed some plumbing done."

"You didn't."

"I told him who I was."

"Told who?"

"Gerald."

"How'd you know it was him?"

"I guessed," I said, "on the basis of the fact that it sounded just like him."

A smile broke over him then, and he shook his head and turned on some music. Frank asked luck to be a lady tonight, and Angus sang along.

I was nervous about going into Wylie's apartment—having ducked out of their tunnel—and stuck my hand in Angus's when we walked inside. He squeezed, then let go. Stan and Berto glanced up, looking unaffected by their stint in jail. I asked how they were doing, and Stan said, "We're out on our own recognizance." Sledge dutifully licked my hand. Irina smiled at me and said, "Look who's here, Psyche," and the baby stared at me as if I were a stranger. So, for that matter, did Wylie. Everybody was sitting around talking, and to my surprise nobody seemed distressed by their failure to keep people off the mountain for very long. They wanted to know if I'd seen their "event" on the news and made fun of Panther for being such a media hog. Every face had a rosy glow. Even Wylie looked happier than I'd seen him in ages.

Now they were talking about whether to take the day off. Wylie was against it, arguing that "the revolution doesn't come with *vacation time*," but was outvoted and backed down with little protest, which I took as a sign of how good he was feeling. Stan and Berto wanted to hang out and drink beer, and the rest of us decided to go for a hike.

Angus drove. The sun shone with a riotous purity, picking out sparks of bright metal in the streets and glinting off cars, the world seemingly lit and mineral, rampant with gems.

We stopped at a grocery store near the university, where shopping carts were scattered across the asphalt expanse of the parking lot. Angus and Wylie got out. A man in a cowboy hat was leaning against the Pepsi machine outside the sliding doors, panhandling. I watched Irina change Psyche's diaper in the backseat, putting the dirty one in a plastic bag from the back of the van.

"I take it you don't use disposables," I said.

"Goodness no! I'll clean that one when we get into the mountains."

"Oh," I said.

"Lynn," Irina said gently, "there is shit in nature. Humans shit. Animals shit." In her accent it sounded like "sheat," and somehow more elegant.

"I know, I know," I said, leaning back in my seat and closing my eyes.

"What we have to get away from," Irina said, settling herself and the baby in the back, "is this idea that we are separate from nature. We are natural too, with bodies and smells, just like the animals do."

I kept my eyes closed and listened to her lilting European intonations while ignoring the words of her harangue. Eventually I heard the car door open and felt a breeze rush into the van.

The Missing Person

"You should've seen that dumpster," Wylie said. "A cornucopia of provisions. Cheetos, day-old muffins, melted cheese on pizza boxes."

"Please say you didn't get our picnic from a dumpster."

"I was going to," he said. "But Angus thought you'd prefer some first-time-use food."

"Angus," Irina said, "I think you are getting soft."

"I know it," Angus said, and started the car. Before long we were in Tijeras Canyon, the road winding between the mountains, Angus humming as we drove, Wylie and Irina chatting quietly in the backseat, Psyche gurgling along with them. I felt a tightening in my chest, heat and air compressing in my lungs, then realized what it was: I was happy.

On the road to the Crest the traffic was thinner and we swung around to the east side of the mountains, the trees now thick and green. Angus parked at a trailhead, and we started hiking.

Tiny brown birds flitted in the juniper scrub. Rustles in the underbrush, scissors of movement far ahead, glimpsed only out of the corner of your eye: the world narrowed to things like this. The sun beat down on the steep, rocky trail. I started to sweat, and my legs hurt. Irina was in front of me, her legs flexing with muscle as she climbed, and gradually she got farther and farther ahead. At a small lookout point I stopped to catch my breath, the mountain falling below me, banded with the switchback curls of the trail.

Then Angus stepped up beside me, holding out his Nalgene bottle. "You look like you could use some water."

We smiled at each other, and I had a long drink. In the sunlight his skin looked blanched, white and shadowless, overexposed. I handed the bottle back and said, "I thought you said you always wear a hat."

"Always," he said, "except right now."

"Hey!" Wylie shouted from up ahead, and we started back up the trail, which soon sank into shadow and was carpeted with pine needles. After a minute or two I saw bright swatches of clothing through the trees. Wylie and Irina were standing off the trail, looking at a washing machine, square, white, half-rusted, suspended on its side in the act of falling down-hill. Its chrome dials were black, absent any markings or instructions. A word I'd always liked in high school ambled into my brain: "erratic," the word for boulders swept into new territories by the movements of glaciers.

"How do you think it got here?" Irina said.

"Somebody dumped it," my brother said. He tried opening the lid, but it wouldn't budge.

"Litterbug," I said.

Wylie found a stick, wedged it under the lid, and lifted it, releasing a terrible, thick, sick-making smell. I backed away and covered my mouth with the tail of my shirt.

"Oh, no," Irina said. She covered up the baby and moved well up the trail, and I followed. But the smell was still with us, so I motioned for her to keep going. I didn't know what Wylie and Angus were doing back there, and didn't care. Finally we stopped in a sunny place where the air smelled fresh and waited for them.

"What was it?" Irina asked when they caught up with us.

Wylie was looking at Psyche. "It was a cat," he said.

"With kittens," Angus added.

"What? How did a cat get in there?"

"I think it got dumped with the machine," Angus said. "At the same time."

"But that machine's all rusted," I said. "Wouldn't the cat already be, you know, disintegrated?"

"Oh, dear," Irina said.

"That's what I said," Wylie said.

"But with the door closed," Angus said, "it's almost a seal. That would slow down the process."

"But it wasn't a seal," my brother said, "because there was rotting."

"I said almost."

"I don't know, Angus," Wylie said. "I think the cat was feral. It just climbed in there to have its kittens, then the door slammed shut and trapped them."

They stood there for a few minutes, calmly discussing the chemistry of rot, the population of feral cats in the Sandias, recent weather patterns and their likely effect on corpses in the wild. I started to feel sick again, and, without speaking, I took off up the trail, my stomach churning.

Wylie caught up to me and we hiked together without saying anything.

"What did it look like?" I asked him after a while.

"You don't want to know," he said.

Looking at him, I thought about the animals piled up in the pale blue basin of the old washing machine; I thought also of a famous painting I'd once seen, an elegant oil of a hare on a wooden table, dribbling fresh blood, in a gilt frame. Irina's words about shit ran through my mind, and so did the naked self-portraits and paintings executed with menstrual blood I'd studied, and Eva Kent's paintings, and so, finally, did the face of my father as he lay in the coffin my mother had chosen, recognizably himself and yet not, his skin plumped with embalming fluid and his cheeks rouged with the undertaker's makeup. You can celebrate the body all you want, I thought, you can sing hymns to its presence, its shit and stink, but it will only ever betray you in the end. I touched Wylie's arm.

"It'd been taken over," he said.

"What do you mean?"

"Maggots," he said. "Blowflies. Other insects. They take over the body."

"That is so gross," I said.

"It's beautiful, if you think about it." All of a sudden, his eyes were glowing with enthusiasm. "It's egalitarian in concept. We act like the human body is the center of the universe, but it decays and gets reabsorbed into the system, just like that cat and its kittens, just like everything else. It loses its boundaries, its privileged status."

"Wylie."

"We don't like to think about it, but that's only symptomatic of our power-driven—"

"Wylie, shut up, for God's sake."

"What's your problem?"

"Just *shut up,*" I said.

At that moment I smelled smoke, and Wylie started walking fast in front of me. Before long I saw a red cloth hanging from a juniper tree, and the burning smell clarified itself into a joint. A couple of hippies were sitting on a boulder in front of a rocky overhang, a scenic overlook behind them. I recognized the place then, and wondered if Wylie had brought me here on purpose. It was another place we used to hike to, when we were kids; one time we'd even spent the night here, Wylie and I in one tent, our parents in another. It occurred to me that this was probably where Wylie stayed when he lived in the woods.

The girl had long hair gnarled into dreadlocks that twisted down her back like vines. The boy had thin dark hair that fell into his eyes; he'd taken off his shirt—the cloth hanging from the tree—and was sunning his pale, sunken chest.

"Hey, how's your life today, man?" he said calmly to Wylie.

"Could be better, could be worse," Wylie said.

The hippie held out the joint between his thumb and his index finger. It was thickly rolled and coated at the end with saliva that sparkled visibly in the sun. We both shook our heads. The sweet, acrid fragrance of pot mingled with the scent of juniper and the heat and the buzz of insects all around us, and I started to feel faint.

"You guys want some jerky?" the girl said.

"No, thanks," I said.

"It's homemade, from all-natural cows."

"No, thanks."

"Okay, that's cool," she said. She took the joint and breathed in deeply, still smiling at us with her mouth carefully closed.

When Wylie stepped closer to them—wanting to take in the view, I guess—the boy took offense. "Hey, man, what're you doing?"

"I just wanted to have a look," Wylie told him. "We came here a lot when we were kids."

"Well, that's sweet and everything, man, but we're hanging here right now, you know what I mean? It's kind of our personal space at the moment, and I'd appreciate it if you didn't invade."

"Yeah," the girl said.

"We just want to take a look," I said.

"I totally respect that, but no way," the boy said. He stood up and faced us, his chest stuck out defiantly. "Don't make me get rough with you guys." At this, Wylie snorted. The girl nodded, sitting cross-legged on the rock, smoking the joint and chewing a stick of homemade jerky at the same time.

I stared at these ridiculous people and started to cry. "It's just a fucking *view*," I said, embarrassed and choking, and what I meant was this: of my father there was nothing left, and in the taxonomy of his absence I could list only his grave marker and places like this where he'd once been and the fading memory of his voice saying my name, and these were paltry things. Snot bubbled out of my nose, and I sniffled it back in.

"Let's just go," Wylie said.

He set off at a brisk pace, and I had to jog to keep up with him. I kept sniffling and wiping my nose, my shoulders spasming, my breath coming in hiccups.

Finally he turned around and said, "Stop it. I mean it. Stop it."

"I'm trying."

"Try harder."

"Sorry," I said.

"Don't say you're sorry," Wylie said, looking away. "Just deal with it."

"Yeah, okay, I'll deal with it," I said. "I'll go find myself a cave to live in, and eat trash from dumpsters, and stop talking to Mom, and plan absurd guerrilla actions. That's exactly what I'll do."

"You think the actions are absurd?" he said.

"Wylie, of course they're absurd."

He scowled at me for a few seconds, then shook his head. "You're so full of shit," he said. "You think I'm the one who avoids things? Who lives in New York and hardly comes home for two years? Who takes up with a boyfriend within two days of being back so she can run off with him all the time and not have to be around? Who's been home all summer and hasn't even gone to the grave?"

"I went," I said. "Once."

"Yeah, well." He shook his head again. "If *you're* worried about *me*," he said, "you're out of your goddamn mind."

I lifted my shirt to my face and wiped away my tears and snot. "I feel like hell," I finally said.

"I know," my brother said. Behind us, coming up the trail, were Irina and Angus. They looked red and sweaty and bedraggled, as, I realized, we must have too. Psyche was shifting uncomfortably on her mother's chest, burbling a stream of annoyed complaint, and her skin had broken out in a rash that resembled hives.

Wylie looked at Irina and said, "Is Psyche okay?"

"I think so," she said.

Angus smiled at me, broadly, genuinely. "Isn't this great?" he said.

Seventeen

Halfway down the trail, a trailer park sitting in the scrub came into view, looking haphazard and almost forgotten. I was tired and kept stumbling. Wylie and Irina were walking together, both of them glancing anxiously at Psyche, and I thought I saw something new in the way they looked at each other, their hands nearly touching as they swung back and forth with the rhythm of their hiking. Angus stayed beside me, offering the water bottle every so often. I didn't care what Wylie said, or even if it was true; I would cling to Angus now, and in bed later, without thinking about what it meant or why I was there.

Back at Wylie's apartment, there was beer and gin and music, and I told myself that everything was fine. But it wasn't fine. The August heat made the apartment claustrophobic. Whether because of the heat or the drinking, nobody could seem to agree on anything, except to question everybody else's ideas and commitment. When Berto suggested working with Panther's organization, he was shouted down. Wylie's philosophical statements had people rolling their eyes, except for Irina, who nodded in encouragement even when it was unclear what he was talking about. Angus leaned against the back wall, smiling at all of this discord, sharing his bottomless gin and tonic with me.

Then Wylie stopped in the middle of a sentence and asked him, "What the hell's so funny?"

"You are, buddy," Angus said.

"What's that mean?"

"You always have this need to dress things up," Angus said. "As if that makes things more important."

"Leave him alone," I said.

"You're not even part of this," Wylie told me.

Looking back and forth at the two of them, I decided to shut up.

The talk dragged on into the night, becoming more impassioned and less intelligible. The room smelled bad, and drinking was making the group less festive rather than more. The dog slept in a corner, snoring hard, an option that was starting to look better and better to me. Outside, the din of the cicadas rose to a fever pitch. Wylie sat in a corner muttering to Irina, his skinny legs tucked beneath him, Psyche asleep against his chest, a little fist flung up against his collarbone. I fell asleep, my head on Angus's shoulder, and when I woke up everything was still the same.

Just after two, Angus stood up and stretched, which somehow brought a hush over the room. He spoke quietly, as if to himself, though he clearly knew everybody was watching him. "You know what makes me happy?" he said, then walked over to the window and pulled the duct-taped curtains aside to look out into the empty Albuquerque night. "Human extinction. We'll be gone before long. We'll ruin ourselves. No matter what anybody in this room does."

"Dude, you're depressing me," Stan said, sprawled on the floor.

Angus shook his head. I watched him idly, feeling flushed and a little dizzy from the gin. "It's not depressing," he said. "It's a real consolation. When I can't sleep at night, that's what I think about. We're a blip on the screen, except you know what? There *is* no screen. We're the ones who invented blips and screens, and soon enough they'll be gone too. And thank God."

"That's a rosy view," I said. "Why even bother then?"

"Realism isn't the same thing as paralysis," Angus said, smiling around the room at everyone. "Besides, we might as well have a good time. What we need to do is take away the blip and the screen for a little while. What we need is a *major event*."

"No shit," Berto said.

Wylie leaned forward, still holding the baby. "A paradigm shift," he said.

"A military action," Stan said.

"A photo op," Berto said.

Angus gazed at me with his bright blue eyes. "What did you say at the beginning of the summer?"

"Me? About what?"

"About Albuquerque."

Tired and drunk, I frowned at him. I felt like I was being put on the spot, and didn't like his showboating. "That it's hot in summer?"

He shook his head.

"Full of chain restaurants? Hard to spell, for people who don't live here? Located in the middle of nowhere?"

"Exactly," Angus said.

"I have no idea what you're talking about," I told him.

Neither did Stan and Berto, judging from their blank expressions. But Wylie was nodding already, his mouth set in the straight line of concentration which for him, I was starting to learn, expressed greater happiness than a smile.

Irina said, "When I first came here, I thought it was the end of the world. In a good way. Like Mars."

"It's not the end of the world," I said, slurring the words a little, "but it definitely feels like it."

"Not enough for me," Angus said

"Are you kidding? Albuquerque's the *capital* of nowhere." My tone made Stan and Berto exchange glances. "I mean, and that's part of its scruffy charm," I added lamely.

"She's right," Irina said.

"Well, it's time to *really* make it the capital of nowhere. Give people a little time to think."

"Time to think," Wylie said. From his lack of scowl and his rigid posture, it seemed like he loved whatever ideas this conversation was giving him.

"Lynn," Angus said, "you're a genius."

"If you say so," I said, and passed out.

When I woke up everybody was gone, even Sledge. I couldn't imagine how I'd slept through the night, in a room full of drunk and stinking people, but the throb in my head gave me a clue. There was such a thing as too much gin. I opened the front door and gazed out at the capital of nowhere. Grocery-store circulars and plastic bags rustled in tree branches. The hood of the Caprice was splattered with bird shit. My stomach was uneasy, and the taste in my mouth was sour. The heat was an insult to the body. Everything was brown and dead, and I couldn't imagine hating anything as much as August in Albuquerque. I wanted to know where everybody was and why I'd been abandoned. I was in a very bad mood.

I was about to shut the door when a taxi—a rare enough sight anywhere in Albuquerque—pulled up in front of the apartment building. Then Daphne Michaelson got out of the cab and paid the driver, looking crisp and unfazed by the heat. She was wearing a navy-blue dress with a white belt, white stockings, and open-toed shoes. Her nails and lips were lacquered in red. Not a single hair was out of place, and when she climbed the stairs up to the landing I could smell the distinct flowers of Chanel No. 5.

She smiled at me, brightly, and said, "I'm looking for Wylie Fleming. The phone book says he lives here."

"He isn't here," I said, nervously conscious of my own morning-after stink.

"You're the other one!" she said, in the cheery tone of a Girl Scout leader addressing her charges. "I remember your visits to my office."

She stood in the doorway, wrinkling her powdered nose, and gave the filthy room a careful inspection that culminated in a head-to-toe look at me. Glancing back at the sleeping bags and tool racks, she raised her tweezed eyebrows, and I realized that at some point I'd stopped paying attention to the weirdness of the place.

"Can I get you something to drink?" I said.

"No, thank you," she said. "I can't stay long. I have many appointments." She laughed again, a trilling and artificial laugh that sounded rehearsed.

"If you say so," I said.

She opened her white leather handbag, took out a compact, and checked her perfect makeup in the mirror, then smacked her lips together and smiled, satisfied. I felt like I was in an old movie, something starring Lana Turner. Maybe a young Frank Sinatra would come looking for her.

"Mrs. Michaelson," I said, "does your family know you're here?"

It was the wrong thing to say. Daphne glared at me, and to compose herself she took out the compact and reapplied her lipstick, giving it a disturbing thickness. "I am occasionally allowed to chaperone myself," she said.

"All right."

"Even at times to dress myself and call taxis. Like a grown woman. Which, incidentally, I am."

"I know you are. Listen, I'm sorry. What can I do for you? I'd offer you a seat, but, well, there aren't any."

"That's quite all right," she said with gracious hauteur. "I've come to discuss our problem of mutual interest. But we can do it standing."

"Problem?"

"Problem, situation, what have you," she said.

"What situation are you talking about?"

"My husband and your mother," she said. "You think I didn't know? There isn't enough medication in the world. The question is what we will do about it. Now that you're on my side we can do something. Once you came to my office, I knew you were on my side. Now, do you think you can get a gun?"

"You're kidding."

"Why would I?" she said. "Let me outline a few small plans." She pulled a small black notebook from her bag and opened it to a page filled with looping, childish handwriting.

"Mrs. Michaelson," I said, "I wanted to ask you about my father. Do you remember the things you said to me before? I felt like you were trying to tell me something."

"This is not about your father," she said.

"But did you ever see him with a woman with long dark hair? What about—"

"This is about David and that whore."

It took me a second to register what this meant, and another second to figure out how to respond. "Um, please don't call my mother a whore," I said.

Daphne's eyes flashed at me, and the notebook trembled in her hands. "Drunken travel-agent whore," she said, drawing out each syllable with evident relish.

"Okay, that's it." I gestured toward the landing. "Time for you to go. I'd call you a cab, but we don't have a phone here."

"I'm not leaving."

"Yes you are."

I walked out onto the landing, as if to show her how, exactly, this might be accomplished, but she didn't follow. I looked back to where she stood framed in the darkness of the apartment.

"You'll have to drive me," she said. "I spent my last dime on the taxi ride here."

I drove Daphne, in silence, back to the Michaelsons' house, where nobody was home, and followed her inside. The doors to the bedrooms were open, and in one of them was an entire wall of trophies, shelf upon shelf of little gold and silver men, knees bent, arms bent to hold bats or sticks or balls. The Michaelson kids, I had to admit, were pretty good at what they'd chosen to do, which was more than either Wylie or I could say. Daphne went into her room, sitting down in her chair with a magazine, and didn't seem surprised when I stepped inside. I wasn't exactly sure what to do, but leaving her alone didn't seem like the smartest thing. I don't know what I expected—a cache of pills piled behind the curtain, or a purse bristling with razor blades—but everything looked exactly as it had before.

Daphne crossed her legs and looked at me severely. "I'm quite disappointed in you," she said. "Perhaps I'll have better luck with Wylie. He always was the one with gumption."

"Gumption?" I said.

"And personality. You, on the other hand, have no personality, and I am highly disappointed." She was staring at me fixedly, more Joan Crawford now than Lana Turner, and then she leaned forward and started scratching her right ankle with manicured fingernails.

"Look, I'm sorry," I said, wondering if she bought her own clothes, or sent David out for them, or simply wore the same outfits she'd bought when she was less ill, back in the seventies. She kept on scratching. By now she was tearing rips and runs in the sheer white hose, but she didn't appear to notice. "Are you all right?"

"No, I'm not all right. I'm disappointed. That's what I keep telling you."

"Right. But you also seem kind of, well, itchy."

Daphne lifted her hand and gazed at it in momentary wonder, then raised it to her cheek and started scratching there. I noticed the droplets of blood swelling through the torn hose at her ankle, and angry red streaks smearing the makeup on her cheeks. I went over and held both her hands in mine.

"Please stop that," I kept saying, as if she were a child or a reasonable person.

"Disappointed!" she kept saying back. Then she pulled away from me—she was much stronger than I ever would've guessed—and cowered behind her chair, looking as if she thought I might shoot her. Momentarily annoyed that she was afraid of me, of all people, I went into the kitchen and searched around for phone numbers. In the directory by the fridge I found the number of David's law firm, but he wasn't there, and I didn't know what kind of message to leave. I also didn't know where Donny or Darren might be. For some reason, whether habit or the absence of any other options, I opened the fridge door, as if help might be waiting for me there. There were four rotisserie chickens and about a side of beef. Then I heard a car pull up in the driveway.

When Donny came through the front door, his doughy face was almost unrecognizable, marked grimly by stress, and only his blue, knee-length surf shorts seemed familiar. For a second, standing in the hall, he looked eerily like his father. I could see him struggling to come up with an explanation for my presence, and failing.

"Your mom's here," I said, "and she's a little upset."

"A little upset!" Daphne called from her room. "Ha!"

I trailed Donny down the hall, and saw her, back in her chair, tearing pages from a magazine and stacking them on the floor. Even her mania had a certain order to it.

"Mom?" Donny kneeled down next to her. "It's okay. Dad's coming."

"Oh, now *that's* a relief," Daphne said. "All my problems are solved."

Donny looked at me. His big muscled arms were on his mother's lap, the weight of them holding her still. "She hasn't done this in years," he said.

"I'm the star of this particular show," Daphne insisted.

"Hold on, Mom," he told her. He left the room and came back with a large glass of water and a palmful of pills.

She studied him with the exact expression of a dog that has misbehaved while its owners were away: guilty and anticipating, even craving the punishment. She took the pills all at once, gulping them down dry, then drinking the water as a chaser, splashing a lot of it down her chin. "Ah," she said afterward, smiling up at him.

"Good girl," he said. "Let's get you cleaned up." He took her by the arm, as if she were a physical invalid, and walked her into the bathroom without paying me even the slightest bit of attention.

I wandered back into the living room, wondering whether I should stay or go. I could hear the shower start, and murmuring voices. Then the phone rang, and after a while I picked it up and said, "Hello?"

"Who is this?"

"It's—Lynn. Lynn Fleming."

"Lynn, it's David. Is Daphne there?"

"Yes, she's—she's in the shower. Donny's helping her get cleaned up. He gave her some of her pills."

"Oh, thank God," he said. "What a crazy goddamn escapade. She hasn't done this in about a decade."

"That's what Donny said."

There was a moment's silence, during which I could hear traffic and car horns, and I guessed he was out looking for her somewhere. Then he said, "What are you doing in my house?"

"She came to Wylie's apartment, and I was there."

"What the hell did she go there for?"

I closed my eyes and said the only thing I could think of. "It's all my fault," I told him.

"I imagine you're right," he said, and hung up.

Finally the shower shut off and Donny led his mother into a bedroom. Feeling like I should leave, but unable to make myself do it, I sat down and listened to their muffled voices. Daphne was giggling, a sweet, girlish sound with a seductive tinge to it. Several minutes later Donny came out and sat down on a couch opposite me, seemingly not surprised that I was still there.

"Your dad called," I said. "I told him she was back."

He nodded. "Darren's out looking too."

"Where do you even start when something like this happens?"

"Anywhere," he said. "Hospitals, police, shopping malls. She likes malls."

He picked up a remote control from the arm of the couch and turned on the television, muting the sound. It was set to

ESPN and showing golf. A man in a blue sweater vest missed a putt and smacked his palm on his forehead. Donny tsked at the screen.

"Did she do this when we were kids?" I said.

Without moving his eyes from the screen, Donny shrugged and slumped down on the couch, his head resting on the back of it, his muscular thighs spread parallel to the floor.

"I dunno," he said. "I do remember one time, at your party. Remember? The one when your mom had that big piñata? Oh, my mom was pissed."

I didn't understand this, although I had vague memories of that party, which was full of drunken adults. I was fourteen and already acutely embarrassed by how my parents and all their friends behaved. Wylie was twelve, still on the pudgy side, and into skateboarding; he had an asymmetrical haircut all my dad's friends from work teased him about. At one point everybody started warbling along with the radio, which was such a hideous display that I had to retreat to my room. I didn't even remember the Michaelsons being there. "She was pissed off because of the piñata?"

"Dude!" Donny said, talking to the TV. After a second he said, "No, she was pissed off about my dad and your mom hanging out too much at the party. And I remember your dad—you know how he talked, we used to call him the Professor—he was all 'Daphne, why don't we discuss this rationally,' and my mom was all 'Fuck rationally!' I remember your dad's face, it was like he never heard anybody say 'fuck' before, ever. Anyway, then she took off and it took us a whole day to find her. In Grants. Can you believe that? *Grants.* It's like an hour and half away. My dad asked her what the hell she was doing there and she said, 'I always wanted to have a drink in Grants.' After that they upped her meds."

"I don't remember any of this," I said.

"You always were a little out of it," Donny said. "No offense. Wow, look at that stroke. That's beautiful. That's sport."

"What do you mean your dad and my mom hanging out?"

"Oh, you know."

"No, I don't know."

"Hanging out. Same as they do now."

I pictured the two of them watching *The Manchurian Candidate* in their bathrobes at my mom's condo. Surely, if they'd been doing that at my parents' house, I would have noticed. Yet as I thought back on things, a whole phalanx of scenes lined up, neat and orderly, in my mind: my mom having David over to fix the car or to help with some household chore while my dad was at work, because he was always at work; my mom going on early-morning walks around the neighborhood, I thought by herself, or telling my dad to take Wylie and me out for the day, on a hike or a picnic in the mountains. I felt like a duped lover. I was the last to know.

I told Donny I had to go—"See ya," he said—and left the house in a daze. The next thing I knew I was going eighty on the highway with the windows down, and a trucker in the next lane waved at me, tanned and friendly, showing me all the missing teeth in his smile.

Eighteen

When I pulled up at Worldwide Travel, I felt like I hadn't seen the place in years. When I stepped gratefully into the frigid air-conditioning, Francie looked up at me without recognition and went back to her computer, squinting at her monitor with her blue-lidded eyes.

"Francie," I said.

She looked at me again and said, "Lynnie! I didn't even recognize you, honey! Are you all right?"

"Everything's fine," I said.

"Do you want to go wash up? Your mom's with somebody just now."

The door to my mother's office was closed, and I wondered if David was in there with her. I nodded at Francie, then went into the bathroom, and what I saw in the mirror wasn't pretty: hair matted from sleeping on a grimy floor; face smudged with dirt and probably spilled gin; a T-shirt that was wrinkled and stained. In the small room I could tell that I really needed a shower. I took a long look at myself and shrugged. "You're turning into Wylie," I said out loud. Nonetheless I washed my face and patted my hair with water, smoothing it somewhat, though there was a ratty tangle at the base of my neck. I felt deeply, impossibly calm. I thought I'd feel that way forever, but my mother came through the door, and then I knew I wouldn't.

She stood before me in the fluorescent light, the lines of her face etched almost blue in the severity of its glow. She'd gotten a haircut recently, and her straight, neat hair was clipped even closer and more neatly than usual around her ears. I found myself staring at her blue-striped blouse, which was made from a slightly sheer fabric that showed the contours of her bra. The thought of her and David together while my father was alive kept flashing in my brain, unwanted and too loud, like commercials on TV. It was one thing for her to have taken up with a married man out of her widowed grief and his impossible home situation; it was quite another for it to have started years ago, in the past, when there weren't such excuses. I couldn't be generous about it; I could hardly even allow the thought of it into my mind.

"You should be ashamed," my mother said.

"Ha!" I said, sounding weirdly like Daphne Michaelson. After this I started to choke and had to take a drink from the sink. I felt dizzy, too, all of a sudden, and kept clutching the sink after I was done drinking.

"That poor woman hasn't had an episode in years," my mother went on. She was standing so close to me that I could smell the clean, slightly medicinal scent of her lotion or deodorant.

My stomach churned. I couldn't remember when I'd last eaten, or what it was. "I don't feel good," I said.

"Nor should you," my mother said primly. "David told me you've been harassing her. She's not a well woman, Lynnie. You can't just treat people any old way you like and not expect there to be consequences."

I stared at her. The fluorescent lights seemed to buzz and twitch, veering from white to blue to white again, the tiles swimming on the floor. I lifted my hand from the sink and then, still dizzy, put it back again. "Any old way?" I said.

"What about you, Mom? How do you treat Daphne Michaelson? What are you, her best friend?"

My mother shook her head. She was prepared for this, I could tell. "Don't start with that," she said. "You're an adult. Not a child."

"I don't feel good," I said again.

She went into a stall and closed the door. I could hear her pee, then the sharp quick sound of her pulling down the toilet paper. The whole time I stared at myself in the mirror, wondering if I was going to throw up.

"You live in a dream world," my mother said from the stall. "You worshipped your father, I always knew that. And you thought everything at our house was perfect. So I never wanted to disillusion you. But Arthur, you know, was—"

"Mom," I said. I went into the cubicle next to hers, closed the door, and threw up, my knees on the cold tile floor. It was a sour, nasty mash that held the lingering aroma of gin. I felt simultaneously hot and cold, disgusted and relieved. Small bright lights of many colors popped and sparkled at the edge of my vision. I wanted very much to lie down on the cold tile and take a nap.

"Are you finished?"

"I don't know." I reached up and flushed the toilet.

"What's wrong? Do you have the flu? Should I take you to the ER?"

"I don't think so," I said. My stomach was still in restless motion, but it seemed to be slowing down. I could see her navy-blue flats under the stall door; they walked to the sink and came back, and she held a damp paper towel below the door. I took it and wiped my face and blew my nose. I contemplated standing up, then thought better of it.

"I never worshipped him," I said, although it occurred to me, as I said it, that I had. And all my memories of being ashamed of him or angry at him were lame attempts to disguise this inevitable truth. I'd always accused Wylie of trying to be just like my father, but in the stall, looking down at my bare legs, I felt that everything I'd ever done—including leaving home and studying art history, a field as far away from physics as you could get—was meant to defy or provoke him, to overcome, in any way I could, the limits of his attention.

"And I didn't think everything was perfect," I said, quieter now. The flats waited, silently. "I just never thought it was *that bad.*"

"Don't be dramatic," my mother said, and heaved a great sigh. "It was somewhere in between."

I felt another wave of nausea tumble through my stomach like clothes in a dryer, and didn't say anything. The flats left the room.

When I went to her office fifteen minutes later, she was gone. Francie said she'd left to run some errands, but I suspected she was over at the Michaelsons', helping David and his sons deal with Daphne—a scene I couldn't exactly picture, and didn't want to, either.

Back at her condo, I let myself in, and slept through the bright hours of the day.

I woke up in the afternoon, ravenous and weak. I ate half a pint of ice cream, took a shower, then finished the other half. I wondered where Wylie et al. had gone, and why I always had to track them down like the younger child wanting to tag along and play. They were probably tunneling beneath the city, planning to suck all of Albuquerque into the lava flows or something. I felt lightheaded and strangely cheerful. It seemed like vomiting in the bathroom in front of my mother had done me a world of good.

The Missing Person

An uncharacteristic cloud had settled over the sky, turning the light in the condo to silver. It made me miss New York, its grayness and rain and subways, and Michael, and even the pain of losing him. A person can get nostalgic for anything, as long as it's in the past. I wandered around the house looking at pictures. There was my parents' wedding picture, Chicago, 1974: my mother smiling widely between dark red lips, my father looking dazed, as if stunned by his own good fortune. But maybe he was only stunned. There were hardly any other pictures of him around, and most were of Wylie and me. In every recent picture, I noticed, we had the same smile, even, practiced, and not at all genuine, as if really smiling were a childish habit we'd put away forever.

I stared at *The Wilderness Kiss* for a while, its brilliant dark colors, the woman and man locked in a kind of combat with the desert looming behind them. My mother was right; I'd never thought about the reality of my parents' marriage, what violence or heartbreak was contained in it, and with what consequences. Why was having a child—the son pictured in *The Ball and Chain*—so painful to Eva that it drove her insane? Studying the man in the picture, the one cradling his own mother, I saw in his thin, dark countenance a resemblance to both Wylie and Lincoln Kent, the yoga instructor.

As I gazed at the paintings, I pictured my father with Eva on those late nights when I'd thought he was at the lab, and then bringing her work home to my mother in an act of almost brutal defiance. He must have known about her and David. He knew, and Eva was his revenge. *Rose red, romantic red, red in the afternoon.* But he wouldn't leave my mother for her, even after she became pregnant, because of me and Wylie. And Eva went crazy, crazy enough to set fires and destroy her own work, just as crazy as Daphne Michaelson, alone in her house while her husband and my mother watched television together.

I had an almost dizzy feeling, as if I were standing at the

edge of a towering cliff, and picked up the flyer from Blue Butterfly Yoga. Lincoln was teaching Ashtanga that afternoon at four o'clock. I drove up to Santa Fe, where I sat in the Caprice with my eyes on the door to the yoga studio. Only a few cars were parked in the lot. Blue Butterfly was housed in a strip mall along with a New Age bookstore, an ice cream parlor, and the coffee shop I'd noticed before, each establishment elegant in fake adobe. Behind the strip mall rose another one; they were lined up, block after block. I hadn't eaten much besides the ice cream, and my stomach rumbled. At five-thirty people started filtering out of the yoga place. Glowing and relaxed, carrying mats and bags, they were all wearing tights or tight shorts and tight tops, clothes that covered their bodies like sausage casings. I had the windows down, and as they filed away I could hear snippets of their conversations, comments regarding numerology and nutrition, the cancerous death of a woman's aunt ("It's like her anger ate her up inside, literally"), and the difference between Reiki and Fendelkrais, as physical disciplines go. Lincoln Kent came out last and locked the outside door. He was wearing long black leggings and a red tank top, and with his straight posture and well-molded shoulders he looked like a ballet dancer on a short break from class. His features were small and perfect, and his short hair, fashionably cut, was dark brown, like Wylie's and mine. Everything about him was well formed and exquisite, like a Christmas ornament or a Hummel figurine.

I got out of the car and approached him, hoping that he wouldn't recognize me. "Excuse me," I said. "I'm lost. Could you help me?"

"Ah, tourists," he said, pointing with a well-muscled arm. "To get to the Plaza, you need to head that way."

"Actually, I'm looking for a place called Enchanted Mesa. I'm supposed to visit my great-aunt and I misplaced the address."

He smiled and took me by the arm. "I go to Enchanted

242

Mesa all the time. It's right around the corner. I can even walk you there, if you don't mind a couple blocks."

I thanked him profusely, and he led me down the street as I tried to figure out what to say to him.

"I think it's a lovely facility," he said confidingly, "and I did a *lot* of research. How long has your great-aunt been living there?"

"Um, not long, I don't think," I said. "What about your relative?"

"For ages and ages," he said. "The quality of care is excellent. It *is* a little hard to find, but once you've been there you won't have any problems."

We stopped in front of an adobe apartment building, by the front door with a small plaque that read ENCHANTED MESA. In a parlor to the right, a few old people in armchairs were staring disconsolately out at the bushes. Down the hallway some plinky jazz standard was being played on a piano. The place had the plush carpeting and smoothly recirculated air of an expensive institution, and the flowers on a stand in the hallway were real. But the scent of potpourri in the air wasn't quite strong enough to disguise the smell of ammonia and feces beneath it.

Squeezing my arm, Lincoln Kent marched up to the reception desk, where a middle-aged woman with short red hair and purple lipstick greeted him by name.

"Hi, Bernice," he said. "She's looking for her great-aunt. Would you help her?"

This was worse than crashing advanced yoga.

Bernice smiled at me. "What's her name?"

"Sylvia Beachman?" I said. This was my great-aunt, who lived in Evanston, Illinois, with my great-uncle Davis and three dachshunds. Every Christmas she sent me a card and a ten-dollar bill.

Bernice frowned and typed away at the computer.

I turned to Lincoln. "Thank you so much," I told him. "I don't mean to keep you."

"Hey, my pleasure. Peace. Bernice, I'll go check on her while I'm here."

Bernice waved without taking her eyes off the screen, and he wandered off down the hall. "I'm not seeing a Sylvia Beachman," she said.

"That can't be right," I said.

"Well, I know everybody in here, and I've never heard of a Sylvia Beachman."

"That can't be," I said. "She writes me all the time. This is Enchantment Mission, isn't it?"

"Enchant*ment Mission*?" Bernice raised an eyebrow. "This is Enchant*ed Mesa*. I don't know about any Enchantment Mission."

"Oh, man," I said. "I don't believe this."

"You've never visited her before?"

"I'm from New York." I leaned forward. "Listen, do you mind if I just go find Lincoln and tell him what happened? He's been helping me."

Bernice looked me up and down and decided, apparently, that I wasn't a threat to the elderly.

"Room 325," she said wearily. "Sign in here."

I walked down one carpeted hallway to another, past the open doors of shared rooms, the sounds of competing televisions broadcasting game shows and local news. An old woman in a light-blue cable-knit cardigan sat weeping in a doorway, her mouth rigid with pain or sadness, the thin wisps of her hair trembling in concert with her sobs. Some old people were playing cards in a lounge whose windows faced the side of the Blue Butterfly strip mall. Through one window I could see a teenaged girl wiping down the counter of the ice cream parlor, and from this context her smooth, tanned skin and long legs looked profane, or dreamlike, or both.

The Missing Person

Inside room 325, Lincoln Kent and a woman were sitting in facing chairs. From the photograph I'd seen, she was recognizably Eva Kent—but aged, decrepit, blank. Her dark hair was shot through with gray and hung limply to her chin. She was wearing baggy pink pants and a white shirt with a flower pattern; the sleeves fell to her wrists, but the skin on her hands was mottled red and white as if ravaged by some disease: the fire. She slouched in her chair, hunched over her low, large breasts. There was no trace of the ferocious pregnant woman with the center part and the burning cigarette, or of the woman in the painting with a slash of red across her face. In fact there was no trace of anything at all. Lincoln was reading to her, but she didn't seem to be listening, only staring into space. Her room was generic, artless, plain, and it smelled bad. Whatever she had once been, I thought, she wasn't an artist now.

The sight of her took me aback, and I realized how much I'd been counting on talking to her, asking her about my father and her work and life, on getting all the answers I'd thought she could provide. I walked down the hallway, bought a Coke from a machine, and pressed the cool can against my face. A nurse came by and smiled at me sympathetically.

"Eva Kent," I said. "What's wrong with her, exactly?"

She shrugged and bought a Dr Pepper. "Brain chemistry, I guess."

I stood there for a minute or two, not sure what to do next.

Then Lincoln came down the hall, smiling at me. "Hey, did you find your great-aunt?"

"Not exactly," I said.

He put his hand on my arm, again. "She didn't—"

"Oh, no," I said. "It turns out I have the wrong place, is all. I messed up. It's not the first time."

He bought a can of iced tea. "Don't be so hard on yourself," he said sweetly.

"How was your visit?" I asked him.

"Well, with my mother," he said, "it's hard to tell." As he sipped his tea, he raised one leg and placed his right foot against his left knee in a yoga pose, looking completely relaxed.

I gazed intently at his delicate features and dark hair. I still couldn't figure out how to ask him what I wanted to know. "Is your father in here too?" I said.

"Oh, no," he said, with a pleasant, musical laugh. "Just my mother. I'm reading Buddhist texts to her right now. I don't know if she finds it uplifting, but I do."

"Has she been here long?"

"For as long as I can remember," he said. "My godfather, Harold—well, unofficial godfather—he put her in here when I was just a kid. I used to hate visiting her, but now I find it kind of restful. I try to think of it as a means of contemplation." He was sounding like he had in yoga class, his voice low and rhythmic, almost a chant.

"What about the rest of your family?" I said. "Do they come too?"

"I don't have much family." Lincoln put his leg down and hoisted up the other, and at the same time—with the can of tea in his right hand—twisted his arms up above his neck. "My mother didn't have many relatives, and my dad died when I was twelve."

"He did?" I said. "Are you sure?"

He raised an eyebrow at the question, then laughed. "Yeah, I'm sure. He was this crazy hippie who lived up in Madrid, and in his last will and testament he left me and my mom a lucky horseshoe and his VW minibus. It didn't even run."

I stared into his tranquil eyes. A crazy hippie with a lucky horseshoe: this was the last thing I'd expected him to say. I felt an intense, burning anger toward Harold, for leading me astray; it seemed like his fault I was here. I wondered why on earth he'd lied to me—and then it occurred to me that he might not have known about the crazy hippie. I remembered Eva's note from California, after she'd run away: *Dear Harold, I know you will take care of things.* Maybe she'd known that Harold would take better care of her son if he thought there was no one else to do it.

"Hold this for a second, will you?" Lincoln asked. I took his drink, and he did a backward bend and then a forward one, sweeping his head down between his outstretched legs. When he came up again his face was red.

I wanted to contradict his story about the hippie father; but on what evidence, and for what reason? Beyond the paintings themselves, I had no reason to think that my father and Eva had even known each other, much less that he'd played any part in her illness. Anything can make a person go crazy: grief, anger, brain chemistry, life.

As I looked at the yoga instructor, the lines I'd drawn—from Eva to her paintings to my father to me—turned to vapor and disappeared. Eva had probably never met my father, and hadn't gone crazy because of their affair. Nor had Daphne Michaelson been trying to tell me anything at all, except that she distinctly preferred certain shades of red lipstick over others. I'd invented all of it. I'd started out wanting to construct a story about the paintings for Michael, and wound up tailoring it to myself. "Sometimes I think I'm the one who's crazy," I said out loud.

"Honey, everybody's crazy," Lincoln said. "The only sane person I know is my cat. Good luck with your great-aunt, okay?" Then he took back his drink and walked away down the hall.

Outside the sun still shone, heavy, inescapable, and my eyes started to water in the parking lot and wouldn't stop. The

Caprice fired up with a knocking sound, and the engine gave a low moan when I pulled out. For the second time this summer I went to my father's grave, which was every bit as inadequate as I remembered it: the sickly, brown-tinged grass, edging into dirt at the sides of the cemetery; the shiny red granite of new-fashioned tombstones, some with photographs airbrushed on them, the dead smiling and youthful, never anticipating to what purpose the pictures would be put. Or maybe they were smiling because they knew that their grip on the living would never be released; they'd maintain their mystery forever; they'd never have to answer any questions. As I was thinking this, a flock of crows landed a few graves in front of me and began to pick and tear at the grass, their ragged black feathers shiny in the light.

In the mid-distance rose the Sandias, their reddish-brown peaks outlined crisp and wild as in a painting by Eva Kent. She and Daphne could have quite a party together, I thought. My mother was the only sane woman I knew, and her sanity was so conspicuously neat and controlled that I was starting to wonder about her, too. This summer was crowded with crazy women and caretaking men, with parents who made their children uneasy, with condos and apartments and institutions, with homes that were not what they'd once been. And everywhere there were fathers, or awkward yet unavoidable substitutes: David Michaelson; Harold Wallace; even Wylie doting fatherlike on Psyche. The days were full of fathers, and none of them was mine. Grief roiled across the world, forever rippling its surface; that, I thought, was the permanent wave. When a feeling's that tenacious, what can you do but say hello to it and keep going? I turned away to find my mother and tell her, as best I could, that I was sorry.

Nineteen

The Caprice shuddered whenever I went above sixty-five, its chassis shaking like a child with a high fever: a new and disturbing symptom. In the rearview mirror I could see a thin band of black air moving across the sky, and when I rolled down the window, the ashy smell of a fire wafted faintly through the car. This whole state was as dry as kindling, ready to light. I could barely remember the last time I'd seen rain.

The curtains were drawn at my mother's house and I saw shapes moving behind them—my mother and David, no doubt, waiting for me to come home, make my apologies, and face my punishment. Maybe I could spend a week at his house, doing chores as a means of reparation, like the child I truly was. But as I opened the front door, from the kitchen came the sweet sounds of Frank Sinatra, tinkling glasses, and loud, low, horsey laughter. Wylie, Angus, and Irina, with Psyche in her sling, were all making themselves drinks, and the entire contents of my mother's well-provisioned refrigerator were emptied onto the counter. Sandwiches were in the making; fruit was being peeled and eaten. As a group they smelled delightful, soapy and fresh, their cheeks red and shiny from recent showers.

Angus was leaning against the far counter, using his finger to stir a glass of what I knew must be gin. His clothes were as tattered as ever, his skin as freckled, his hair as red. "Knew you couldn't stay away from us," he said.

I looked at him, flushed with annoyance. For the first time since that day in June at Wylie's apartment my body had no reaction to his; no heat on my skin, no ripple down my spine, no sensations elsewhere, either. It was an unsettling feeling, like an alcohol buzz wearing off too early in the evening.

He smiled at me and lifted his glass. "Cheers," he said.

Wylie, who'd been facing the other direction, turned around and nodded. Irina came fluttering toward me, her face flushed, and kissed me on the cheek. Psyche cooed and hit her fist against Irina's collarbone, and when I touched her cheek she looked at me, her eyes wide open, and laughed. Her skin looked rosier than usual, and I wondered if everyone had been out hiking again. Then they all started talking at the same time.

"Can I fix you a drink?"

"We're here making preparations."

"Your time is perfect, we are just making ready."

"Ready for what?" I said.

"Oh, our biggest project yet," Irina said. "It is very exciting. We have been planning many aspects of things."

The baby now cooed in earnest, hitting Irina again.

Irina laughed and said, "She wants a cocktail, like everybody else has."

"Cute," I said.

Irina gave her some apple juice, and she sucked happily at the bottle. On the stereo, Frank decided it was just one of those things.

"Where's Mom?" I asked Wylie.

He shrugged. "Haven't seen her."

"Have you talked to her?"

"No."

"I messed up with Daphne Michaelson. She went kind of crazy—even crazier than she was before, I mean."

"Well, that's no surprise."

"What's that supposed to mean?"

"That you're kind of messed up."

"Pot. Kettle. Black!"

He shrugged again, his lips pursed.

"Here's your drink," Angus said, materializing at my side. The ice swayed and bumped in the glass, a thin, elegant lime slice floating between two cubes.

"I didn't ask for that."

"I brought it anyway," he said, and kissed me on the cheek. "Now if everyone has food and drink, it's time for a meeting of the high council, and I propose the backyard as our secure location."

"Well, if the high council's meeting, I'll take my drink and go elsewhere."

"Oh no," Wylie said. "You're coming."

"I'm pretty sure I'm not on the high council," I said.

"You are now. That's why we're here."

I looked around at them. Irina smiled at me encouragingly. Angus winked, and I thought, Who winks anymore? Nobody *winks*. I paused to take a long, slow swallow of gin and tonic. "Look," I said. "Just because Angus wants me around doesn't mean I have to be part of your little capers."

"I want you around," Wylie said. "I'm the one who said we should come get you."

"What? Why?"

"Because you need us," he said. "We're good for you."

By the time everyone had taken their sandwiches and drinks to the patio furniture in the small, square backyard, Stan and Berto had shown up with a case of beer and two bags of take-out from Taco Bell. They sprawled on the ground spurting hot sauce from little flat packets into their foil-wrapped burritos.

The sound of children splashing in a backyard pool carried from somewhere down the street. I sat down on a plastic lawn chair in the shade, and Irina sat next to me, feeding the baby a biscuit that she gnawed and slobbered on happily. I waited for Angus to call the meeting to order, but it was Wylie who started talking first. Since the closing of the Crest, he seemed to stand taller, scowl less, and talk with greater ease, or maybe I'd started listening to him more. At any rate, everyone was paying attention.

"Now is the time for all good people to come to the defense of their country," he said. "The mountains are catching fire while the city spreads at their feet. If you saw a murder being committed, you'd rush in to stop it; your conscience would demand it. It's time for us to rush. We can't let the summer pass without a grand gesture. People say that gestures accomplish nothing, but they're wrong. If we abandon gestures, we abandon the fight to assert what we believe."

"Hear, hear, man," Berto said. Irina clapped prettily, one arm around the baby, the other arm reaching around to meet it. Angus, who was lying propped on one elbow in the grass, clapped too, but I could see a kind of smirk in his smile, as if he were an adult watching a child ride a bicycle: half proud, half waiting for him to fall. And Wylie seemed to know it; despite his ease in speaking, I could tell he was watching Angus watching him.

I sipped my drink. The breeze that ruffled my hair was almost cool, with August moving toward September. In the days of unceasing sunshine, in my visits to various crazy women and my nights with Angus, I'd almost forgotten that summer would ever end. Looking at my brother, I thought that he was right: I was messed up, and he had it together, with a life built on his beliefs. At least he actually had beliefs.

"Wylie," I said, "I still don't really know why I'm here."

He smiled at me then, genuinely, for the first time in recent memory. "You have to drive," he said.

Wylie and Angus were consulting a pad of paper covered in mysterious diagrams that reminded me of the plumbing model I'd seen over martinis. Maybe they were going to break into people's houses and start installing low-flow toilets. It was early evening. I could smell the spicy smoke of piñon wood, people so eager for fall that they couldn't wait for an actually cold night. Angus came over and sat down next to me against the back wall of the condo. He put his arm around me, and I let him. On my other side the baby huddled against Irina for warmth; she kept turning and squirming restlessly, and knocking her head against Irina's chest as if she couldn't get close enough to her body and whimpering. Everyone was talking, their lips thick with spittle, the words tumbling out fast as the evening shaded into darkness. All around us lights went on in houses, and the habitual blue glow of televisions. The baby started crying and Irina took her inside, bouncing her up and down in the sling.

I wondered where my mother was, if she was coming back soon, if she would forgive me when she did. I stood up and almost lost my balance. "I'm going to bed," I said.

"Oh no you're not," Wylie said. "We've got work to do."

"Now?" I said.

"Of course now."

"Wylie, I really need to talk to Mom."

"After," he said.

So I found myself driving my brother's car through the neon-lit streets of Albuquerque, with the whole group chattering and happy, except for Psyche, in Irina's arms beside me, who kept squirming and muttering angry complaints. Nothing her mother did could soothe her.

"Maybe you should take her to the doctor," I said.

Irina shook her head. "Everything will be fine," she said, smiling sweetly.

I drove to Wylie's, as instructed. The place looked different, and I noticed that the dog was gone.

"Where's Sledge?" I asked Irina.

"With a friend of Angus," she said.

"What friend?" I asked, but she didn't answer.

The walls, previously bare, were plastered now with topographical maps of New Mexico, region by region, its mountains graphed in pale green ink, shot through with thin strands of blue rivers and red roads, the old Spanish land grants neatly labeled. I walked the room, passing from map to map, the contours of the state traced before my eyes in awesome detail; it seemed like a crazy thing for a human hand to have accomplished, to have charted each rise and dip and curve of the land. On the last map, by the kitchen, was Bernalillo County, and the Rio Grande washed across the sheet. Albuquerque spread red and pink at the center of it, the land parceled into tiny geometrical squares. In the context of the green blobs that defined the wilderness around it, the city looked belated and sad, a cluster of cubbyholes and closets and shoeboxes that people called homes. With my finger I traced a route from Indian School to Central, then over to this apartment. Wylie came and stood beside me, and together we looked at the map, the foothills where our childhood home stood and the edge where, high in the Sandias, Bernalillo County gave way to Sandoval.

After a few minutes of loading the van with backpacks and boxes of tools, Wylie, Berto, and Angus climbed inside it. As they left, Angus kissed me good-bye and whispered, "Stay close." I said I'd try, and got behind the wheel of the Caprice. Without Berto beside him, Stan seemed a bit lost, crossing his arms and frowning at me when I met his gaze in the rearview mirror.

"Where are we going?" I said.

"Just follow the van, please," Irina said.

I trailed the van through light evening traffic onto the interstate, switching lanes every time Angus did, worried that I'd lose them. These maneuvers continued even when there were no cars to pass, and I suspected he was just playing a game, smiling and watching me follow in the rearview mirror. Irina sang "The Itsy-Bitsy Spider" over and over to Psyche, the repetition—like some inventively childish form of torture—driving me insane. I kept glaring at her, to no avail, but after a while she switched to a Czech melody whose words, at least, I couldn't understand, and Psyche's irritated babble finally subsided.

"Where are we going—Bisbee?" I said. Nobody answered.

We were west of town when the van signaled for an exit onto a rough, one-lane road. The car jostled and shuddered, and Psyche woke up and started crying again. I sighed, staring out at the dark, empty land around us and the black silhouettes of power lines snaking along the horizon. When I followed the van onto a dirt road, the Caprice bucked in protest, and rocks sprayed across the windshield. On Irina's side the glass began to spiderweb.

"Shit," I said.

"Are we here?" Irina said.

"How should I know?" I said. The road weaved and turned back on itself, heading up into hills. It was too dark to see very well, and the car kept bouncing into ruts or scraping its bottom against the dirt and gravel. The shuddering kept getting worse, even at this low speed. I gripped the wheel at ten and two, as if this would prevent anything bad from happening. At one point the headlights flashed over the bloody remains of a deer or antelope, and I veered around it. Five minutes later, I parked beside the van in front of a cabin that was cobbled together out of adobe and two-by-fours. Sledge stood outside, barking, and next to him was Gerald Lobachevski.

I got out of the car and stretched; my right leg was numb. Wylie climbed out of the van and waved at me as Angus and Gerald disappeared into the darkness. I walked back down the road and looked up at the sky—it was a true New Mexico black, flecked with bright stars. There was just enough light to limn the contours of the desert below, indeterminate and lovely. The land rose and fell like breath. I sat down on a long flat rock. Outlined around me, somewhere between object and shadow, were cacti and boulders and squat juniper scrub. I could feel the edge of a chill in the air.

From above I heard the murmur of voices and the flat scuffle of shoes, and moments later Angus and Gerald came walking slowly toward me, their heads swaying together rhythmically as if they belonged to a single animal. Angus was talking, but I couldn't make out the words. "Ache back," I thought I heard him say, not once but twice, and I wondered what language or code he was speaking. Gerald wasn't saying anything at all. I knew they couldn't see me, so I coughed.

"Well, hello there," Angus said. "You remember Gerald."

"Hello, Gerald."

"Wylie's sister," Gerald said flatly.

"That would be me," I said. He turned around and walked back to the house. "He's so gracious," I said to Angus.

"I know it." He sat down next to me on the rock, and I moved over to a less smooth and comfortable part, resenting him and trying not to, our hips pressed close together. I have slept with this ragged, red-haired person, I thought, *multiple times.* His freckled skin was practically glowing in the dark desert night. An owl hooted in the quiet. Angus put his hand on my knee, then turned and kissed me full on the lips. It was a fine kiss; there was nothing wrong with it; but it was not what it had been at the beginning of the summer. Somehow, and so soon—a fact that burst sadly inside me—I had gotten used to Angus Beam. I pulled my head away and stared down at the ground as he put his arm around me.

"Let's go back," I said, and stood up. Just then a thin, plaintive cry rose through the air. "Is that a coyote?" I said.

Angus laughed and said, "No, it's Psyche."

Inside the cabin, in the gloomy light of a camping lantern, Stan and Berto were looking freaked out as the baby screamed her head off. Wylie and Irina were bent over a blanket on the floor, making shushing and humming sounds, but Psyche ignored them, wrapped up in her own distress, and I thought I detected a certain satisfaction in her wailing. Her face was screwed up tight and red, with a kind of rash on her forehead; when I got closer, I could see it had spread down her neck and shoulders all the way to her little hands.

"Did you try feeding her?" Angus said.

"Of course I tried feeding her," Irina said, looking sweaty and worried, her accent suddenly thicker.

"I think she has a fever," Wylie said.

Angus crouched down next to them, balancing lightly on the balls of his feet and touching her pudgy shoulder. After Wylie finished changing her diaper, Irina picked her up and said, "I'm taking her outside."

From the other side of the room, Gerald growled, "Ridiculous to bring a baby up here."

"You be quiet," Wylie told him.

"He's got a point, man," Berto said.

"What's she supposed to do with it?" Stan muttered. "She can't just leave it behind."

"I'm just saying, man," Berto said.

"You drag that baby around like a dog," Gerald said.

Irina was staring straight at him, ignoring everybody else, the baby wailing over her shoulder.

Gerald's voice was harsh and rasping with scorn. "You're like a girl with a doll."

"I'm her mother," Irina said.

"She's compromising this whole operation."

"She will stop soon," Irina said, "I know it."

"You don't know anything," Gerald said, louder, glaring right back at her. "It's a game to you."

Irina was scowling, her face transformed without its trademark smile. "You could help," she said. "She is yours too. You could help me!"

"I told you I wouldn't," he said flatly.

"You son of a bitching!" Irina said wildly. "You!" Then both she and the baby were wailing, a high and awful noise like bagpipes or cats.

"Oh, shut up," Gerald told her.

"You shut up," Wylie said, standing there with his fists clenched.

Angus unfolded himself from his crouch and lifted his palms to calm the two men. Gerald turned away, shrugging, and Wylie glowered at Angus—an equal contest, it seemed to me—but then subsided, shaking his head and relaxing his fists.

Cradling the baby in her arms, Irina walked resolutely outside, where we could hear Psyche's shivering cries and her mother's shaky, delicate singing in counterpoint harmony. Wylie glanced around, his face torqued with worry, and then went outside. Before long, the howling grew thinner and higher, falling away in the dark, until it was only a sliver of sound.

Twenty

The lamp swung back and forth, pushed into motion by the door Wylie had closed behind him. Sledge had gotten inside, and now started licking the backs of my calves, so I scolded him away to the far corner of the room. Angus and Gerald spread out maps and sank deep into private conversation. Closer to me, Stan and Berto were arguing with each other, muttering and shaking their heads like some old married couple with longstanding disagreements.

"You can't go around shooting cows," Stan was telling him.

"Why not?"

"Because what did they ever do to you?"

"Yeah, but it's ranching, man," Berto said. "It's completely messing up the ecosystem."

"That's some crazy shit you're talking."

Angus clapped his hands and everybody snapped to attention—relieved, it seemed to me, to finally get started.

"We're going to shut this city down," he said.

Grinning, Stan and Berto nudged each other, and I went outside to find Wylie and Irina, following the trail of Psyche's distant crying, stronger as I approached. I kept tripping in the dark, but I finally came upon Wylie and Irina walking in circles, his arm around her wide back, his voice soothing and calm.

"How is she?" I said.

"Oh, Lynn," Irina said. "I think the baby is sick."

"No kidding," I said.

"Hey," Wylie said sharply.

"Oh, come on," I said. I didn't like the idea of being on the same side of the fence as Gerald Lobachevski, but in this case I was. My voice seemed to boom in the empty mountain air. "When you have a baby, take care of it. I mean, if nothing else you should take care of your child."

"Leave her alone," Wylie said, grabbing me by the arm and shaking it, hard.

Irina sniffled—a sharp, anguished intake of breath—and I realized that I'd made her cry again. "I am always left out," she said. "Not tonight." She fumbled with the buttons on the front of her brown sack dress to offer her breast, but Psyche wouldn't nurse. Then she began to rock the sling and pace back and forth across the road, constantly murmuring something, not quite words and not quite song, that sounded like "oh hasha hasha hasha oh." Her voice filtered through the clear night, mournful as prayer and steady as grief. Wylie walked over to her and they leaned against the peeling, shadowy bark of a juniper tree. The baby's cries were agonizing to hear. Wylie brushed some hair from Irina's cheek, and Irina nodded at whatever he was whispering to her.

Angus came out, stepping lightly down the path, apparently having no problem whatsoever seeing where he was going, and again I was struck by how swiftly and easily he moved, seemingly unburdened by gravity or any other force. He put his hand on the small of my back. "We're ready to go," he said. "I want you to drive Irina and Psyche home."

I nodded, but Irina stepped forward, and even in the dark I could see her flushed cheeks and wild eyes. "No," she said. "I have come this far. I have been here for everything. I am not going to miss the most important action of the summer."

"Irina, the baby," I said.

"She is fine. She is fine."

Angus smiled at her, gently. "The baby's more important."

She shook her head. "You always want to rid of me. It is like Lynn said before. I am always excluded from the boys' club. You are like little boys playing in a fort in the wood."

"Irina, be sensible."

"Let her stay," Wylie said, walking forward from the darkness. "If that's what she wants."

The two of them faced off again, my brother dark and scowling, Angus still smiling gently. I was starting to wonder if his smile was some sort of condition.

"We can't have a crying baby in the middle of this," Angus said. "I'm sorry, but that's just common sense."

Wylie sighed then, and I knew Angus and Gerald had won.

"I'll drive them to the hospital," I offered.

But when I turned the key, the Caprice gave a harsh, metallic rattle and wouldn't turn over. I thought of how badly the car had been shuddering, and cursed myself for not having told Wylie about it earlier. He was sitting next to Irina in the back, the baby huddled between them, but I couldn't see his face in the rearview mirror.

"Won't start," I said.

"I can hear that," Wylie said immediately. "What have you been doing to my car?"

"Driving it."

"Driving it *how*?"

"Wylie, it's not my fault."

"How can it *not* be?"

"This car is old. Old cars have problems. That's just the way it goes."

"This car will last indefinitely in an arid climate with proper maintenance."

"You're being ridiculous."

"You *broke* my car!"

"Look, there's Gerald's car," I said. "We could borrow that."

"Absolutely fucking not."

Angus and the others were standing at the back of the van, conferring. I thought of all the tools and fluids and aerosol cans he had in there, even the BB gun, and wondered what they needed for whatever they were about to do.

"Listen, you two," Irina said. "Listen." The baby had stopped crying. "Psyche," she said, "we can stay."

In the end, we squeezed into the Plumbarama van with Angus, our hips and shoulders pressed together as we drove over the bumpy terrain. The smells of the desert breezed through the open windows, the clean, spicy scent of night-flowering plants, the funkier aroma of animals, the acrid trace of something burning in the distance. I sat between Angus and Irina, who was in Wylie's lap, and Stan and Berto were in the back. I had no idea what time it was, but instead of sleepy I felt almost preternaturally alert, rested and ready, as if I'd been sleeping my entire life up till now. Psyche was quiet, finally, asleep in her mother's arms, and Wylie glanced down at her constantly, checking on her condition. Gerald was behind us in his own car, accompanied only by the dog.

"Where are we going?" I asked Angus, but he didn't answer.

The van jolted and shook over the dirt road, the headlights bouncing through the blackness. A strange kind of elation came over me, to be driving through the night away from the city and everything else; it was an almost religious feeling, tranquility and excitement in equal measure.

Angus rummaged around beneath his seat and then handed something to me. Holding it up to my face, I saw it was a roll of duct tape.

"Run some around your shoes and pass it around," he said. "It disguises treads."

I nodded, ripped off a silvery swatch, and handed the roll to Stan in the back, then looked at Wylie. "Where are we going?" I said.

He frowned. "Are you going to start complaining again?"

"No," I said, and it was true. "I just want to know what we're doing."

Angus grinned and said, "Hold on," then swerved off to the right, from the dirt road to no road at all, as I bounced between him and Irina. He turned the lights off and drove straight across desert, dirt and rocks rattling beneath the wheels. After a few minutes he stopped and we climbed out, so far as I could tell, in the middle of nowhere. When my eyes adjusted, I saw Gerald and the dog getting out of the sedan and, overhead, thick, horizontal lines that stretched out and disappeared into the horizon. Power lines.

"This is so weird," I said.

Wylie came up beside me. "Its beauty is in its simplicity. We don't need bolt cutters or submersible pumps or tunnels. We just need a match."

"You're going to burn down the lines?"

"It's not the fire that does it," he said. "Smoke particles conduct electricity. They short-circuit one line, then the next line gets overloaded, then the next one, then the next. One domino falls against another until the whole city goes dark. It isn't the fire that does it. It's the smoke."

"You're starting a *wilderness fire*?" I said.

"Fire suppression's an ill-advised program to begin with," he said. "If we allowed natural fires to burn, the brush wouldn't accumulate to the point where a wilderness fire is devastating."

"But what if it spreads?" I said. "What about people?"

"It won't," he said firmly. "Trust me."

Shadows walked ahead of me as I stood there noticing everything: the stalks of desert grasses swaying in the night wind; the howl of coyotes, plaintive and distant; the black ash of night and the pinpricks of stars. In front of me the shadows melted into darkness and I couldn't see them anymore. I breathed in and out. I was alone.

Then Psyche started crying again, in real pain, it seemed to me. This is ridiculous, I thought, she needs to go to the hospital. I ran until I caught up with Irina, who was kneeling by a boulder and frantically shushing the baby. Psyche's face was splotched and yellow, a shade skin should never have. She was coughing hard between her cries, her head pressed to Irina's chest, and it sounded like she was throwing up. Then, ahead of us, sparks exploded into the night in a small, brilliant spray: the fire was set. The flames reminded me of the sparklers Wylie and I used to run around with on the Fourth of July, and there stole into my mind an image of my father leaning against the back of the house, a cocktail in one hand, watching us chase each other, his face lit by the flicker of a dwindling sparkler. My mother, inside in the kitchen, was shaking her head and watching us, too, from the window over the sink. Remembering this moment, the unbridled simplicity of the holiday, our backyard, our family, I felt unmistakably happy and then, just as unmistakably, terrible. Which was worse, I wondered: enduring the wash of loss over your life, or surviving long enough to feel its ebb? Wylie thought I stayed away so I wouldn't have to feel the pain of it, but this wasn't true. I hadn't come home so I wouldn't have to recover.

The fire flared and smoke rose in a loose gray column

toward the power lines as Psyche's sad aria carried into the
night. I wanted to see her in the oasis of a hospital waiting
room, bathed in the antiseptic brilliance of fluorescent lights,
doctors in white coats dispensing pills, giving injections, and
placing the medals of the stethoscopes, round and reassuring,
over her tiny heart.

Angus materialized beside us. "Just wait," he said. "Soon
the real fun starts."

"What's that?" I said, looking at him.

"Oh, this is just the tip of the iceberg," he said.

"Angus," I said, "I have to take the baby to the hospital. I'm
taking the van."

"No way. Just wait fifteen minutes until we're done. We
need the van."

"Then I'll take Gerald's car. Get me the keys."

"Yeah, right," Angus said, and laughed. I felt like he
would've laughed at anything I said. In the distant glow of the
fire his smile looked wet.

"I mean it," I said. Psyche sounded like she was gagging on
her own vomit, then started crying again.

"She's right," Wylie said. I didn't know where he'd come
from.

"Gerald will never give her the keys."

"He will if you ask him to," Wylie said.

"I think you have a misguided sense of our dynamic,"
Angus said.

"Oh, shut up," Wylie said, walking right up to him and
standing there, nose to nose.

I knew he wanted to punch him, and it seemed like a fine idea
to me. There was a whispering sound behind me, buzzing in my
ear like an unwelcome bug, and when I finally took a moment to
listen it resolved into Irina's voice. "Angus, she is right, we need
to go now. Angus, Angus, Angus," she kept saying, as if she'd

forgotten most other English words. Then I smelled tobacco and cologne, and Gerald was standing beside me.

"Are you provoking all this noise," he asked Angus, "or are you letting it happen?"

Angus didn't answer.

"The baby's really sick," I said to Gerald. "We need your car."

"No."

"You're not being reasonable," I said, looking back and forth between him and Angus. "If you let us have the car, we'll take the crying baby away and there'll be less noise. It's a win-win situation."

"Win-win," Angus repeated softly. "Gerald—"

"No."

"Come on," I said.

"Listen to her," Wylie said urgently.

"You can't have the car. But you do have to shut the baby up until this is done."

"For God's sake, why?" I said.

Gerald ignored me, looking at Angus. "You know we need the car."

Wylie took a swing at Gerald. Somebody stepped on the dog's tail, and he howled, along with the baby, and Irina started sobbing. Wylie and Gerald were truly fighting now, grappling and punching, grunting and heaving with breath. I'd never seen Wylie fight before and hadn't known that he could. I sprinted back to the van and rummaged through the tools and trash until I found the crate I was looking for and pulled out the BB gun.

The thought of Angus firing it into the wall now seemed like years ago, and it aroused in me a strong, sexual sense of regret; then the wind delivered the sounds of Psyche crying, and I ran back to the tumult and pointed the BB gun at Gerald Lobachevski. "Give me the keys," I said.

He ignored me completely. Wylie'd just hit him on the cheek, and Gerald had pushed him back, and they were sizing each other up in that strangely polite way men have when they're trying to decide who'll go on the attack next.

I could see Irina's shadow and the shivering, sickly, wailing shadow that was her child. "Wylie," I said, louder. "I'm going to shoot him. Stand back."

"What?" Gerald said.

"Where'd you get that gun?" Wylie said.

"This is New Mexico," I said. "Everybody has a gun."

Angus's eyes focused on me, and I knew he remembered the same day I did, the long afternoon in the motel, the soft sounds of television, our two selves slipping together on the sheets. "You better watch it, Gerald," he said then. "That's my gun."

I was holding the gun out in front of me with my arms locked like they do in movies. My finger on the trigger was shaking. I thought this should feel like a dream, but it didn't; it all felt gloriously real, each second defined, as it passed, in miniature splendor. "Pull the keys out of your pocket," I said, "and hand them to Wylie."

Gerald dropped his fists and looked at me with what I had to admit was considerable dignity for a man faced with a gun he didn't know was loaded with BBs. "Don't be stupid," he said to me.

"Show me the keys," I said.

He shrugged, and did.

Wylie stepped forward and grabbed them. "Let's go," he said.

Wylie drove. Psyche was quiet, a silence that now seemed ominous. Irina was quiet too, and when I asked how she was doing—she was sitting in the back—she didn't answer. I asked her again.

"I am worrying," she said tightly. Her shadowed face had an ugly red sheen; her breath was labored and her voice hoarse. She was sick, too.

"Wylie," I said.

"I know," he said. The car bounced and jostled on the dirt road, then turned velvet-smooth—it was an expensive sedan— as we sped onto the highway. After several minutes I could see the city's loose beginnings ahead, farms and spread-out houses and the flow of gas stations. Beside the road the land sloped away to sheer nothing. Somewhere in that nothing, I knew, fire was catching in the desert grasses, a flower of spark blossoming into the air, the smoking particles fizzing and popping like a lightning storm. Ahead of the car the lights of the city stitched an uneven seam against the hem of the night sky. The world took on a funhouse cast, dense with terrible possibilities. We raced past a gas station, and inside the brilliantly lit interior of the Quick Mart a man stood behind the counter smoking and gazing out at the night.

Then, in front of us, the cluster of electricity and faint halo of neon around Albuquerque went dark, like a candle blown out in a single breath. The city vanished.

"Yes," Irina said.

Never in my life had I seen so many stars.

Twenty-One

Irina was chattering behind me in some kind of dizzy, sick euphoria, and I snapped at her to shut up and Wylie told me to shut up and then we all did for a while. Darkness settled over everything, and the car's headlights seemed barely able to penetrate it. It was like black fog, and Wylie kept braking suddenly at the shocking discovery of a stop sign, a cat prowling, another car. He kept off the main streets, wisely, steering us through neighborhoods where people stood in front of their dark houses talking to their neighbors or on their cell phones, whose tiny screens flared like lit matches as we passed.

On Indian School Road, I saw a man standing in front of a tall building, shaking his fist at it in reproach. Outside a nightclub, people had circled their cars in the parking lot and were dancing in the ring of headlights, their radios turned to the same booming station.

In another parking lot, a crowd had gathered round a bonfire in a garbage can, warming their hands over it as if the night were cold, which it was not.

"We're almost there," Wylie said.

I saw a few flashlights and candles, and with my window rolled down I could hear distant yelling and what sounded like breaking glass; if looting had broken out, it wouldn't have surprised me. I realized that Irina had been quiet for a long time, and when I looked back her head was laying against the seat at an awkward angle and I couldn't tell if she was asleep or unconscious. The baby, too, was silent in her sling.

"Wylie," I whispered. "We've got to hurry."

"I know," he said.

But around the next corner we came upon a scene of malevolent chaos. In front of a gas station several cars were parked in the middle of the street, doors open and lights on. One had a dent in the passenger side and steam issuing from its hood. Along the curb other cars had stopped, some drivers honking their horns, and a crowd had gathered, though for what purpose, exactly, was unclear. Some people were banging on the dark windows of the gas station, others were yelling, and there were several fistfights. The road was completely blocked, and Wylie slowed down, trying to decide what to do. I heard a window shatter, and Irina leaned into the front seat.

"What is happening? Are we at the hospital?"

"Almost," Wylie said. "Everything's going to be fine."

"Who are all these people?" Irina said wonderingly. I was asking myself the same question. They looked monstrous and intent, their faces contorted with anger, but I couldn't figure out what they wanted or where they'd all come from.

Wylie pulled into the gas station and drove around the back of the building, but then a police car pulled in on the far side, cutting us off, and a voice on a megaphone told us to turn off the engine and step out of the vehicle.

"Shit, shit, shit," Wylie said.

"What is this?" Irina said. "Wylie, we can't stop. We have to go to the hospital."

"Hold on," Wylie said. "We have to deal with this first."

We stepped out of the car and faced two blue-uniformed officers, who in the red swirl of the cruiser's light seemed just as monstrous as the rioters out front. I saw two other patrol cars pull into the lot, the cops looking anxious as they commanded the crowd to disperse.

"We need to get to the hospital," Wylie was explaining. "We have a sick baby over here."

One of the officers glanced at Irina and Psyche and nodded. The other, though, came around to my side of the car and played his flashlight over the interior.

"Please, there is no time for this!" Irina shouted, her voice breaking with panic. "We have to go now!" She was bouncing in place and sobbing, clutching Psyche to her chest.

"What are you people doing back here? And what is *that*?" the officer said.

His beam, I saw, was fixed on the pistol on the front seat.

"What are you doing with that weapon?"

"It's a BB gun," I said.

The cop looked at me as if this was everybody's excuse. "That doesn't answer my question," he said.

"What are you waiting for?" Irina yelled, and people all around us stopped whatever they were doing to stare. It was possibly the loudest shout I'd ever heard. "My baby needs a doctor!"

"Planning on doing a little shopping tonight while the lights are out?" the cop said.

"With a BB gun?"

"You want to scare people, all you need is the appearance of a weapon," he said. A universal wisdom, apparently, since Angus had said the same thing. I just shrugged. He went around to the back of the sedan and told me to open the trunk, which I did.

"What's all this?"

"I don't know," I said. "It's not my car," I said.

"Where'd you get it from, then?"

"A friend of ours."

By this time Irina was completely hysterical, and Wylie wasn't in much better shape. I had a dreary, dazed feeling that things were going from bad to worse, which was confirmed by the officer's reaction when he looked in the trunk.

"Jesus," he said. "We'll take that baby to a doctor, and then you people are going to answer some questions."

We wound up with a police escort to the hospital. The building had power, and coming into its stark fluorescence made us all blink like moles. An orderly or a nurse—someone wearing pink scrubs and carrying a chart—took one look at Irina and Psyche and said, "Come with me." Wylie and I filled out the paperwork, and he kept trying to persuade the desk clerk that he should be allowed to go back and check on his friend and her baby.

The cops wanted to question us but were constantly interrupted by urgent calls on their radios. From the unending crackle of the dispatcher and the frantic repetition of police codes, I could tell that the city was verging on chaos.

"We're not going anywhere," I told the nicer officer. "We'll be here for a while if you want to come back." His partner shot me a dirty look. "We haven't *done* anything," I said, but he looked completely unconvinced.

The officers argued briefly, over the radio and with each other, then wrote Wylie a ticket for reckless driving. He started to protest, but then thought better of it, and the police left, promising they'd be back.

Outside the electric doors of the hospital the city stayed dark. A man came in leaning on another man's shoulder, moaning that his leg was broken. In the waiting area a woman in a flowered dress held her son's head in her lap and her daughter sat next to them, squinting intently at a hand-held video game that beeped and sang as she played it. A short man in his forties, who I guessed was her husband, stood at the counter explaining their situation to a young receptionist.

"We can't afford to buy my mom's insulin from the pharmacy," he was saying, his hands palms-up on the counter. "We got no health insurance and the guy in the South Valley only charges five dollars."

"You buy illegal medication, you take your life in your hands," the receptionist said. She didn't look much older than seventeen, and on her bare shoulder was a small, elegant tattoo of a woman's face.

"Five dollars," the man said. "Instead of like fifty."

"Some guy tells you it's insulin, and you believe him?" she said. "You can't trust these people." She shook her long, shiny hair, dismissing him, and picked up the phone. The man watched her for a moment, then walked slowly back to his family.

In the corner a man in a red suit was shaking, as if being constantly electrocuted; his suit buttons rattled against the plastic chair, and every once in a while he shouted out random obscenities. A couple of homeless people sat wrapped in layers of clothes and blankets, and there were several families with young children and a man with a cut on his forehead who apparently spoke neither English nor Spanish and couldn't understand the receptionist. It was the county hospital, and everyone in the room seemed used to waiting a long time for any kind of service at all.

Wylie came back shaking his head. "They wouldn't let me in," he said. He looked like hell. Dust ringed his eyes and striped his cheeks; his face was all dark circles and hollows, his nose and cheekbones jutting out.

"We'll just have to wait," I said, and tried to smile.

"I didn't know you could shoot a gun."

"I'm glad I didn't have to."

"What was it, a BB gun?"

"Yeah."

"How'd you know it was there?"

"I know a few things."

He nodded. "I guess so," he said.

Time passed and passed, and then it was two in the morning. I drank three Cokes and felt brittle and jittery and wide awake. The man in the red suit let loose an elaborate string of swear words, beaded with shrieks and gasps, and the mother covered the ears of her sleeping son with the palms of her hands. Two young white junkies walked in—a boy and girl, impossibly skinny, wrapped in blankets, the visible swatches of their pale skin festooned with sores and scabs—and asked the receptionist about a friend of theirs named Buster. A doctor came out and informed the man whose mother had taken illegal insulin that she'd be all right. After the doctor left, he sat down, put his head in his hands, and was wracked by three or four dry, heaving sobs. Then he looked up at his wife and children, and his face was perfectly calm.

The doors to the ER hissed open, and the same cops walked up to us. "Did you think we'd forgotten about you?" the mean one said. He was gray-faced and smelled strongly of cigarette smoke. He held out his hand, and I thought the gesture was curiously graceful, almost chivalrous, until he gripped my wrist, hard.

"You're coming with us," he said, jerking me to my feet.

"What?" I said. The other cop was talking to Wylie, who was telling him that we hadn't heard about Irina and the baby yet and had to stay at the hospital.

"Hey, lady, focus on me," my cop said. "You and I are talking here."

"What's going on?" I said.

"We need to ask you a few questions about that car of yours."

"Gerald's car?" I said. "Is this about taking Gerald's car?"

"Are you telling me the car's stolen?"

"Well, he can have it back *now*," I said.

The man in the red suit yelled, "That's right, motherfucker!" and I glanced at him, grateful for his support. Everybody was watching. Wylie and his cop were undergoing the same talk and the same dance, face to face. The next thing I knew, we were being marched outside to the patrol car, my cop gripping my elbow and reciting my rights, his posture again almost chivalrous. The night air blew a current of exhaust from somewhere in the invisible city. In the intersection below us a cop had set up a spotlight and was directing traffic, his white gloves lit eerily in its glow. Without electricity the darkness took on new gradations of gray, navy, and mauve.

At the police station they led us into different rooms for questioning. My cop kept talking about "materials" in the trunk, which I didn't know anything about and couldn't get them to explain. He wanted to know what we'd been doing all night, and I didn't want to say. Keeping my mouth shut was remarkably easy, and the cop became incensed, yelling at me and pounding his fist on the table. I didn't think that anyone who smoked as much as he evidently did could stand to be that angry without risking a heart attack. I looked down at the ground, feeling like a kid in high-school detention.

"All right," he finally said. "I'll let you stew in a cell for a while. That should change your mind."

The cell was jam-packed, with hardly enough room for me to squeeze in, but everyone ignored me except a prostitute with long red nails and a purple leather miniskirt. She offered me a cigarette, which I accepted, and told me that her friend had OD'd in a motel room on Central but was going to pull through, maybe.

"Tonight's gone all crazy," she said. In her high-heeled boots and teased-up hair she towered over me. "The whole city got no lights, and I'm like, what the fuck is this?"

"Yeah, I know," I said.

"I mean, what the fuck *is* this?"

A woman in the cell gave a high-pitched moan, and Psyche's face flashed in front of me then, red and twisted. I hoped desperately that she was all right.

Still muttering, the hooker flicked her cigarette across the floor, where it skipped over the concrete like a stone on a lake. Then she stamped her high-heeled foot in a fit of petulance and said, "Fucking Albuquerque. City can't do anything right."

The cell stank of urine and body odor and smoke. As the sugar high from my Cokes wore off, crashing me into exhaustion, I started to reconsider my high-minded position. So what if the police found out where Wylie and Irina and I had been? We'd left before the main event anyway. But saying anything about this would amount to turning in Stan and Berto—and Angus. I couldn't do it. Gerald, maybe, but not the others.

Another cop came into the holding area and called my name. Tall and thin, he had a neatly trimmed mustache and carried himself with an air of gravitas.

"I'm Lieutenant Duran," he said.

"Pleased to meet you," I said.

"You're in a lot of trouble, missy."

I looked at him, not believing that anybody still used the word "missy." It was one more element of the evening that I couldn't believe. It was three in the morning, and my patience for everything was wearing thin.

He guided me by the elbow and led me upstairs to a plain,

windowless room. On the table were clear plastic Ziploc bags filled with wrenches, cutters, and handsaws, all the usual apparatus of vandalism. The whole world was swimming into the surreal. I wondered where Wylie was, how they were treating him and what he was saying, when we could leave.

"Explain," the lieutenant said.

"Explain what?"

"What you were planning on doing with all these items."

"What, the stuff in the bags?" I said. "That's not mine. I have no idea what those things are."

"We found these items in the vehicle you were driving, so you'd better start explaining."

"Right, but what I'm trying to tell you is that those things aren't mine. Whatever they are. Just like the car, right? The car isn't mine, and neither is this stuff."

The lieutenant pulled me over to the table, roughly, and I tried to focus on the items in the bags. I felt like I was looking at some child's science experiment, a carefully designed project whose point was nonetheless obscure. I could see blueprints showing what looked like pipes and tubes and valves, everything that controlled the heating and circulation. A switch flicked in my head. Heating, ventilation, and air conditioning: HVAC. That, not "ache back," was what Angus had said to Gerald. Near the top of the blueprints I saw the name Sunrise Casino. There was also a brochure for the Shangri-la golf course, the site I'd passed so many times on my drives to and from Santa Fe. Feeling Lieutenant Duran watching me, I closed my eyes and contemplated a number of possibilities that made me feel light-headed.

"I think I'd better call a lawyer," I said.

There was only one lawyer I knew in Albuquerque. From a pay phone in the hallway I called my mother's condo. On the fourth ring she answered, her voice groggy and slurred.

"Mom," I said, "is David there?"

. . .

They came and got me from the holding cell an hour later. Practically delirious with fatigue, I'd had to struggle to keep myself from falling asleep with my head against the hooker's shoulder, not that she seemed to mind. I was brought to another windowless room, where David Michaelson and my mother were sitting in two folding chairs behind a table. She looked as tired as I'd ever seen her, and I wanted to take her away from this place immediately. David, on the other hand, was spry and alert, erect in his chair. He was wearing a plaid shirt, blue jeans, and cowboy boots and eating a Milky Way bar, snapping off pieces cleanly with his teeth.

Wylie was led in, his arm gripped by a grim-faced cop. My mother wouldn't meet our eyes; she just kept looking at David as if she hoped that he'd step in and fix the whole situation. I was looking at him the same way. Wylie was staring at either the floor or his duct-taped shoes.

"Thanks for coming," I said to David.

"Well, a client's a client, that's what I like to say," he said cheerfully. "We'll need a room to consult," he told the cops. He looked down at his half-finished Milky Way, then closed the wrapper around it and stowed it in his pocket with an expression of regret.

"You can use this one, but she won't be allowed in with you," one of the cops said, nodding at my mother.

"I'm their mother," she explained, not in the proudest tone I'd ever heard.

The cop shrugged, and without raising his head—or his voice, for that matter—Wylie asked her to go to the hospital and check on Irina and Psyche.

"Those your girlfriends, son?" the cop said. "They mixed up in this too?"

Wylie scowled and didn't answer.

An officer was summoned to drive my mother to the hospital. David Michaelson kissed her gently on the cheek and looked her straight in the eye. "We'll be over there in a New York minute," he said, then winked at me. "Right?"

I didn't know what to say to that.

After our mother left, David offered us the rest of his candy bar. Sitting across the table from him, Wylie and I shook our heads. I felt about ten years old. With his head deeply bowed, Wylie looked to me like someone about to be hanged.

"So, kids," David said. "Why don't you tell me what happened, from the first of it to the last."

I stared at him blankly. When was the first of it? Was it Wylie's e-mails, his long-winded manifestos, his disappearance into the dumpsters and mountains? Or was it the second I stepped off the plane in Albuquerque, into its thin desert air, the smell and sun of it, the sweetly irresistible, scab-picking pain of home? It was impossible to answer the question.

"Answer the goddamn question," David said.

"Wylie, you start," I said.

He shifted in his seat, never looking up, and muttered, "Fuck off. You called him, you talk to him."

"Who else did you want me to call? Your buddy Gerald?"

"Who's Gerald?" David said.

"This is all your fault," Wylie said.

"How do you figure that?"

"It was your idea to take the car. We could've waited to go to the hospital."

"You stole a car?" David said.

"We couldn't wait to go to the hospital. You know that. For God's sake, Wylie, grow the fuck up."

"You grow up."

"Oh, fuck off."

David stood up. "You all don't seem especially eager to discuss your situation with me," he said, turning to the door. "In which case, I'll be going."

"Wait," I said, looking at Wylie and then at him. "Please stay."

In the end I told him the entire story, at least as I saw it, and it took a long time. David reached into his back pocket—I expected another Milky Way—and pulled out a small notebook in which he took careful notes, every once in a while stroking his mustache. Eventually he brought out the leftover candy bar and finished it, sitting there chewing amiably, as though he couldn't think of any better place to be in the middle of the night than at the police station, listening to his mistress's children describe a summer's worth of antics. I thought that he knew I owed him, which irked me very much. But it was also true.

After I was done, Wylie gave his version of events, filling in a few details. If he knew more than I did about Angus and Gerald's plans—the blueprints in the car, the Shangri-la—he didn't let on, and I believed him.

After posting our bail, David drove us to the hospital, where our mother was waiting in the lounge along with a new set of deranged, uncomfortable-looking people. She looked at Wylie and me with an expression I couldn't identify.

"Any news?" David asked her.

She shook her head.

"Can I see them?" Wylie said.

"They said not yet."

When David asked if she cared for a soda, jiggling the change in his pocket, she looked at him as if he'd just offered her some crack cocaine. "Why don't you go home, David?"

"I don't mind staying."

"You don't need to," she said. "It's late."

"I don't mind."

She pressed her hand against his. "I know you don't."

He shrugged and ambled out, his shoulders round and slumped, and seeing this dismissal made me feel sorry for him for the first time.

My mother sat quietly reading a magazine, every once in a while politely covering her mouth during a yawn. I kept waiting for her to explode, but she didn't. Wylie wandered outside. When I followed him out there, I found him just finishing smoking a joint with one of the blanket-wrapped junkies, who wandered off when I walked up.

"Where do you think Angus is?"

"Is that all you can think about?"

"I have room in my head for more than one person," I said.

The sky was paling, slowly but surely, its murky black ceding to blue, the city around us still without power. My mother emerged from the hospital and stood next to us, not saying anything. There was a dismal silence. Then Wylie started crying, his shoulders shaking as he just stood there. She had to reach up to put her arm around his shoulder. Across the thoroughfare in front of us, three bulky shapes drifted along, and I realized it was the skinny, blanket-wrapped junkies, reunited, I guessed, with their friend Buster. The three of us watched the three of them, not talking, just waiting together to see what the day would bring. In time the edge of the sky took on a puzzling cast, swollen with color like a bruise, and I was so tired I didn't realize at first that it was the sun, rising.

Twenty-Two

I woke with a start. I'd fallen asleep on my side, lying across two orange plastic chairs, with an ache down my side corresponding to their contours. My mother and brother were nowhere to be seen. Outside the clear sliding doors of the ER I could see the gentle brilliance of early-morning sun. New nurses were coming on duty, busily chatting about the craziness of the blackout. From what they were saying nobody suspected that the fire, by now extinguished, had been started on purpose; the group's most successful gesture, I thought, was also the one that everybody took for an accident.

"But did you see all the stars?" a nurse said. "I wish the lights would go out more often."

"You would," another nurse said, and they both laughed.

I sat there in the lounge rubbing my face. There was a rattling sound by the doors that made me look up. Behind the glass I saw as in a dream the tousled red hair of Angus Beam.

I stood up and went outside, the city's apartment buildings and offices and traffic glittering in the morning sun, the slight coolness in the air hinting at fall. August was ending, the summer was ending, everything was ending.

"I thought we should have one last cocktail," Angus said.

"It's like seven o'clock in the morning or something."

"I know," he said. "But I'm leaving."

We looked at each other. His freckles seemed to multiply

before my eyes. I'd forgotten how blue his eyes were, how white his smile. "Let me guess," I said. "Bisbee, Arizona."

"How'd you know?" he said, and grinned.

We walked down the unscenic driveway toward the parking lot, the sun glinting off the fenders of cars. In the distance I could hear traffic and planes, the city awakening.

"I'm leaving too," I said. "Going back to New York."

It sounded as if I were saying it just because he was leaving, but I wasn't. I hadn't realized that I was going back to face Michael, school, the fortune-teller across the street, but once I said it I knew it was true. I was never going to be the kind of person I'd thought Michael could make me—art-world sophisticate, graduate-school operator, easy, slick sharer in romantic affairs—but that didn't mean that I could just abandon the city and everything I'd started there.

Angus and I sat down on a bench located on a cement island next to the parking lot. Judging from the quantity of cigarette butts scattered on the ground, this was where the smokers from the hospital congregated. I tried to think of what to say to him, about sex and emotion and about how all touch means something, even if that something is not exactly love.

He held my hand. "How's Psyche?"

"She's in intensive care," I said. "She has an upper respiratory infection and smoke inhalation and I'm not even sure what else."

"That sounds bad."

"It is bad," I said.

He blew a soft sigh from between his lips.

I leaned against his shoulder and closed my eyes. I felt like I could sit there forever, in a moment without past or future, the bright light warming my eyelids. "You were going to rob the casino, weren't you?" I said. "While the lights were out. I heard you talking about the ventilation system. HVAC."

"Could be," he said.

"Why?"

"For the money."

"Angus."

"Well, okay," he said. "Theoretically speaking, a lot of money could prevent the development of the Shangri-la golf course. There's a lot of state requirements that a golf course has to meet. Impact statements have to pass. Zoning and regulations. A lot of officials have to approve various permits and licenses. And officials, you know, are susceptible."

"You're kidding. That would never work."

"You're probably right."

"It's a good thing you didn't go ahead with it."

"Yeah," he said, "a good thing."

The tone of his voice made me open my eyes, and he was looking away. I knew they'd gone ahead and done it anyway, and that at the beginning of the summer I would've said it was ridiculous and reckless and stupid and wrong, and that now I wasn't so sure. I thought of all the times I'd driven past that sign, the pure bare bones of the land beneath it, of the way the world looked when the lights of Albuquerque went dark. The sweet sounds of Frank Sinatra slid into my head. *Night and day, you are the one. Only you beneath the moon and under the sun.* "I can't believe you did it," I said. "You're completely insane. Out of your mind."

Angus laughed. "And you're funny," he said. "You stand outside of things, and hold people to standards you're allowed to change at any time. I like that about you."

It was the least charming compliment I'd ever received, and it made me smile.

"You're completely insane," I said again.

"I know it," he said. "Shut your eyes." He pushed gently on my shoulder until I was sitting upright, not touching him, then kissed me on the mouth.

The Missing Person

The color of the sun behind my eyelids mingled, in my mind, with the redness of his hair and the flush of his skin, and with the memory of my blood rushing as we moved together. And I waited even longer than I had to before opening my eyes, to be sure that he was gone.

When I got back to the ER, a horrible shriek was coming down a hallway, a woman sobbing and shouting unintelligibly. The nurses at reception were acting as if nothing was happening while family members in the waiting area whispered and exchanged panicked looks as they tried to guess whether the voice was one of their own. To me it sounded like Irina.

I ran down the hallway to an open door. The shrieks were piercing and Czech. Irina was sitting up in bed wailing and banging her fists against the mattress on either side of her body, her round, pretty face twisted and splotchy, and her body wasted and frail. Wylie was standing beside her, trying helplessly to catch her fists as she flailed away. A doctor was looking on with an expression of detachment that unnerved me. The only person whose head turned when I came in was my mother, who was crying. She took my arm and led me out into the green hallway.

"They couldn't save Psyche," she said, and I started crying too.

After death, a great numbness, like a coat of ice over a pond. My mother and I made room in the condo for Irina and Wylie to move in. They stayed in the room I'd been using, and I slept on the couch in the living room. The days that followed, for all their grief and horror and shock, resembled my childhood more than any in recent years: living again in a house full of people, eating meals and doing dishes together, maneuvering around one another for showers. Irina was a shadow of herself, and we all thought, Wylie especially, that she would not survive the loss. He was with her every second, holding her hand and looking at her, as if the fact of being *seen* would somehow keep her alive. And maybe he was right; she did not die.

On a brutally hot afternoon Psyche was buried in the same cemetery that held my father. My mother had made all the arrangements, and the four of us stood under a tent as the unfathomably small casket was lowered into the ground. So far as I knew, Stan and Berto and Angus and Gerald weren't even aware of what had happened. Irina's eyes looked dead in their sockets. The earth was dry and cracked, and a breeze blew sandy grit into our faces. Except for the priest, nobody said anything. There was nothing to say.

We kept on rising, eating, and sleeping through the final days of August. It looked like life but wasn't, really. The Sunrise Casino reported a substantial theft, and the Shangri-la golf course was put on hold pending environmental review. David Michaelson managed to persuade the police that Wylie, Irina, and I bore no responsibility for any materials in the car we'd borrowed; what Gerald told them, I didn't know and didn't care to ask. I recovered the Caprice and took it in to be repaired. When my mother went back to work, I asked her to book me a plane ticket to New York, and she did.

I wrapped Eva Kent's paintings in bubble wrap and brown paper, and arranged to ship them back to my apartment. I wanted to hang them there, as a reminder of the desert, the summer, and, most of all, my father.

As I was finishing the packing, I decided to call Harold Wallace, who picked up the phone on the second ring and sounded happy enough to hear from me. "I'm taking the paintings back to New York," I told him.

"Going to write that little paper of yours?" he said.

"My *dissertation*," I said, offended until I remembered that I hadn't exactly behaved like a paragon of art-historical scholarship around him. Then I sighed. "I'm not sure it'll be about Eva, but I am going to write it."

"Well, you know I'm not really retired," Harold said. "I still represent a select group of wonderful artists. You may want to take a look sometime."

"Thanks," I said. There was a silence on the line, in which I imagined him slipping into one of his reveries, in his white living room. "Listen, I saw Eva." Harold still said nothing. I thought about telling him about Lincoln and our conversation about his father, but what would be the point? "I won't go see her again," I added. "Or bother any of you. I just wanted to tell you, well, that I really do love her work." I waited for a long couple seconds, wondering if Harold was even there, until he spoke.

"Me, too," he said.

Throughout all this time, Wylie and Irina stayed in their room most of the day and night. They were both losing weight, their clothes seeming to grow larger and larger. I was afraid for both of them, and yet I didn't know what to say that could make them feel any better.

In my dreams, Psyche burbled and sang and waved her fat, sweet arms, and then there were crashes and screams and cars careening off slick roads into the chaos of an unlit night. Waking in tears, I tried not to imagine what Irina dreamed about, or thought when she awoke.

I missed Angus, his quick smile, his skin, how happy he

always was to see me. I wished I could have stayed with him forever in a world without New York or Bisbee, without consequence or regret; a world of cheap motels, cable television, gin, and sex. I tried to picture what he was doing now, where he was, who he was with. Lying in bed one early morning, just past six, I asked myself what seemed like the most important question: how does anyone get used to the ends of things?

I got up and took a cup of coffee outside. The days that week had been hot and windless, but in the early hours the air was cool, almost chill. I decided to go for a drive. The streets were still empty, and the first chile-roasting stands were setting up along the major boulevards. Everything looked washed out and pale, under a kind of brown cloud, and fighter jets from the base boomed overhead, two by two.

I pulled up in front of the Michaelsons' house. Since my last visit, the people who lived in our old house had painted the shutters purple and added a stained-glass dragonfly to the display of butterflies on the front wall. A few tiny hummingbirds were dive-bombing the red sections of the dragonfly, thinking they might find sustenance there. David came out wearing a blue bathrobe and leather slippers. His hair was a mess. He bent down stiffly to pick up the newspaper lying folded on his front lawn. As he straightened up, he saw me sitting there in the car, lifted a hand, and waved.

I got out and started up the walk.

He stood there without looking down at the paper, which impressed me; most people can't just stand in one place and watch somebody walk up to them. He didn't move a muscle. Beside him, in the unmanicured front yard, a prickly pear cactus spread thick and purple with fruit that was starting to rot. Another pair of fighter jets came roaring overhead and disappeared into the cloudless horizon.

"How's your mom?" David said once I was standing in front of him.

"She's all right, I guess," I said, noticing there were circles beneath his eyes. I'd assumed that she saw him during the day, or at the very least spoke to him on the phone. "You haven't talked to her?"

"She said she needed some time with her family."

Nestled somewhere inside the prickly pear an insect was buzzing angrily. I put my hands in the pockets of my jeans. "Aren't you her family too?"

David looked surprised and amused. "Ha," he said. His robe was falling open in the front, revealing thick chest hair. He stuck the newspaper under his arm and readjusted the robe.

"I came to say I'm leaving," I said.

"Is that so," he said.

"Yes, it is."

"Well," he said, "don't be a stranger." He laid a hand lightly on my arm, a brief but deliberate touch, then stepped back inside his house.

When I got back to the condo, my mother was drinking coffee in her neatly pressed work clothes. She smiled when she saw me, a haggard, joyless smile.

I sat down at the table opposite her and watched her make toast. "I just got back from David's."

My mother, applying butter to her toast with a knife designed specifically for that purpose, seemed intent on spreading it to a scientific degree of evenness. Her face was still frozen in a dazed smile that looked even more bereft than the contorted features of grief.

"Did you hear what I said?"

"I heard you."

"How come you haven't been talking to him? You can't just act like he doesn't exist."

She sat down and started to eat, taking small, neat bites that reminded me of somebody, although I couldn't at first place it. Then I realized: it was David. I watched as she chewed, swallowed, and sipped coffee.

"I've been busy," she finally said.

I made a snorting sound and contemplated that dazed smile, wondering if she'd had that same expression in the aftermath of my father's death. But of all those days and weeks I could remember nothing at all.

Wylie came out of the bedroom, poured himself a cup of coffee, and sat down next to me at the table. Hairs from his long braid were frizzing all around his head, golden in the morning light. He looked older and terribly, wrongly thinner.

Our mother stood up and wiped her lips, and I thought she was leaving for work, but instead she moved behind Wylie, unfastened his braid, and spread his hair over his shoulders. Slowly, as I watched her, she rebraided his long, fine hair, smoothing out all that was loose and errant, and refastened the elastic at the bottom. And Wylie let her do it; he let her.

Days passed, and Irina began to move about the house during the daylight hours and sleep through the night, and there grew a semblance of regularity to things. She and Wylie took evening walks around the neighborhood, moving at the slow pace of invalids and holding hands. I saw that heartbreak wasn't going to kill her, any more than running away from home to live on the street of a foreign city had, and that behind her smiling tenderness, her misleading innocence, was hidden a hard determination to survive. I saw, too, that Wylie was there whenever she reached out her hand, to catch it. He would not let her drift away, the way the three of us had after the death of my father, and I admired him for that.

The Missing Person

In the end I asked my mother to go with me to my father's grave. She nodded and said, "I usually go before work." It was cool the morning we drove to the cemetery, the light still silvery and weak. Albuquerque was just waking. The city's few junior skyscrapers rose up against the flat expanse of suburbs; cars shot fast along the broad freeways; houses stood low and solid in their lots. The world was going on.

We passed the emerald fairways of a golf course, where men were already out playing, and turned into the cemetery, an altogether paler green. We stopped first at Psyche's grave, where fine shoots of grass were beginning to come up through the fresh dirt, then walked slowly over to my father's.

"Does David ever come here with you?" I asked.

My mother looked surprised, and for the first time in days that numb smile left her face.

"Why would he?"

"I don't know," I said. "Maybe he'd like to."

"I never thought about it."

"Well, it's up to you," I said.

She handed me a flower to put on the grave. On the power lines ringing the cemetery small birds sang a little two-note song. A thin fingernail of moon still hung in the pale sky, the Sandias blue in the distance. I thought of my father hiking with Wylie and me in the mountains, his big hands and hairy knuckles moving quickly as he built a fire, the tilt of his head and the flicker of his eyes and the low, unmistakable rumble of his laughter, and Psyche's voice whispering above and below it all. My mother and I held each other until it was time to leave.

It was my mother, also, who took me to the airport a few days later, after I'd said good-bye to Wylie and Irina. We drove past the pine trees along the university streets, the reflective windows of strip-mall stores, the freaks and fanatics on Central Avenue. In Brooklyn, I knew, the psychic was waiting, busy at work, the neon hands of her sign shaping a symbol meant to represent the future, but I was in love with Albuquerque then: the sun shone indiscriminately over the city, its kaleidoscope of color and noise and car exhaust and trash, the mix and din of the present day. As the nose of the plane lifted, shifting us all back in our seats, I watched the small, receding jewels of lawns and swimming pools and the vast brown wash of the mountains. The woman beside me opened the slick pages of a fashion magazine with an audible snap. We flew east, toward the green of the Midwest, our connecting flights and final destinations, and quickly, quickly, the desert disappeared.

A NOTE ON THE TYPE

The text of this book was set in Sabon, a typeface designed by Jan Tschichold (1902–1974), the well-known German typographer. Based loosely on the original designs by Claude Garamond (c. 1480–1561), Sabon is unique in that it was explicitly designed for hot metal composition on both the Monotype and Linotype machines as well as for filmsetting. Designed in 1966 in Frankfurt, Sabon was named for the famous Lyons punch cutter Jacques Sabon, who is thought to have brought some of Garamond's matrices to Frankfurt.

Composed by NK Graphics
West Chesterfield, New Hampshire

Printed and bound by R. R. Donnelley & Sons
Harrisonburg, Virginia

Designed by Pamela G. Parker